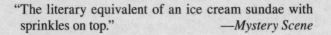

Praise for Meri Allen and the Ice Cream
Shop Mysteries

"The literary equivalent of an ice cream sundae with
sprinkles on top." —*Mystery Scene*

"Populated with well-drawn characters living in a viv-
idly described New England town." —*Booklist*

"Foodie mystery fans will be hungering for more."
—*Kings River Life*

"Allen's writing is detailed and entertaining."
—*Fresh Fiction*

"Who knew ice cream and murder would go so well
together?" —Book Frolic

"[*The Rocky Road to Ruin*] is a fun small town mystery,
complete with two fun cats as supporting characters."
—*Red Carpet Crash*

Fatal Fudge

SWIRL

ICE CREAM SHOP MYSTERY #3

By Meri Allen

St. Martin's Paperbacks

First published in the United States by St. Martin's Paperbacks, an imprint of St. Martin's Publishing Group.

FATAL FUDGE SWIRL

Copyright © 2023 by Meri Allen.

All rights reserved.

For information, address St. Martin's Publishing Group, 120 Broadway, New York, NY 10271.

www.stmartins.com

ISBN: 978-1-250-26710-8

Our books may be purchased in bulk for promotional, educational, or business use. Please contact your local bookseller or the Macmillan Corporate and Premium Sales Department at 1-800-221-7945, ext. 5442, or by email at MacmillanSpecialMarkets@macmillan.com.

Printed in the United States of America

St. Martin's Paperbacks edition / July 2023

10 9 8 7 6 5 4 3 2 1

Acknowledgments

Many thanks:

To writer friend Tammy Euliano, M.D., for answering my medical questions without batting an eye or reporting me to the authorities;

To eagle-eyed librarian Jenny Ellis, for catching a whopper of a typo; and

To Maddie and the team at St. Martin's, who help me keep it cozy.

More than kisses, letters mingle souls.

—*John Donne*

Once is happenstance. Twice is coincidence. Three times is enemy action.

—*Ian Fleming*

Fatal Fudge

SWIRL

Chapter 1

SATURDAY, The Day before Halloween

"Nothing like reading other people's mail." Flo Fairweather's sky-blue eyes sparkled as she smothered a luscious hot fudge sundae with light-as-air whipped cream. "I hope we find some juicy gossip."

Her sister, Gerri Hunt, huffed. "Reading the Collins family letters is historical research of first-person documents, not gossip."

Flo topped the sundae with a cherry and winked at me as I stuffed a waffle cone with sweet candy apple crumble ice cream. I handed it to a young customer dressed as Dracula and hid a smile as he struggled to lick the cone through his plastic fangs. Since Halloween fell on a Sunday, Penniman was celebrating all weekend long with a two-day fall festival on the green, and many revelers had made their way to my Udderly Delicious Ice Cream Shop for a treat.

"So, Riley, you'll do it? Organize and catalog the Collins family letters for us?" Gerri continued as Dracula's family left the shop.

I was being roped in by an expert for the position of

volunteer librarian at the Penniman Historical Society. I'd known Gerri long enough to know that resistance was futile but to be honest, I agreed with Flo. Reading somebody else's letters, even two-hundred-fifty-year-old letters, would be fascinating. "I'll have time after we close for the winter."

That time was approaching fast. Udderly was decorated for Halloween with orange twinkle lights, scarecrows, and several jack-o'-lanterns. One of my teen employees, Brandon Terwilliger, had given me a pumpkin carved with images of ice-cream cones and a black cat in honor of my rescue, Rocky. All week, my staff and I had dressed in costume. Today Flo was a daisy, in a green sweatshirt with a hood ringed with white felt petals, a perfect costume for the sunny, retired kindergarten teacher. Gerri, the intimidating retired principal of Penniman High School, had opted for a faux-bejeweled crown—no delicate tiara for her. Instead the crown topping her jet-black bouffant was in the style of those worn by the Imperial Russian court. I sported a white cowboy hat embellished with rhinestones sent from an Udderly fan in Texas, who loved my peach ice cream so much he had me ship a gallon of it to him from Connecticut.

"I wonder why Diantha's donating the letters?" Flo mused. "I heard she'd found some valuable ones."

Gerri gave us a knowing look. "She's sending us the dregs."

"There may still be plenty of interesting stuff," I said. "It's nice of her."

"I have another word for it," Gerri scoffed. "Her family's had the Inn on the Green since the Revolution, but she bugged out of Penniman after high school. Now she flounces back here after living in Los Angeles for forty years, all Lady Bountiful, because she's expanding the Inn and opening a new restaurant. She wants to curry favor with the locals she abandoned."

"As if there's anything wrong with her giving us her papers and money," Flo said, "though the real issue is Diantha made it known that she wants to be president of the Penniman Colonial Dames and she's not even officially a member yet." The Dames, Penniman's version of the DAR, dressed up in colonial garb and organized an annual wreath laying at the war memorial. Flo said sotto voce, "And you know who's president." She mouthed, *Gerri*.

Gerri scooped a mint chocolate chip cone for a customer then turned to me. "Her application is under review." I don't know which was frostier, the ice cream or Gerri's tone. "Obviously her family's old, but she has to validate her pedigree, er, ancestry, to get in."

Her slip of the tongue brought to mind my best friend Caroline Spooner's spoiled Persian show cat, Sprinkles. Well, former show cat—she'd been kicked off the circuit for biting the judges, which just goes to show, pedigree isn't everything.

"Hello, ladies!" a deep voice called from the kitchen workroom. I joined Rob Wainwright, a stocky middle-aged man with a steel gray crew cut. No Halloween costume for Rob; he was dressed in a bright teal-blue polo shirt and khaki pants. Inn on the Green was embroidered on the chest pocket of his shirt, and the short sleeves revealed dozens of tattoos Rob had gotten during his years in the navy. The anchors, palm trees, and other nautical images were usually covered by the tailored blue blazer he wore as manager of Diantha's luxurious inn. His years in the navy had given him a variety of skills, and he also served as a handyman for the historical society.

Rob hefted a cardboard box onto the worktable. "Diantha sent me with the papers she's donating."

"Thank you for bringing them, Rob." Gerri gave him a regal nod.

"You know I like to help, Your Majesty," he chuckled and gave me a hopeful look. "And coming here means I can get an ice-cream cone."

"If you don't mind being a guinea pig, you can try the first batch of one of my new flavors, spiced eggnog."

Rob rubbed his hands together. "Fire away!"

I wrapped a freshly made waffle cone in a napkin as I went to the shelf in the shop's enormous freezer where I stored small batches of trial recipes. For the new recipe, I'd infused eggnog and cream with some grated nutmeg, allspice, and a bit of cinnamon for a spicy base, then added an extra kick of Madagascar vanilla. I scooped up a generous portion, pleased with the creamy consistency, and handed it to Rob.

"On the house," I said.

His eyes lit up as he tried his first lick, then another. "Oh, this one's a keeper. Many thanks." He turned toward the door. "Sorry, I have to run. You ladies have a good day."

"Before you go," Gerri called, "did you fix the leaky faucet at the historical society?"

"I'll head there next. But you can only coax so much time out of those old fixtures. That sink needs replacing, and soon." Rob waved goodbye as he stepped outside.

"Another cost for the society." Gerri shook her head, causing her crown to tip. "We'll have to do another fundraiser."

"Diantha Collins mentioned another donation"—Flo threw a careful glance at her sister—"When she's back from her honeymoon."

"Buying her way in," Gerri sniffed as she straightened her crown. "Let's see what's in these papers first. I'll bring them to you when I'm done, Riley."

While Gerri put the box in the vast trunk of her Lincoln Continental, Flo returned to the front of the shop and I stepped into the office to check the shop email. My breath caught when I saw a message from *"Gelataio, Inc."* On a whim, I'd applied to take a gelato-making class with the top school in the world. I clicked open the email.

Dear Ms. Rhodes,
We are pleased to inform you that you have been accepted . . .

I jumped to my feet with a whoop. I'd been accepted—me, the new manager of a small one-shop operation in a tiny town in northeast Connecticut. I sat again and read the rest of the email. There was space in their December class. I checked the details, rereading the message to make sure I hadn't made a mistake.

Flo poked her head through the office's beaded-curtain door. "You sound happy. Good news?"

"I was accepted into the gelato-making class!"

Flo rushed to hug me, the flower petals of her costume brushing my shoulder, then she leaned toward the computer screen. "It says you can do the class in New York or"—she clapped her hands—"they're offering a class in Rome? The Eternal City! How wonderful would that be? You love to travel!" She whirled to the doorframe and shouted, "Gerri, Riley was accepted into the gelato class!"

Inwardly I sighed. Nothing would please me more than traveling to Italy for a gelato-making class. Italy was the home of gelato, after all. But Rome. . . . I'd never told anyone but Caroline about the professional and personal disaster that had befallen me there. Still, I wasn't going to let those bad memories ruin the moment.

I jumped around the office with Flo—she hops when she's excited—and accepted a hug from Gerri. "I have to think about it," I said.

"What's to think about?" Flo said. "I'd be packing my bags."

I laughed, but turned so she couldn't see my face; both sisters were way too perceptive. "Gotta get through Diantha's Halloween wedding first."

As an extra revenue stream for the shop, I did special-request ice-cream cakes for parties. My friend Mary Anne Dumas, head pastry chef at the Inn on the Green, had contacted me when Diantha asked for a Halloween-themed ice-cream wedding cake.

Mary Anne and I had both run track at Penniman High School. Though we hadn't been close—she was a senior who ran short distances and I was a freshman who ran cross-country—we'd reconnected at a Penniman Women in Business Club meeting after I moved back home five months ago. After culinary school, Mary Anne had trained with some of the most talented pastry chefs in the state before returning to Penniman to take the job at the Inn with head chef Dominic Dominello. He'd appreciated her talents and more, and a year after she'd started working at the Inn, they'd married. After seven years together, they'd divorced this past spring and he was now marrying Diantha, a personal blow and professional complication for Mary Anne.

I took Diantha's boxed triple-layer ice-cream cake from the freezer and set it in a special carrier with dry ice. I lifted the lid and Gerri and Flo bent close, disappointment evident as they saw the unadorned orange top layer of the cake.

"Don't worry, Mary Anne's going to decorate it with vines and black roses made of buttercream and fondant, and there's an amazing wedding-cake topper," I said. "The bride and groom are Día de los Muertos skeletons."

"Day of the Dead figures for a wedding?" Flo shivered. "Creepy!"

"The top layer's pumpkin spice?" Gerri pointed a regal, disapproving finger.

"The layers are pumpkin spice, chai latte, and fudge swirl, the bride and groom's favorite flavors," I said, "and the fillings are bitter chocolate ganache and caramel cookie crumbles."

Gerri rolled her deep set black eyes. "I don't remember everyone from high school, but I do remember even then Diantha was crazy for Halloween."

"That's putting it mildly." I thought of the black chai-latte layer of the cake she'd specifically requested. I'd used culinary-grade charcoal to get the color—thank goodness the stuff was flavorless. Getting the balance of flavors and colors for the wedding cake had been a fun, creative challenge.

Gerri snorted. "What's Dominic? Husband number six? Seven?"

Flo and I exchanged glances. Gerri'd been married three times herself.

Gerri lowered her voice. "Everyone knows Diantha's marriages don't last long and Dominic has a wandering eye."

Flo folded her arms. "Who's gossiping now?"

Chapter 2

I smoothed my hair into a high ponytail, making a mental note to get it cut. I'd been so busy I hadn't been to a salon in months, and my normally shoulder-length had grown several inches too long.

I drove Sadie, the 1978 orange VW square back wagon I'd inherited from Caroline's mother, Buzzy, into Penniman where every road leading to the town green was backed up and every parking spot taken. Costumed crowds streamed into the Halloween Happening Fall Fair on the green and filled the sidewalks. All these shoppers would mean great business for my dad's used bookshop, The Penniless Reader.

I turned into the parking lot behind the Inn and squeezed Sadie into a spot next to a white stockade fence that shielded a dumpster. Skirting a huge expensive-looking motorcycle with a plate reading MRLY, I climbed the stairs to the service entrance of the Inn.

A guy stopped me at the back door, pointing to a sign that said QUIET PLEASE, WE'RE FILMING, and I waited on the porch surrounded by stacks of empty cardboard liquor boxes and Styrofoam coolers. Dominic and Mary Anne did weekly social-media cooking segments that often showcased Dominic's talent for molecular gastronomy, entertaining segments that mixed science and food.

Mary Anne, in a black dress with a plunging V neckline and a vampire cape and hood, peeked into the hall and waved me into the Inn's expansive kitchen to stand behind the film crew. Her wavy black hair was pulled into a bun as usual and topped with a bat-shaped barrette. She was petite and curvy, with a round face and large, deep brown eyes that today were worried and bloodshot. I smiled thanks but wondered why she wasn't on camera as usual.

At the brightly lit wooden butcher-block worktable in the middle of the kitchen, Dominic joked as he poured cream into a bowl. Broad-shouldered, with a jovial round face, he was dressed as a zombie chef with a foam butcher's knife through his toque. By his side was a striking woman wearing an evil-queen costume complete with black snood and purple horns.

"Diantha, dearest, hand me that spoon," Dominic said.

So that was Diantha Collins, Inn owner, socialite, heiress, and potential president of the Penniman Colonial Dames. I threw a sympathetic glance at Mary Anne.

Diantha had sparkling ice blue eyes highlighted with dramatic dark brows. A strand of honey gold hair escaped her headdress and her bloodred lips were parted in a showstopping smile. Lovely as she was, there was an imperious quality to Diantha's carriage, her sculpted jaw. She'd chosen a perfect costume.

A cloud of fog swirled around the bowl, and I realized Dominic was making liquid nitrogen ice cream.

"As you can see," Dominic said, "you can use liquid nitrogen or dry ice or different smoking techniques to make your Halloween fun."

"Always pushing the envelope," Diantha gushed, her voice musical and deep.

"That's me! But seriously folks, you must be careful when working with dry ice," he said. "Strangely enough, something that's this cold—109 degrees below zero—can burn you like a flame. Plus, it gives off dangerous gases, so you must work in a well-ventilated space." He pointed to the open window. "Having said that, it's a blast! Show everyone the finished product, Mar!"

Mary Anne pasted on a smile and stepped up to the table, showing off a dish of the frosty treat. I wondered how she could hold her emotions in check and smile. Not only had Diantha replaced her in Dominic's heart, she was replacing her on camera too.

The man holding the camera said, "That's a wrap."

"Thank goodness, these lights are melting my fake blood." Dominic clapped Mary Anne on the shoulder, ignoring her wince. "Halloween episode in the can."

"Time to put my feet up." Ignoring Mary Anne, Diantha gave Dominic a quick kiss and left the kitchen, the train of her gown sweeping behind her. Dominic and the camera operator headed into the hallway, leaving an assistant to take down the equipment and clean up.

Mary Anne tugged me into a quiet, narrow pantry off the kitchen lined with shelves of dinner ware, serving pieces, and stacks of table linens. Removing her cape, she sagged onto a low stool. I cast my eyes on the floor-to-ceiling shelves, pretending to admire the antique pieces, while Mary Anne took several deep breaths to compose herself. "Dominic posts a video for his fans every Sunday. He'll be a bit busy tomorrow marrying Diantha so we recorded it today." Her dark eyes shimmered with tears and she pinched the bridge of her nose. "As you saw, she'll be replacing me in our video show too, the show that was my idea."

Mary Anne crushed the cape into a ball and threw it onto a shelf. "Riley, I didn't want a divorce, but what could I do? I had to accept that he didn't love me anymore. There was only one of us in this marriage for a long time." Bitterness tinged her voice as she rose and peeked into the kitchen. "It didn't help that I didn't have thousands of dollars to give him so he could open a new restaurant. Come on. They're done."

Mary Anne led me back into the kitchen where I unpacked the cooler and set the boxed ice-cream cake on a shelf in the walk-in freezer. I shut the door and joined her at the butcher-block island, where she showed me sketches of her plans for the cake's decoration.

"Amazing," I said.

She smiled sadly.

"Are you really okay?" I said. "This must be so hard for you."

She ran her fingers along the wood's scarred surface. "You told me I didn't have to help with the wedding just to prove I was okay with it. You can say I told you so."

"I'd never say that." I squeezed her hand.

Mary Anne sighed. "I thought I'd be okay with this, but now Dominic's really stabbing me in the back."

"Not a wise thing to do with the chef who's handling your wedding luncheon," I said.

Mary Anne snorted. "I should've listened to your advice. I never should've agreed to cater the wedding of my ex-husband and his new wife." A mischievous glint appeared in her large brown eyes. "Don't worry, I overcharged them so much. I'm greedy! What can I say? I need the money."

To my quizzical look, she shook her head and glanced at a wall clock over the sink. "Let's talk tomorrow. Be sure to go out through the front door when you leave so you can check out the decorations in the dining room. The Inn's closed to everyone but the wedding party. I've got to get through dinner service—thank god I have an assistant to help." She lowered her voice, "Though he wasted no time ingratiating himself with Dominic and gunning for my job."

She threw a glance toward the pantry door and barked, "Marley!"

A whippet thin guy in a white chef's jacket burst through the pantry door so quickly I was sure he must've been listening. His hazel eyes darted guiltily as he smoothed his reddish-brown hair, which was pulled into a low ponytail, and gave us a curt nod.

"Riley Rhodes, meet Marley Wagner, a graduate of the Culinary Institute of America. He started here two months ago and"—her voice dripped honey—"has already impressed everyone."

"Hi." Marley gave Mary Anne a wide berth and went into the freezer.

I gave Mary Anne a quick hug, then exited through the pantry door into the Inn's cozy, low-ceilinged dining room. The room had been readied for the private dinner, with one long table covered with a black and gold tapestry cloth, gold chargers set at each place, and a Halloween tableau using Día de los Muertos skeleton figures running down the center. Tall candles on black cast-iron holders gleamed above a miniature haunted cardboard village and skeletal wedding procession.

It was charming, whimsical, and gothic, and I marveled at the intricate figures. Not what I'd do to celebrate my own marriage, but to each her own. Maybe by the time you were on your sixth wedding, you wanted something different.

I walked through the entry hall of the Inn, recently

renovated with a sleek design that had removed many of the cozy colonial touches I remembered from my library-school graduation dinner. The two-story lobby was welcoming with the Inn's signature sky-blue walls over white wainscoting. Nods to the Inn's history were subtle: a couple of colonial-style hooded capes on pegs by the door, an oil painting of the town green, a single Windsor chair by an antique credenza, a homey antique coat rack where guests still hung their coats.

The Inn's library was one of my favorite spaces, and I decided to see what changes had been made there. As I crossed the lobby I noted the stack of beautifully wrapped wedding gifts and cardboard mailing cartons on the credenza. Diantha and Dominic's friends were certainly generous.

Voices came from the library and I remembered that the Inn was closed to everyone except wedding guests, so I retreated into the dining room. With all the gifts sitting out, I didn't want it to look like I was casing the joint. Footsteps stopped in the hallway.

A man's voice, a good-natured tenor, said with a laugh, "You do realize that Mom's a Black Widow?"

Mom? Did he mean *Diantha*?

The voice continued with a laugh. "She inherited when Dad died, and when Charles and Juan-Carlos and Lloyd and Darius died. Maybe we better warn Dom—"

"Come on Coop, you know they all died of natural causes," a deeper, raspy voice cut in. "That's what happens when your husbands are pushing eighty when you marry them. But now the black widow's changed her MO and is robbing the cradle. Once they're married and she changes her will, Dominic'll be the one doing the inheriting. Mom's already warned me that"—his voice changed to Diantha's imperious plummy tone—"it's time to stand on your own two feet, darling."

Coop said, "What are you complaining about? Emilia inherited all that money when her parents died."

"Keep up, Coop," the second voice answered. "She's pouring it all into the hydro plant and school and hospital in Africa."

"Your wife's a saint." There was brief silence. "So you won't be able to float your favorite brother a loan? I need financing for another project."

I heard the door open as the deeper voice continued. "It's not my money, bro, and I'm barely making any bank. My contract with my sponsor's up at the end of the year. Doesn't matter. I'll be too busy digging wells in Africa to spend any money."

Coop said, "Not like there will be much money left to inherit anyway. Mom's bankrolling Dominic's new restaurant."

The deeper voice swore. "We're all screwed."

Chapter 3

As the door of the Inn closed, I let out the breath I'd been holding. I didn't know who was worse, Diantha for how she ignored Mary Anne or Diantha's kids for seeing their mother as an ATM. Though maybe Diantha deserved it. Maybe she was a terrible mom. Listening to that conversation made me even more grateful for my kind, loving dad.

I peeked around the corner, noted the coats on the rack were gone, and crossed under the gleaming chandelier to the library. From my previous visits to the Inn, I expected a fire crackling in the fireplace and guests relaxing in the two wing chairs flanking the hearth, but the fireplace was cold and the snug room was stuffed with more gifts for a bride and groom who probably didn't need anything.

Cold October night air stung my cheeks as I stepped outside onto the broad porch of the Inn and closed the door behind me. A sign swung from the doorknob: CLOSED FOR PRIVATE EVENT. As I turned I almost stumbled over Rob, who was swearing as he crouched over a small machine.

"What's that?" I asked.

"Fog machine." He scooted aside, and after a moment, a soft white fog flowed out of the device and streamed down the steps. "Diantha wants to set the mood while she hands out candy," he said, his voice tinged with admiration.

When Halloween landed on a Sunday, Penniman schools encouraged trick-or-treating on the Saturday before the holiday. "Look at this." Rob pointed to two large baskets tied with orange ribbons that overflowed with full-sized candy bars in wrappers printed with the Inn's logo. "That woman's attention to detail's second to none."

I had to agree. "She's done a beautiful job."

"And so did you." Rob winked. "I'll be back for more of that spicy eggnog ice cream."

"Thanks." I zipped my down jacket to my chin and descended the Inn's wide stairs, enjoying the sunlight streaming from the windows and the artful arrangements of mums and pumpkins flanking the door. Mary Anne passed the dining room window, her expression tense, and I felt a pang of sadness for my friend.

In the deepening twilight, I hurried down the sidewalk to Dad's bookshop, enjoying the swish of my steps through the dried leaves as I threaded through groups of chattering kids in costume. Because most of Penniman was rural, the houses too spread out and the roads too narrow for trick-or-treating, the merchants around the green gave out candy during the Halloween Happening festival. Lights and music flowed from the tents set up on the town green across from the shops, and golden light shone from the shop windows.

A life-sized, headless mannequin wrapped in a cloak sprawled on the bench by the front door of Dad's shop. The mannequin's right arm rested on the back of the bench, and in his white gloved hand he held a copy of

The Legend of Sleepy Hollow. A pumpkin head with a ghoulish grin illuminated by a flickering flameless candle was set next to him. I had to admire the decorating handiwork of my stepmother, Paulette, another woman with exceptional attention to detail. I moved aside so tourists could snap selfies with her Headless Horseman.

A bell jangled as I stepped into the warmth of the low-ceilinged shop, expecting a greeting from Dad. Instead, he and Paulette were deep in conversation with two men at the counter.

More shoppers than usual jammed the narrow aisles of the already-snug shop, but one person stood out against the backdrop of bookshelves. Paulette was a former nurse who'd worked part time in the shop and went full time after she retired and married Dad. She's lovely— champagne blonde hair, cornflower blue eyes, slim and elegant as the cashmere sweaters and subtle diamond jewelry she preferred, and tonight she was especially lovely dressed as Glinda the Good Witch complete with a pink basket of candy.

She and Dad were definitely a case of opposites attracting, Paulette gregarious and Dad shy and good-natured. Dad, named Nathaniel Hawthorne Rhodes by his bibliophile mother, generally wore plaid flannel shirts, corduroy pants, and tortoiseshell glasses, and had a mass of untamable graying brown hair. His only concession to Halloween was a white lab coat and some Albert Einstein glasses—he already had the mad-scientist hair.

Inwardly I sighed. I had to admit she was good for him. I just wasn't used to sharing him, even though he and Paulette had been married for five years. Of course, I hadn't lived here in Penniman until this summer when I came home for Buzzy's funeral and stuck around to run the ice-cream shop.

Dad had been a history teacher before he opened The Penniless Reader after my mom died when I was three. I'd worked in the store before I could ride a bike. Dad may have flouted some child-labor laws, but I loved every inch of the quirky little shop.

Paulette loved it too, and was clearly besotted by my dad. She was now giving him the adoring look that meant if he'd only say yes she'd be the happiest woman in the world.

"Oh, Nate, won't it be fun? Such great publicity for the shop!" Paulette clasped Dad's hand.

"It'll be one for the books," Dad chuckled.

I groaned—Dad and his puns—as Dad shook hands with the two men flanking Paulette. "We don't get these opportunities every day."

My heart jumped. Penniman had been buzzing about a visit from Skylark Films' location scout for weeks. He'd been in touch with Dad and Paulette about using the store as a set for their new rom-com, *Bound for Love*, about a bookseller and a librarian who fall in love. Was the deal sealed?

One of the men with Dad and Paulette turned toward me and gave a smile that hit me like a wave of sunshine and testosterone. Despite the parka, he was all California surfer charm, with sun-bleached honey blond hair, tanned cheekbones, and a wide toothy grin. I recognized Cooper Collins though it was years since he'd starred in *Family Magic*, a television show about a family of scientists who have kids with magical powers. Like every twelve-year-old in America, I'd had a crush on the handsome tween wizard.

I returned his smile. With difficulty, I pulled my eyes away from his dazzling baby blues and noticed for the first time that the crowd in the shop was mostly women, all holding books that none of them was reading. Their attention was fixed on the hunk in front of me.

Dad waved me over. "Riley! Come meet the directors of the movie."

"Remember I told you about the location scout who came through here a few weeks ago?" Paulette beamed. "This is him, Cooper Collins. Skylark picked the shop for a scene!"

"Call me Coop." He put out his hand and I pulled myself together enough to shake it. The child star was now working behind the camera? I recognized his voice as "Coop" from the conversation I'd overheard at the Inn. "I'm the location scout for Skylark. This is our director, Charles Worth."

"Call me Chip. Nice to meet you." A slight guy with a round face and gold-rimmed glasses, Chip's tenor voice had a New York edge, and wasn't one of the voices I'd heard earlier at the Inn. "Actually, Coop's assistant director on this one. He did suggest Penniman, and how could anyone resist?" He waved his hands. "The green, the covered bridge, all this New England charm. Plus, Penniman's the ancestral home of the Collins family."

Dad turned to Paulette. "The Collins Homestead's around the corner from the Inn, just down the road a quarter mile, and the family still owns the Inn on the Green."

The eavesdropping crowd stirred as it absorbed this information.

For all the prominence of the Collins name in Penniman, I'd never put Diantha Collins together with the child star.

Cooper said, "We'd come back east to the Inn for family holidays, and for many years my brothers and I went to school right down the road at Magistrate's

School, but I haven't been here in years. It's great to come back."

I marveled at the discretion of Magistrate's School. If any of the girls in Penniman had known Coop was a mere two miles down the road at Magistrate's, they would've stormed the walls.

"And this bookstore's perfect. There are a lot of"—Chip hesitated—"unique bookshops, but this really has character. Homey. The Skylark feel. Perfect for the shoot." He jutted his chin toward the fireplace where a fire crackled in the stone hearth and a swag of dried Queen Anne's lace and hydrangea decorated the mantel. Next to it was a coffee and tea bar, free to all readers, stocked with yard-sale china cups. An overstuffed chair where any customer could relax in the warmth of the fire was occupied by a woman in a Family Magic sweatshirt who was filming Cooper on her cell phone.

Paulette stepped directly in front of her, blocking the woman's view with her broad pink skirt.

"You know what we need?" Chip stroked his narrow chin, "A cat, a bookstore cat curled up by the fireplace—"

Paulette waved her wand, her eyes gleaming. "We have a cat! She was a show cat, a fluffy white Persian!"

Dad's shaggy eyebrows flew up over the rims of his thick metal-framed glasses and we shared a horrified look.

"Wait a second, Paulette." I raised a warning hand, but Paulette plowed on.

"Her name is Sprinkles!"

It was true that Sprinkles was a beautiful Persian, but the aging queen was a bountiful ball of white fur, delinquent behavior, and certain trouble. I knew because I'd lived with her in Caroline's farmhouse for the past five months and the darn cat never missed an opportunity to try to trip me down the stairs.

I tried to keep my voice level. "Paulette, I don't think that's a good—"

"Oh, pretty please!" Paulette clasped her hands, which gave the effect that she was going to bat me with her magic wand. Dad had told me Paulette was desperate to be an extra in the film, and it looked like she was willing to go to any lengths—no matter how dubious—to ingratiate herself with the filmmakers.

I tried to stay calm in front of Cooper but inside I was screaming, *Are you nuts?* Aloud I said, "You know Sprinkles, and besides she's Caroline's pet. You have to ask her."

"We're stuck and could use her," Cooper said. "The animal actor we usually use decided to have kittens."

"Riley, you know how much Caroline adores Skylark movies," Paulette said. "This way she could be part of one." Translation: This way Paulette could be part of one.

Chip nodded. "We can arrange that." He and Cooper turned to me with expectant looks.

This combined charm offensive, especially the friendly entreaty in Coop's beautiful blue eyes, rendered me speechless. *Caroline did love Skylark movies. Cooper Collins wanted Sprinkles.* I felt my resistance crumble, and my momentary silence gave Paulette her opening. "So happy to help." Paulette gave me a smile but the expression in her eyes said a house would fall on me if I disagreed.

I managed a single nod.

Cooper looked at his watch. "Great. Hey, Chip, we've got to get going."

"Thank you again," Chip said as he and Cooper shook hands with us all and headed for the door.

"See you bright and early on Monday," Cooper said.

The shop bell jangled again as Cooper and Chip left, and I watched them cross to the green and disappear into the crowd at the Halloween Happening. A wave of customers whooshed out of the shop in pursuit as a crowd of chattering children dressed as miniature superheroes surged in with plastic pumpkins held out at arm's length shouting "Trick or treat!"

Paulette's starstruck expression didn't waver as I wheeled on her. "Don't you remember Sprinkles was kicked off the show circuit for biting the judges?"

Dad took the basket from her hands and gave each kid a handful of candy as Paulette and I squared off.

"Oh, she'll be fine." Paulette turned side to side, making her skirt swish. "You know how she loves attention. She'll rise to the occasion."

I raised my hands in surrender. "If Caroline agrees, and as long as you wrangle Sprinkles," I said, "I wash my hands. It's your rodeo, Paulette." Or funeral, I thought.

Sprinkles and I had a complicated relationship, which was currently an uneasy truce. Because Caroline worked in Boston during the week and came home on weekends, I took care of Sprinkles. If she didn't rely on me for food, I wasn't one hundred percent sure she wouldn't succeed in killing me one day.

"Don't forget you're coming over for your birthday dinner Monday night," Dad said, waving as the children whooshed back out.

"Looking forward to it." My birthday was October 31, but because both Dad and I had shops to run on the busy festival weekend, we decided to celebrate on Monday night, November 1.

Paulette ignored us as she texted, no doubt asking— no, telling—Caroline that she'd offered Sprinkles' services for the movie. I sighed. Like everyone else, Caroline was dying to be part of the movie and, I recalled, had had a poster of Cooper Collins on her bedroom wall. I hoped her usual common sense would prevail and not the pull of a schoolgirl crush.

The fans who didn't follow Cooper and Chip surrounded Dad and Paulette and peppered them with questions. I wanted to shake off my irritation with Paulette, so I gave them a wave and crossed the street to the green, dodging a hay wagon full of kids pulled by two gentle old horses.

The familiar sights and sounds of the festival soothed me. The green was lined by booths and white tents—I passed a fortune teller, many tables full of clever arts and crafts, several games of chance and skill, and even a dunk booth. I breathed in sweet and salty aromas as I passed booths selling candy apples and popcorn.

A crowd jostled in front of a booth where a teenage girl dressed in an authentic-looking colonial-era costume complete with an apron, mobcap, and cape carved pumpkins to order. If not for her glasses and the neon-orange tips of her dark hair, she could've stepped out of a history book. A sign pinned to the back curtain of the booth read LUCRETIA'S PERFECT PUMPKINS in script that reminded me of John Hancock's signature on the Declaration of Independence. I stopped with the crowd to marvel at her pumpkins decorated with intricate carvings of cats, witches on brooms, crows, and other spooky motifs.

"Mommy! I want a dinosaur like me!" a child in a T-rex costume cried.

"Is that possible?" the mother asked.

The young woman nodded and as I watched she deftly cut and shaved the pumpkin's skin into a mirror image of the miniature T-rex hopping up and down before her.

When she finished, she placed a flameless candle inside and the child squealed with delight.

Next, I stopped by the silent-auction fundraiser for the Penniman High School Lock-In. The night before Halloween had always been Mischief Night, when kids pulled pranks and toilet-papered trees, but after an almost-fatal crash with some drunk teens, the school instituted a lock-in where students celebrated Halloween with an all-night party in the gym. I was gratified to see that there were many bids on the Udderly Delicious gift certificate I'd donated.

Practically everyone was in costume, so when a slim woman in a green duffel coat scurried past me toward the Inn, for a moment I tried to figure out what her costume was. She had a roll of silver wrapping paper tucked under her arm. Harried Shopper? She and I may have been the only people on the green not in costume.

The woman skirted the long line of people waiting at the Inn's steps and disappeared into the shadows around the corner. On the spotlighted front porch of the Inn, Diantha Collins stood in the eerie fog handing out those full-sized chocolate bars. I kicked myself for not grabbing one earlier. Statuesque Diantha in her evil-queen costume knew how to set a scene. At her side, Dominic the zombie chef signed autographs. There were more adults than kids there, jostling for a candy bar and selfie with the celebrity chef.

The strains of "Thriller" drew me to the midway, and I joined the crowd as the Penniman High School band marched by with Brandon Terwilliger leading the drum line.

I sensed someone approach and whirled as a woman dressed in an oversized pinstriped gangster suit sidled behind me.

"Do I blend?" she whispered as she pulled her fedora low over her small, bear-like eyes.

Tillie O'Malley, the loosest lips in Penniman. "You never blend, Tillie."

She guffawed. "Good. No, bad."

There was no hope of Tillie blending in. Curvy and broad shouldered with a booming voice, she favored tropical prints, usually wrapping her jet-black curls in neon-colored headscarves. Though she'd chosen a subtle pinstripe fabric for her gangster costume, she'd accessorized with fuchsia lipstick and beaded drop earrings.

Tillie lowered her voice. "Actually, I'm undercover."

"Undercover?" I asked.

"Security." Tillie nodded toward a woman dressed as a Dalmatian, her arm through that of a guy's wearing a hockey mask and fright wig. "That's my client. Walk with me."

"You have clients?" After she flunked out of the police academy, Tillie got a job as secretary at the police services building, thanks to the affection felt by the town for her father, the beloved former chief of police.

"Jenira Ford," Tillie said as she purchased a bag of popcorn. "She's the Queen of Skylark movies. I've seen all of them, and she's the best."

I'd seen a few myself and knew who Jenira was. A stunning beauty with a mane of dark brown hair and dramatic ebony eyes, the Skylark star always played a sweet but spunky heroine. Now her petite frame was hidden beneath a bulky white fur costume, her face covered with white makeup and black spots, her hair tucked under a hood with black floppy ears.

Tillie offered me her popcorn and I took a handful. "She's dressed as a . . . dog," I said.

"Smart," Tillie said. "No one knows who she is. She

wants to enjoy herself before filming starts. I'm providing security."

I choked. "Really?" *Had Tillie been deputized?*

Tillie's tone grew defensive. "I'm getting tired of the desk job, answering phones, taking messages, filing, while the officers get to go off and do exciting stuff. So when I heard the movie was coming, I was proactive. Skylark called the office and Jack told them they'd work with the movie—you know, traffic safety and direction—but they didn't have enough staff to provide private security. Jenira wanted her own, so I offered my services." She gave me a card: O'Malley Private Security.

"Does Jack know about this?" The words flew out of my mouth before I could think. Of course he didn't know about it. Providing private security without a license was illegal. Jack Voelker was the police chief who was dating my best friend, Caroline. If Tillie and I had a complicated relationship, the relationship I had with Jack was even more complicated—and fraught—because I'd inadvertently stumbled into solving a couple of murders since I came back to Penniman, a job I knew Jack wished I'd left to him. More than anything, I didn't want to be a stumbling block to his relationship with Caroline. It was her first serious relationship; she was so happy and things between them were too good to mess up.

Tillie plucked the card back from my hand. "No, he doesn't know and no one's telling him. I have lots of leave. It's a part-time gig on my own time." She raised an eyebrow. "Besides, you're not one to talk. We have an understanding, right? I don't tell him what you get up to, and you don't tell him what I get up to."

A devil's bargain. I sighed. Tillie had been a very leaky source for me the last times I'd done some digging into Penniman's unsolved crimes, but I felt I'd more than righted the scales by helping solve some big cases. What trouble could Tillie get into, right? This was quiet Penniman.

"No worries," I said.

Tillie munched popcorn and followed close behind the couple as I walked away. My time working with the CIA, doing occasional undercover work, had taught me that she was too close to her subjects. She was probably making them uncomfortable, but on the plus side she did draw attention from them.

My phone buzzed, and the caller ID read INN ON THE GREEN. Maybe it was Mary Anne. Why didn't she call from her own cell? Perhaps the battery died?

"Hello?"

"Riley?" a gravelly voice spoke. "It's Ruthie Adams at the Inn."

Ruthie? My former elementary school Girl Scout leader was a housekeeper at the Inn. "Oh, hi, how are you?" Was Mary Anne all right? I wondered. "Is everything okay?"

"Yes. Well, no." Ruthie heaved a heavy sigh. "I hired two girls to help me with serving and doing the rooms tomorrow and, well, Rob found them trying to take pictures of Miss Ford. She said someone had sold pictures of her to TMZ. Miss Ford had a cow—let me tell you that girl can swear in several languages. She ran my helpers right out the door."

Why was Ruthie telling me this? "Oh . . . that's too bad?"

"Well"—she cleared her throat—"I need someone I trust to help out, and Mary Anne told me you'd be back tomorrow morning to work on your cake and well, I thought you might be able to help me out tonight and tomorrow morning? Rob Wainwright said you can spend the night in one of the guest rooms—"

After the words "guest rooms," her voice faded as
I gazed up at the glowing lights of the Inn. Stay at the
Inn on the Green? The Inn was five star. And even if I
could've afforded it, the Inn was always booked. The
place oozed comfort and romance. The spa was known
to be one of the priciest on the East Coast. The joke in
Penniman was that the Inn was the place rich, cheating
husbands brought their girlfriends. My graduation celebration had been a complete splurge. How could I say
no? Fall hours at Udderly meant the shop opened at one
o'clock, so I was free in the morning.

"I'll do it," I said. "I'll stop home, grab some clothes,
and come over right after."

"You're a lifesaver." Relief accented her words.
"Thank you, Riley."

The warm glow of candlelight beckoned from the
windows of the three-story inn. Diantha and Dominic
stood in the hazy blanket of fog created by the dry-ice
machines. The foggy scene made the Inn more mysterious, even more enticing. A room at the Inn on the Green?
Yes, please!

Chapter 4

R iley, Flo told me you were accepted to gelato school! I'm so happy for you! Now we can buy that gelato machine for the shop!" My best friend Caroline Spooner threw her arms around me as I entered the kitchen of the farmhouse we shared. Caroline lived in Boston during the week, where she worked as an art appraiser for an auction house, and came back home to Penniman on weekends to work at Udderly, which she'd inherited from her mother, Buzzy.

Her hazel eyes glowed behind her oversized tortoise-shell glasses. "You've been wanting to take that gelato class for ages!"

I smiled. "Did Flo tell you where the class is?"

"New York City, right?" Caroline scooped a golden-brown grilled cheese sandwich off the griddle onto a plate and handed it to me.

I joined her at the table. "And Rome."

"Ah." She held my gaze as she took her seat. "I can see where you're torn. But Paolo's gone, right?"

Paolo, the reason I'd lost my job as a librarian with the CIA.

"Riley, aren't you always giving me pep talks about

taking chances, you only live once, seize the day? You have to choose Rome! You love to travel!"

I laughed. "You got me. I'll think about it. Even if I can't make the Rome trip work, New York's always fun."

"You deserve a break." She bit into her crisp, gooey sandwich and sighed. "Though here it is your birthday weekend and you're working tomorrow at the Inn—but didn't that turn out lucky? Diantha Collins' wedding. . . . Think of the drama! I'm sure Diantha's going to make an amazing entrance." Her eyes grew dreamy. "I'd love to spend a night at that Inn."

"With a special someone?" I teased.

A pink blush suffused Caroline's skin to the roots of her unruly shoulder-length, curly brown hair. "Mm, maybe. If Jack ever had a free moment." As Caroline brushed white cat hairs off the sleeve of her sweatshirt, I noticed her fingernails were flecked with crimson and orange paint. Caroline used painting as a coping mechanism whenever she was stressed.

I swallowed my last bite and said, "Are you guys okay?"

Caroline set down her sandwich. "I thought things were going really well. We had that wonderful trip to his family cabin. Sprinkles has even stopped biting him, well, most of the time. But ever since that domestic . . . he's been . . ." She looked away. "Busy."

Two weeks earlier, Jack had been called to a domestic disturbance. I'd read that domestic disputes are one of the most fraught situations for law enforcement, and this one had turned out to be a nightmare. Once he arrived, the woman who'd begged for help suddenly turned on the police and emergency personnel who'd shown up. Her boyfriend had a rifle and had fired several shots, hitting Jack's SUV and a neighbor's house. The woman and her boyfriend barricaded themselves for hours before finally surrendering. Though no one had been hurt, Caroline had panicked when she saw the bullet hole in Jack's SUV. He'd played it down, but ever since, he hadn't been around much.

"It's leaf-peeping time. So many tourists and traffic jams. He is busy," I said, stressing the word "is." "When things calm down, things'll go back to normal."

I hoped.

Caroline gave me a sly look. "Don't you have a date with Liam tomorrow night?"

Liam Pryce was Penniman's veterinarian. Adored by humans and his animal patients alike, Liam had the chiseled features of a model, a heart of gold, and the remnants of an accent from his Jamaican birthplace. I was a sucker for a man with an accent. We'd had one whole date two months ago—I'd invited him to the shop for an ice-cream cone. When I brought Rocky in for shots a week ago, we'd discovered we shared a love of Ethiopian food. One of his assistants was an old friend who mentioned my birthday was coming up, so he'd insisted he'd treat me to dinner at a new place he'd discovered in Hartford.

"Tomorrow will be busy. I'm helping Mary Anne ready Diantha Collins' wedding cake in the morning, then I'm helping Ruthie with housekeeping because the extra help Rob hired for this weekend didn't work out," I filled Caroline in on the Jenira Ford incident as we finished our meal and cleared our plates. "Then I'll do my shift at the shop and Liam and I'll go out after."

"Whew," Caroline said as she loaded the dishwasher. "I'm exhausted just hearing about it."

"I hope I don't fall asleep in my dinner."

Sprinkles padded into the kitchen and wove around

Caroline's ankles, and I remembered Paulette's offer to the filmmakers.

"Did Paulette—"

Sprinkles yowled as Caroline picked her up. "She did! I'm so excited, Riley!"

Her reaction made me swallow the words I'd been planning to say aloud. *Did you talk to Paulette about the movie and her insane offer?*

Caroline snuggled Sprinkles. "It'll be so good for Sprinkles. You know how my pretty queen likes being admired, and when Paulette mentioned Cooper Collins, how could I say no?"

Everyone's starstruck, I thought. I left Caroline and Sprinkles to their love fest, packed an outfit in my travel bag, and drove to the Inn.

I parked behind the building, once again squeezing Sadie into a space by the whitewashed fence that hid the dumpster, some Styrofoam coolers, and more discarded cardboard liquor boxes. This place went through a lot of alcohol, I mused. Well, it was the biggest money-making stream in the restaurant business.

On the other side of the Inn's parking lot was a two-story structure with broad garage doors on the lowest level: the renovated carriage house. A narrow outside staircase led to the second floor, and a small sign reading R. WAINWRIGHT, MANAGER was affixed by the staircase. Even the carriage house was decorated with barrels of golden mums and pumpkins, and white candles glowed in the windows.

As I cut the engine, I saw Diantha on the back steps by the rear entrance of the Inn, still in costume, talking to Rob as he drank from a bottle of beer. I gathered my things and headed toward them.

Diantha's imperious voice rang out, seething with anger. "Enough already! It'll never happen!"

Shocked by her tone, I shrank behind the fence enclosing the dumpster, praying they hadn't seen me.

Rob's voice was a growl; the only words I could make out were, "I'll tell your son."

"Don't you dare!" Diantha spat.

I sidled forward and peered around the corner of the fence.

Rob's voice took on a wheedling tone as he took Diantha's hand in his. "Come on, Diantha, you know we were always meant to be. Don't forget—"

"If you can't handle it, you can find another job and another place to live." She jerked her hand away and stormed inside. Rob swore and hurled his bottle at the dumpster. The glass shattered and a stream of the tart-smelling liquid puddled near my shoes. I froze, fearing he'd come down to clean up the broken glass, but instead he ran a hand over his cropped hair and followed Diantha inside, letting the door slam shut behind him.

Was Rob declaring his feelings for Diantha on the eve of her wedding? Talk about bad timing. The uncomfortable exchange unnerved me. I glanced around the parking lot as I took several deep steadying breaths.

In the sea of late-model SUVs were two rental box trucks with out-of-state plates. Curious, I climbed up on the running board of one and peeked in the passenger-side window, tilting my head to read a clipboard on the seat: a cover sheet read "Bound for Love: Schedule."

Ah, of course, some of the film crew must be staying here. I wondered if scenes were also planned for the Inn. Talk about a setting that had all the ingredients of a Skylark movie: charm, history, romance, fall leaves, twinkle lights . . . I turned . . . dumpster and broken glass.

I pasted a smile on my face, ready to pretend I hadn't witnessed the uncomfortable scene between Diantha and Rob as I shouldered my bag and knocked on the kitchen door. No one answered, so I slipped into the empty kitchen, set my bag by a coat rack at the door, and followed the sound of music and laughter through the pantry and dining room to the lobby. The pile of gifts had been removed from the credenza, which now held only a single potted orchid.

Rob Wainwright emerged from a hallway past a sign that read SPA/POOL/MEETING ROOMS.

"Hello, Riley, nice of you to help Ruthie out. She's been here since seven this morning." Ruddy cheeks and a sheen of perspiration in his graying crew cut were the only remnants of the previous emotional scene. Now Rob cut a distinguished figure in tan slacks, pale-blue button-down shirt, and navy blazer with a blue embroidered patch on the breast pocket. The design was a miniature of the Inn.

Ruthie Adams, wearing a blue maid's smock over jeans rolled up at the ankles and Crocs, joined us. "Riley, you're a lifesaver! So nice to see you." Though her shag-cut chestnut hair was threaded with gray, the petite woman's dark eyes were bright and she still exuded the bountiful energy I remembered from years ago at camp.

"I can't say no to my Girl Scout leader." I smiled as she gave me a hug and helped me into a blue housekeeping smock as we chatted and caught up.

I followed Ruthie back through the kitchen to a housekeeping closet in a service hallway that led past an office and restroom into the lounge.

My heart tugged when she yawned and pressed her hand to her lower back. Ruthie had to be in her sixties. She caught my concerned look and gave me a playful grin. "I get up with the larks, I'm not used to staying up with the owls," she chuckled.

Music and raucous laughter rang from the lounge where guests crowded the bar. Ruthie and I backtracked through the kitchen, dining room, and lobby to the library.

The snug room had been cleared of gifts and requisitioned as a staging area where baskets of small, wrapped favors covered worktables. Ruthie thrust a cardboard box into my hands and opened another, releasing the rich scent of deep dark chocolate. "Specially made chocolates, decorated like sugar skulls. Don't they smell heavenly? We'll put one on every pillow at turndown, and then wedding guests get them as party favors tomorrow. Diantha's set some aside for staff too. They're tying the knot in the Grand Parlor."

I followed Ruthie into a long, narrow room off the lobby. A podium was set up under an arch of dried hydrangea, orange and pink roses, and ivy, in front of a fireplace bedecked with pumpkins, ribbons, and mums in fall colors. Two dozen delicate gold-painted chairs were set up for the guests.

"Wait till you see her flowers tomorrow." Ruthie sighed as she picked up a wayward rose petal, then turned to me with a mischievous gleam in her eye. "Want to see her wedding dress?" She tugged me to the sweeping main staircase.

"Are you sure this is okay?" I threw a glance toward the entrance to the lounge, where I could see Diantha, still wearing her slinky Maleficent costume, in a circle of admirers, holding court while raising a glass holding a drink, colored blood red, with dry ice fog spilling over the rim.

"My last drink as a single woman and then I promise I'll get my beauty sleep," Diantha crowed. Her admirers raised their glasses. Marley and Dominic stood at the bar, serving drinks from a punchbowl that overflowed with dry-ice fog.

"They're busy," Ruthie whispered. "Besides, when you're a maid, you can go anywhere. No one pays you any mind."

As we turned the corner to go upstairs, we almost ran into a slim guy with sun-streaked, shoulder-length brown hair dressed in slouchy jeans and an oversized t-shirt. He stood with his foot on the bottom stair, holding a large gift box with a white bow on his hip as he looked at his phone.

"Taking that upstairs to the gift room, Sam?" Ruthie said. "You don't have to. I'll get them all later."

"Please don't worry about it, Ruthie. This one's heavy and the elevator's not working. I saw it on the reception desk and thought I'd put it in the library, but that room's full of decorations." I recognized the deep, raspy voice from earlier when he'd been talking to Cooper.

Ruthie smiled. "Thank you. Oh, my manners. Sam Collins, this is Riley Rhodes, she's helping me today but she also manages the Udderly Delicious Ice Cream Shop. Sam's one of Diantha's sons."

"Nice to meet you," I said.

"Hi. Emilia and I'll have to stop by. She loves ice cream." Sam slid the phone in his pocket and shook his hair away from his eyes, revealing a silvery, long-healed scar along his jawline and wide blue eyes. With the easy grace of an athlete, he balanced the box on his hip with one hand and made an "after you" gesture up the stairs with the other. With the gesture, a gold ring with a heavy red stone flashed on his hand, the only skin on his arm without tattoos.

We passed the second floor and continued up the stairs to the third. "We're renovating the whole south wing and most of the north on the second floor. Third floor's all suites," Ruthie said as we climbed. She turned to Sam and asked, "How's Emilia doing? Poor thing looked exhausted when you got here."

"Hey, thanks for helping me make her that smoothie. Yeah, jet lag's rough and we had a long flight. Didn't think we'd make it in time for the wedding." As we reached the third floor, Sam pulled his phone from his pocket again and shifted the package under his arm onto a table next to a golden mum plant. "Excuse me, gotta take this," he said.

"I'll unlock the gift room door for you. Have a good night." Ruthie took a ring of keys from her pocket and unlocked a door with a brass plaque that read LILAC.

We continued down the hallway to a door at the very end where "Dianthus" was etched on a brass label above the doorknob.

Ruthie threw a glance down the hall where Sam stood texting. Instead of using the old-fashioned key she'd used earlier, she pressed a modern key card to a pad and held the door open for me.

"Ruthie, should we be up here?" I whispered as we went into the room.

She winked and shut the door. "Nothing to worry about. Diantha's staying on the second floor in her old room tonight." It dawned on me that years of working in a hotel had given my former Scout leader no scruples about going into people's private spaces.

We stepped into an expansive suite with a sitting room, bedroom, bath, walk-in closet, and separate dressing room.

Ruthie pointed to a white dress on a form in the walk-in closet, a surprisingly sexy ensemble with a white leather biker jacket over a white silk minidress embellished with pearls.

"It's very pretty," I said, nonplussed, "but I expected something more formal for her wedding dress."

"Nah, not that one." Ruthie waved dismissively. "That's for getting the license at Town Hall. No, *this* is her wedding dress."

She walked through an adjoining door into the small dressing room. In the center was a mannequin in a black strapless ballgown with a floor-length tulle skirt. The lace lingerie-look, boned bodice was all glittering sequins, black embroidered hearts and—I looked closer—appliques in the shape of bats.

I met Ruthie's eye and we burst out laughing.

"To each his own," she said.

I gathered used towels in the bath as Ruthie folded a salmon-colored sweater left on the end of the bed. She put it on a shelf in the walk-in closet with a rainbow assortment of dozens of other sweaters, each stack of sweaters in a different hue.

"Diantha says she's always wanted a Halloween wedding and she's been too busy getting permits for the new restaurant to do much planning," Ruthie said. "She'll do the photo op at Town Hall later."

"Aren't you supposed to get the marriage license first?" I asked.

Ruthie shrugged. "All she cares about is the ceremony tomorrow and the photos." She gave me a look that blended bemusement, affection, and pride. "They've been in Hollywood too long. It's all show business with that family."

Just as we were turning off the lights, I noticed that a pillow was missing from Diantha's bed. Ruthie followed my gaze. "I put it in her Little Room downstairs. She always uses the same pillow."

We moved on to the next suite. As I turned down the

bed, Ruthie set the elaborate skull-shaped chocolates on each pillow and regaled me with stories about the show-biz guests who had stayed at the Inn. "Oh, I've had fun working here."

"How long have you worked here, Ruthie?"

She waved her hand. "Forever, it seems. I picked up extra money helping with banquets and such while I taught school. I kept it up after my husband died and my granddaughter Lucretia came to live with me." She avoided my eyes and fluffed a pillow with such concentration I could tell Lucretia was a sore subject. "And when I retired from teaching, what would I do? Sit at home and watch the soaps when I can see the stars in person here?"

Each suite retained the bones of the colonial structure—wooden plank floors, sloping ceilings, floral wallpaper in the Inn's signature blue—but the updated bathrooms were luxurious, the bedding fluffy soft duvets in silk and satin. Each room was named for a plant native to the state and each room was also sloppier than the next. Ruthie was a whirlwind as she replaced used towels, wiped spills, and hung clothing in closets.

In the Oak suite, I recognized the parka Cooper Collins had worn. I hung it in the closet, noting a carry-on bag in soft black leather next to a battered leather duffel and huge black suitcase. A laptop and paper script on the desk caught my eye: *"Bound for Love."*

His room had a connecting door to the adjoining suite and the deadbolt was open.

In the next room, Laurel, I flipped the tag on pink luggage. *"If found please return to J. Ford."* I checked the connecting door to Cooper's room. The bolt was closed.

"Beautiful girl. Saw her in one of Skylark's shows," Ruthie said as she bent to empty a wastebasket. "Which one was it? *Holiday in the Hamptons*? *Bakeshop on Peach Tree Lane*?"

Though Jenira had left several glittering pieces of jewelry on her dressing table, what stirred envy in me were the airport tags on her suitcase. I recognized a tag from Rome's FCO Leonardo da Vinci–Fiumicino airport. How I longed to take that gelato-making class in Rome, but too many bad memories made me hesitate.

Ruthie smoothed the bed one more time and admired her work with satisfaction as I put the colorful chocolates on Jenira's pillow.

"These suites are beautiful," I sighed.

"When Diantha had some fancy designers make over the Inn several years ago, she spared no expense. Her husband—I think it was number three? Darius?—left her some money and she used it to move the Inn into a different realm with more luxury, less history." She rubbed her fingers together. "It's been making money hand over fist ever since."

Ruthie showed me the upstairs housekeeping closet where she stowed her cart, cleaning supplies, and linens.

"What about this wing?" I gestured to a hallway labeled NORTH WING.

"I almost forgot. Chip's by himself down there." I followed her past several closed doors to the end of the hallway.

"He's the only one in this wing?" I said as we entered the last room before the Exit door to the stairs. An engraved brass plaque on the door read ELDERBERRY.

Ruthie nodded. "Yes. Chip likes to be somewhere quiet, to do his writing." While the other suites had been messy, the director's room required little more than a turndown and a change of towels. A laptop on the desk and one rinsed glass by the bathroom sink were the only signs of occupation.

"A dream guest," Ruthie laughed, then stowed the cart and went downstairs into the lobby. Ignoring the hubbub of the party, I noticed decorative, old-fashioned skeleton keys on blue ribbons hanging on a plaque behind the reception desk where Rob spoke on the phone. Over each was a number inscribed on a brass plate. The hook under the number One was empty.

"A key's missing," I said to Ruthie.

"Diantha's. It's our old-fashioned security system. Did you notice that most rooms are named for a native tree or flower? We have so few rooms we know which room corresponds to each of these numbers. Number One's the Little Room, Diantha's second-floor bedroom," Ruthie explained. "She probably has it. Only family in the building this week, so nothing to worry about."

Rob hung up the phone and heaved a sigh. "The Inn's answering machine says we're not taking guests this week, but still folks try." He forced a smile and returned to the lounge.

"I'll take you to your room," Ruthie said. "It's not one of the renovated ones, but it's still pretty special."

I retrieved my bag from the kitchen and followed Ruthie up the service stairs to the second floor. She paused briefly to pick up trash from a discreet trash basket at the spot where the hallway turned down the north wing. At the end of the hall was a stairwell labeled EXIT. One door led off the hallway to the right, two to the left.

"We're using only three rooms down here. On the right is Sam and Emilia's room." There was a Do Not Disturb tag on the doorknob, and Ruthie held a finger to her lips. "They didn't know if they'd make it back in time for the wedding, but they were able to book a last-minute flight from Africa. It's a nice room, redone.

Emilia asked for it because it's where they spent their honeymoon. Good thing, because by the time they arrived, Cooper and Chip had commandeered one of the suites for an office and we needed one for gifts. Other people would've kicked about not getting one of the fancy third-floor suites, but Emilia's not like that."

"You're not staying here?" I whispered.

Ruthie shook her head. "I live right behind the Inn. Remember the Collins Homestead? Diantha rents it to me. Gotta take care of Sergio, Engelbert, and Tom Jones."

At my quizzical look she said, "My pups. See you tomorrow in the kitchen at eight?" Ruthie said as she turned the key in the lock under a brass plate that read SPEEDWELL. "This group won't be up early with all the partying going on. I bring Diantha her coffee and newspaper at eight fifteen." She pointed at the door next to mine, where a brass plaque over the knob read LITTLE ROOM.

"See you tomorrow." I returned her smile and closed the door, noting the old-fashioned lock. I could probably pick this lock with a safety pin, but I wasn't concerned. The only other inhabitants were a very drunk wedding party, a disappointed-in-love hotel manager, and, if the stories were true, a few colonial ghosts.

After seeing the luxurious renovated suites upstairs, my room was a shock. The cramped, low-ceilinged room barely had space for the bed and nightstand but as I turned, taking in the Cinderella quarters, I felt myself fall under its spell. This room would be prized by a history buff who wanted to go back in time.

The wooden floor was original, uneven, covered with a thick rag rug. The narrow twin bed was unusually tall, like many in colonial homes, and there was a little footstool to make getting into it easier. I climbed up and sank into luxuriously deep, soft down bedding, which was topped with a pieced quilt in soft faded colors. An old-fashioned bedwarmer, a flat metal pan on a long wooden dowel that would be filled with warming coals and slid between the sheets to warm the bed on cold nights, leaned on the hearth of a narrow fireplace.

A sampler hanging over the fireplace exhorted, "Silence makes a man's heart glad."

The room was spartan, but the bedding was soft and comfortable, so comfortable that I knew if I lingered a moment longer, I'd surrender to it and fall asleep without brushing my teeth.

After readying for bed in the miniscule but beautifully updated bathroom, I pulled back the thick drape covering the window. My view overlooked the parking lot, and I could see down into a very un-colonial dumpster filled with construction debris situated directly under the window of Diantha's adjoining Little Room. Like the dumpster closer to the kitchen entrance, it was enclosed by white stockade fencing.

A flare of light drew my eye. Rob Wainwright smoked a cigarette outside the carriage house, his face illuminated in the strike of a match. Movement near the parking lot entrance made me press my cheek against the frigid window glass to see better, and I saw Rob's head swivel too. Someone in a hooded cape moved out of sight behind a box truck. I shivered. From the cold or the spooky sight, I wasn't sure.

From my room, the music from the party was barely audible. Footsteps thudded overhead and a door slammed deep in the hotel, but it was a soft squeak of floorboards close by that made the hair on the back of my neck rise. I jumped into the bed and pulled the covers up to my chin.

Just in case the Inn was haunted, I wished the spirits

good night, then reminded myself that in any old building, there would be creaky wooden floorboards. In a motion born of a longtime habit, I stretched out my arm to reach for Rocky, then remembered he was at home with Sprinkles. With a flash of satisfaction, I wondered how long it would take Sprinkles to get herself kicked off the movie set. Then I wondered uneasily how Caroline and Jack were managing. Caroline had fallen hard for Jack as soon as she'd met him, and he seemed equally taken with her. They'd successfully passed the going-away-for-a-weekend test.

I turned over and then turned back. Despite my reassuring words earlier, I realized that Caroline was right—Jack hadn't been around much. I reminded myself that he was busy, especially with the film crew here. Things would get back to normal. I hoped so. I didn't want Caroline to get hurt. I let my mind drift and my body melt into the irresistibly soft mattress.

I didn't know how much time had passed when my eyes flew open to unwelcome and complete wakefulness, and I tried to make sense of what had woken me. A clattering sound. I squinted at my phone. 3:00. I heard it again. What was that noise? Had an animal gotten into the dumpster? Had someone fallen? Who would be up this hour, especially after all the drinking at the party?

A breath of cold air rippled the drapes, and I got up to make sure the window was closed. It was, but icy air slid in around the ill-fitted wooden frame. As I tugged the drape I saw a form cross the parking lot. It cut through a spill of light from a lamppost, a white flash and a stream of black fabric. A white hat? A mobcap. It was a woman with a mobcap cutting behind the carriage house. Was I seeing things? I rubbed my eyes, but she was gone. Had I seen a ghost?

I shivered, from the cold floor, the draft, or the specter I'd seen, and jumped back into the bed. How fun if I did see a ghost! I laughed at myself as I pulled the covers over my head. As I snuggled deeper into the warm sheets, I wondered who she was and where she was going. Sleep pulled me into the dark, and as I relaxed the phrase "I'll tell your son" slipped through my mind like a whisper. What secret was Rob threatening to expose?

Chapter 5

SUNDAY, Halloween

The next morning, I followed the enticing aroma of brewing coffee to the Inn's kitchen. Marley Wagner gave me a curt nod that let me know he was wasn't pleased about my presence. I'd forgotten that Marley was working on the wedding luncheon, but after Mary Anne's emotional revelations yesterday I realized the decision was for the best.

"Check on the cake?" Marley said.

Good morning to you too, I thought, and headed to the walk-in freezer. As I stepped inside, my shoes made a crunching noise. Puzzled, I glanced down on a sprinkling of white crystals. "What on earth?" I stopped short. There was a spilled box of salt under the metal shelving, and crystals shimmered on the side of the plastic box that held the cake. My heart hammered with foreboding.

"What is it?" Marley said as he joined me. I took the cake off the shelf with trembling hands. The cover was askew and white crystals spilled as I put the box on the worktable. Marley and I made eye contact as I removed the lid, and my heart fell when I saw the mess inside. A butcher knife stood upright in the cake, the blade embedded in colorful layers of pumpkin spice, fudge swirl, and black chai latte ice cream. The cake had been coated with salt and stabbed into pieces. Marley swiped the crystals that had fallen to the table with a finger, tasted them, and swore.

"Coated with salt," he fumed. "Didn't the Romans salt their foe's fields?"

My stomach lurched as I met Marley's eyes.

"You can fix this," he said. It wasn't a question. He whirled into the freezer with a broom.

"I'll try," I whispered. I glanced at the clock and tore into the pantry—the Inn had an ice-cream chiller and pans I could use to recreate the cake. I'd have just enough time.

As I began to gather my supplies, my hands shook. Chai tea. Sugar. Madagascar vanilla. Cinnamon. "Do you have activated charcoal?" I called. "Diantha wanted a black layer. I don't have time to get back to the shop—"

Marley took a bottle of activated charcoal off a shelf and handed it to me.

"I can't believe you have this," I said.

"When your boss does experimental cuisine"—Marley shrugged—"you have to keep your pantry stocked with unusual ingredients."

I took a deep, steadying breath and opened a carton of heavy cream. *Who could've done this to the cake?*

"Hell hath no fury like a woman scorned," Marley muttered as he wiped salt from the worktable. It was clear he thought Mary Anne had ruined the cake. I pressed my lips together and concentrated on measuring the cream, but unbidden and unwelcome thoughts rose in my mind. *Mary Anne had been upset. Her divorce had been finalized just this spring. Dominic's relationship with Diantha must've begun while he was still married to Mary Anne. . . .*

As Marley reached past me to grab a box of nitrile gloves, I noticed a scarlet burn on his thumb.

"Is your hand okay?" I asked, grateful to turn the conversation away from Mary Anne.

He slid a glove over the angry-looking burn. "Occupational hazard."

I heard a muffled scream, then a woman's shout. "Help!" I recognized Ruthie's voice.

"What now?" Marley groused.

Ruthie banged through the kitchen door, her eyes wild, her chest heaving. I ran to her. "Ruthie, what is it?"

"Come quick!" Ruthie grabbed my arm and pulled me upstairs to the second floor where the door of the room next to mine stood open. Marley followed close behind us.

Ruthie stopped at the entrance to the Little Room and pointed a trembling finger. Behind me, Marley gasped.

Dust motes danced in the shaft of pale morning light that illuminated Diantha Collins on the narrow bed. She lay on her side, still dressed in her Halloween costume, an incongruous sight in the narrow colonial-style chamber. Her hands were contorted like claws on the silky blue duvet.

I rushed to Diantha's side and felt for a pulse, but it was evident she was dead. Her black snood had been pulled aside and tendrils of her honey gold hair spilled over her forehead. Her eyes, still ringed with mascara, were open, her mouth stretched in an awful rictus. The harsh morning light revealed a crosshatch of fine wrinkles in gray skin, but the cheek that rested on the pillow had turned a purplish color. One hand clenched a room key that was looped around her wrist on a silky blue ribbon.

"She was cold when I checked her," Ruthie whispered. "Should I call nine-one-one?"

"Yes."

She pulled her phone from the pocket of her smock and dialed. "I'm calling from the Inn on the Green . . ."

Ruthie's voice faded as I stepped back from the bed, bumping into Marley as he squeezed behind us toward the window.

His hand gripped the sill as he gulped deep breaths of the fresh air that streamed in through the open window. In keeping with the colonial décor, the window was not screened, and Marley's breath puffed in the cold air.

"You're sure she's . . . dead?" he whispered. "Should I close the window?"

I shook my head. "Don't touch anything." Through the shock, I remembered that this was Diantha's wedding day. What a terrible blow for Dominic and the family.

Ruthie started to sob softly and her voice faltered. To my surprise, Marley took the phone from her hand, taking over the call to emergency services. He put an arm around Ruthie's quaking shoulders and led her out of the room.

I started to follow them, but stopped. There was no blood, no sign of injury, but there was something off here, something that made me turn back to the room.

First of all, why did Diantha stay here when she had the most luxurious suite in the Inn?

Trying to ignore Diantha's body, I noted the tray Ruthie had left on the bed at Diantha's feet, the coffeepot and cup undisturbed, a newspaper folded to the crossword page. The only other furniture was a nightstand next to the bed, with just enough surface space for a candlestick lamp and Diantha's phone. The screen was blank and I knew better than to touch it.

I peered into the bathroom. Unlike the one in my

room, Diantha's had a claw-foot tub instead of an updated shower. The tub was empty and only one bath towel hung on the bar, instead of two as there had been in my bath. I scanned the floor, but didn't see it. The hand towel by the sink was unused, the toothbrush was in its holder, and the makeup bag was zipped up. I pulled aside the floral-patterned sink skirt and saw not a speck of dust on the gleaming wood floor. Back in the little bedroom, I opened the door of a tiny closet revealing a spa robe, a silky blue nightgown, and slippers. Diantha hadn't had time to change or even go into the bathroom to begin her nightly routine before she died.

I checked the floor. No towel. Had Ruthie forgotten to put two on the bar?

The sound of emergency vehicles in the distance made me quicken my search, but there was hardly anything in the closet-sized room. I looked under the bed—nothing. As in my room, a sampler hung on the wall above the fireplace, but this one read "In prosperity friends will be plenty, but in adversity not one in twenty."

On the fireplace mantel was a small jack-o'-lantern carved with the images of a skeleton bride and groom. Stepping closer, I noted a little cat carved on the side along with LPP and remembered the girl from the town green. Lucretia's Perfect Pumpkins.

A gust of cold air stirred the drape, and I hurried out of the room.

Chapter 6

A police officer herded Marley, Ruthie, and me to a scrubbed wooden table in an alcove near the kitchen's service entrance. He asked us basic questions—name, address, contact information—then added, "It's all just a formality," his way of trying to calm us. I figured he wasn't from Penniman when I told him I worked at Udderly and he didn't comment. When I say I work at Udderly, most locals reply by announcing their favorite ice-cream flavor.

"Please wait here. We may need to ask you more questions." He flipped his notebook closed and left the room. He must be new, I thought. I'd never leave suspects—because that's what we were—in close proximity not only to an exit door but also cleavers and butcher's knives. I also remembered Ruthie's comment that our maid uniforms rendered us invisible; perhaps they rendered us harmless in people's estimation as well.

I scanned the alcove: hooks on the wall held jackets, and shelves were stacked with crockery and less frequently used cookware like Bundt pans and earthenware tagines. Marley surprised me when he set cups of tea in front of me and Ruthie. He went back into the kitchen, gathering vegetables and herbs from the refrigerator, and I realized he was going through the rest of the prep work for the luncheon. I respected his dedication to duty and envied that he could put his nervous energy to work. No matter the circumstances, there was a family in residence that would need sustenance.

His knife hammered the wooden cutting board as Ruthie sipped her tea and color returned to her pale cheeks. She sniffled into an old-fashioned lace handkerchief, then put her cell on the table and sent a text. I could see the message on the screen as it buzzed with a reply. IT'S 9 AM. I'M STILL IN BED.

Ruthie followed my gaze. "Checking on my granddaughter, Lucretia. I didn't tell her about Diantha. I wanted to make sure she's okay."

"I understand." *Lucretia*. "The girl who carves the pumpkins?"

Ruthie nodded.

I shifted in the chair, thinking with unease about the pumpkin in Diantha's room. That didn't mean Lucretia killed Diantha. Is that why Ruthie texted her? I took a breath. Ridiculous. *Calm down, Riley.* Halloween-mad Diantha bought a nice pumpkin, that was all. It made sense to check on a loved one when something traumatic happened, right?

"Did Lucretia carve a pumpkin for Diantha?" I asked.

Ruthie shrugged, but a smile lifted the ends of her thin, pale lips. "My granddaughter's an artist. She can carve a pumpkin to order in five minutes."

"I saw her at the festival on the green. She's talented." My words felt stilted as the sound of emergency vehicles seeped into our cozy nook.

"What do you think happened to Diantha?" I asked.

Ruthie dabbed her eyes and shrugged. "Heart attack?

Maybe a stroke? I didn't see any blood. She wasn't old, sixty, and Dominic is forty-nine if you're wondering."

I had wondered. I knew Mary Anne was ten years younger than her former husband.

Ruthie continued. "But Diantha had COPD and some heart issues. She never told anyone about that, but I knew. She used to be a smoker, but she gave it up and even took up jogging." Ruthie's eyes welled. "She was so happy about marrying Dominic . . ."

I patted her hand, trying to untangle the shock of finding Diantha's body from my own growing sense of unease. Tillie's bulldog face materialized in my mind. I'd have to wait like everyone else for facts from the forensic report, and then hope that the loosest lips in Penniman would be willing to spill details with me. I hoped she'd be free on my day off.

"Why was Diantha in that tiny room?" I remembered Diantha's massive, luxurious suite. "It was barely as big as a closet."

A tender look softened Ruthie's face. "Diantha loved the Little Room, that's what she named it. When she was a girl and her family ran the Inn full time, they lived in the apartment over the carriage house. Those small, historic rooms on the second floor were rented out if needed, but if they weren't, she loved staying in them, pretending that she was a girl in colonial times. Yes, it's tiny and hasn't been redone, but she liked it that way. That's how I could tell she was serious about a guy. She only showed that room to men she was serious about."

I recalled the single towel on the bar in Diantha's bath. I felt silly asking but said, "Weren't there supposed to be two towels in her bathroom? I only saw one."

Ruthie frowned. "There are always two."

A missing towel . . . such a small thing. Why did it make me feel so uneasy?

The creaking sound of footsteps on antique floorboards made us lift our eyes to the ceiling. The sound of sirens and the arrival of police and EMTs must be the most awful wake-up call for the guests at the Inn.

The back door flew open and Rob Wainwright dashed inside, his bloodshot eyes wide as he shrugged his broad shoulders into his blazer. "What's going on?"

Chapter 7

As Ruthie and I broke the news of Diantha's death, Rob dropped into the chair Marley had vacated. Instead of turning pale, Rob's face grew ruddier, and his breath came in short, violent gasps. Worry creased Ruthie's forehead as she clasped his hand in both of hers.

"Rob, are you okay?"

He jerked his arm away and leapt to his feet so quickly he knocked his chair over. "Sorry, Ruthie, sorry," he muttered then stormed out the door.

I straightened the chair and caught Ruthie's wide eyes. Rob's extreme reaction shocked both of us.

"I'll get you some more tea," I said.

"No." She rose and straightened her smock. "I can't sit still. Oh, the boys must've had a terrible shock, and poor Dominic . . ."

"He's not here, is he?"

"No, he went back to his place last night. The boys told him it's bad luck to see the bride before the wedding. He has a cottage on Penniman Lake." Ruthie wrung her hands "I wonder who's going to break the news to him?"

He'd be questioned by the police, I thought. Of course

Diantha's death could be natural, but the police would do their due diligence. Most murder victims were intimates of their killers. I wouldn't mention that. Instead, I remembered Ruthie's comment about our uniforms making us invisible. Perhaps we could learn more while we took care of the people staying in the Inn.

A murmur of voices from the lounge traveled down the back hallway. "Let's bring some coffee and tea to the family," I said, heading to the coffeemaker.

"Yes, and something to eat." Color returned to her face as Ruthie gathered cups and two trays.

"I'll ask the officer if it's okay." I poured a mug of the fragrant brew, passed through the dining room, and caught sight of the officer who'd questioned us standing in the hall scrolling on his cell phone. I handed him the mug. He seemed surprised but nodded thanks.

"We're going to bring some coffee to the family." I didn't exactly form the request as a question.

He took a sip and jutted his chin toward the lounge. "Guess that's all right. They're gathering in that room by the bar."

"Thank you, officer."

I returned to the kitchen. Marley set some delectable miniature coffee cakes, pastries, and quiches onto one tray and handed it to Ruthie. I took the heavier coffee and tea service and followed Ruthie out of the kitchen, through the back hallway.

The lounge was paneled in dark oak, clubby and snug with a long mahogany bar running along one wall and plush armchairs arranged around low coffee tables. The windows overlooked a small patio walled off from the back parking lot with potted arbor vitae and white lattice panels.

Cooper and Sam huddled together on a leather settee,

Cooper in trim jeans and an untucked blue button-down shirt, Sam in sweat pants and a faded olive green hoodie. He wore the hood up and jammed his hands into its kangaroo pocket. Both looked bleary and shocked. Ruthie set her tray on a low table, and they rose and embraced her. I remembered that she'd worked at the Inn for years and my heart tugged as I realized she'd seen the men grow up.

I almost missed a woman huddled deep in a wingback chair, her knees pulled up and hidden in the folds of a white floor-length terrycloth spa robe. Her thin ash blonde hair was held back from her high forehead by a drugstore clip. This must be Sam's wife, Emilia, the one who'd begged off the party due to jet lag. She looked more than tired; her skin had a grayish cast and was pulled taut on the jutting cheekbones of her mild, narrow face. Her eyes were so heavy lidded that I wondered if she was ill.

I offered her a mug of coffee and she looked up with a warm smile, her eyes a surprisingly lovely emerald green. "Oh no, I can't drink coffee. Is there any tea?"

"I'll get you some." I poured a cup of tea and she took it, wrapping her fingers around the cup, savoring its warmth.

"Thank you."

Chip sat at the bar, leaning his head on his hand as he scrolled on his phone.

I poured a cup of coffee and brought it to him. "Coffee?"

He looked up with a rueful grin as he took the cup. "Thanks, but I'd rather a good stiff whiskey. I guess no one will complain if I make that happen." He gave me a conspiratorial look and reached across the bar to a bottle of Scotch that had been left on the counter and added a generous pour to his cup. He jabbed a finger at me. "Mr. Rhodes' daughter. You were at the bookshop. I thought you ran an ice-cream parlor?"

"Yes, I'm Riley." I nodded toward Ruthie. "Ruthie asked for some help when some staff"—I hesitated— "couldn't be here."

Chip chuckled. "Don't worry, everybody knows Jenira got those girls sacked. All in a day's work for America's sweetheart. Speak of the devil."

Jenira, escorted by an officer, paused in the doorway. A striking brunette from Puerto Rico, her huge brown eyes, softly rounded cheekbones, and sweet turned-up nose had made her the go-to actress for Skylark. Dressed in silver running tights and a matching top and jacket, she put her hands on her hips and scanned the room. "Will someone tell me what the hell's going on?"

Cooper jumped to his feet and took Jenira's hand. "It's Diantha. She's gone. She died in her sleep." *In her sleep?* We didn't really know anything about Diantha's death yet. I looked to Ruthie and she lowered her eyes to the floor. Kind-hearted Ruthie must've said that to soften the news.

Jenira blinked rapidly, her long lashes fluttering, her glossy red full lips forming an O. She'd done her makeup before running. "Oh no, that's awful! What happened?"

"We all just learned the news." Sam lay back on the thick couch cushions and stretched his long legs out on the antique coffee table. "I was out for a jog, Emilia was asleep. When I got back there were cop cars all over. Ruthie found Mom."

Everyone turned to Ruthie. She paled and her hand flew to her throat. "She was in bed when I brought her breakfast tray," Ruthie said slowly, choosing her words. "She looked . . . peaceful."

Hardly. Ruthie kept trying to soften the blow for

Cooper and Sam. She excused herself and the two men hugged her again before she left the room. I followed her out of the room and lingered outside the doorway, stacking and restacking glasses on a bus tray. I wanted to hear what else the family said.

Sam resumed his seat, his body relaxed, while Cooper rubbed his forehead and paced.

"Then why are there so many cop cars here?" Jenira said. "And fire engines?"

"When you call nine-one-one you get everything," Chip tipped more Scotch into his mug. "When there's an unattended death, the police have to check it out."

"Unattended?" Jenira said.

"It means she didn't die in the hospital or under a doctor's care," Chip said. "And I only know that because it was in a script for an episode of *Atlanta 911* I did a few years back." He turned to Cooper. "Was she under a doctor's care?"

Cooper cradled a cup of coffee and didn't look up as he shook his head. "No idea. Dominic would know."

"What about Dominic?" Emilia said in a quiet voice as she set down her tea cup. "Poor guy, this is such dreadful news."

Chip's gaze shifted to me, so I hefted the tray and headed toward the kitchen. As I did, I realized that I hadn't seen anyone shed a tear for Diantha.

Chapter 8

Back in the kitchen, Ruthie slid into a kitchen chair and lay her head on her arms with a groan. Marley looked up from the cutting board in alarm. I set down my tray and hurried to the cop at the door.

"Mrs. Adams should go home," I said. "She's been through a lot this morning."

"Let me talk to the boss." He stepped aside and spoke into his mic. "Chief told me to take her home. He asked you to wait."

Ruthie demurred when the cop came into the kitchen and said he was taking her home.

"Chief's orders, ma'am."

A broad-shouldered officer with a beard and striking gray-blue eyes entered the kitchen. His tall frame made the doorway look too small and he brought with him an air of quiet authority that made the cop talking to Ruthie straighten his spine.

Ruthie folded her arms and leveled a look at the newcomer. "Jack Voelker, I can walk to my own house."

Jack smiled, but didn't waver. "I'll be over to talk with you in a bit, Ruthie."

Ruthie rolled her eyes, but hung her blue housekeeping

smock on a peg and donned a well-worn navy wool pea-coat. We embraced. and she left with the cop through the service door.

"Miss Rhodes." Jack escorted me into the quiet nook off the kitchen.

When we were seated, he said in a low voice, "Well, if it isn't Penniman's own Sherlock Holmes."

Under different circumstances I would've laughed, but emotional exhaustion was starting to replace the adrenaline shock of finding Diantha's body. "Ruthie needed help and asked me to stay overnight, cleaning rooms and then helping with service today. I made a cake for the wedding." Which was now covered with salt and completely wrecked.

Marley brought over a cup of coffee and set it in front of Jack. He looked down his nose at me and said tartly, "Did you tell him what Mary Anne Dumas did to the wedding cake?"

"I, we, don't know for sure it was Mary Anne," I stammered. *Why was Marley so sure?*

Jack's brow wrinkled. "What happened to the cake?"

Marley waved Jack to the walk-in freezer and cut his eyes at me. "I preserved the evidence."

As befits a chief of police, Jack's expression was always hard to read, but the destruction of the cake was so over the top I saw a flicker of surprise on his normally composed face.

I wheeled on Marley. "I thought you tossed the cake in the trash."

A smug smile curled Marley's thin lips. "Oh no, I wanted to bring this to Dominic's attention, and to the police of course. It's beyond unprofessional, maybe even criminal."

Little weasel. He wanted to use this to curry favor with Dominic.

I took a deep breath to steady myself and suppress the urge to punch Marley in his pinched little mouth.

Jack stepped out of the freezer, the movement of his muscular frame driving Marley back on his heels.

"Wait," Marley said as he trailed Jack, "you're going to arrest her, right? Destruction of property, right?"

"If it's your property, you can make a complaint. This isn't the time." Jack gave him a level look that said, *Dismissed.* Marley folded his arms but returned to his cutting board while Jack and I resumed out seats at the table.

"Besides, we don't know for certain if Mary Anne—" I began.

Jack flipped open a notebook and clicked a pen branded Penniman Police Services. "Save the cake story for later. Tell me what happened when you found Diantha Collins this morning."

I took a deep breath and told Jack everything as I mentally walked through the discovery of Diantha's body. "There have been a few odd things. Rob Wainwright came in a short while ago." I nodded toward the back door. "He was awfully upset. I think you should talk to him. He has an apartment over the carriage house."

Jack flipped his notebook closed and put it in his shirt pocket. "I intend to." He got up, avoiding my eyes. "You can go."

"Okay," I said. "See you at the farm."

Jack scratched the back of his neck. "Yeah, well, this situation's going to be taking up a lot of time. Tell Caroline I'm sorry but I'll be busy, okay?" He left without making eye contact.

What was that about?

I hung up my smock and put on my parka as I walked past Marley, who stood at the stove stirring a deliciously fragrant stew. I might not like him, but the guy could cook.

Marley stopped mid-stir and called after me, "Wait a minute! You can't leave me alone with all these people to take care of. Rob's disappeared! Ruthie's gone! The help was fired! How can I be expected to cook under these conditions and no—"

"I have my own business to run," I said. Marley's whine set my teeth on edge.

"Serving help" he continued. "And—" The back door opened and a slender young woman entered. Her black hair had blond roots and ends dip dyed orange. Her eyes were heavily rimmed with black eyeliner, making her ghostly pale skin seem paler. A tiny gold ring gleamed in her nose. I searched my memory—I'd seen her the night before, carving pumpkins. Lucretia Adams, Ruthie's granddaughter.

She hung up a jean jacket embellished with embroidered red and black roses and colorful patches, then gave us an insolent look. "What? My grandma sent me to take down the wedding decorations in the dining room. She said it would be cruel to leave them up." Her narrow shoulders slumped. "And then I'm supposed to go clean the rooms." She heaved a dramatic "they don't pay me enough" sigh and frowned with distaste as she pinched Ruthie's blue smock from the hook.

Marley gawped at the girl. "Will Ruthie be back tomorrow?"

The girl shrugged as she put on the smock. "Dunno. I guess. I have school."

"Good enough," Marley said. "Now I can concentrate on cooking."

I gave the officer at the door a nod and ran down the front steps of the Inn, filling my lungs with fresh, crisp air. Church bells rang as the eleven a.m. Sunday service let out at the Congregational church and the curious faithful strolled across the green to gawk at all the emergency vehicles.

I was halfway to The Penniless Reader when I remembered that I'd parked Sadie behind the Inn. Discovering Diantha's body had upset me more than I'd realized. By instinct, my footsteps carried me to the shop where Dad was turning the sign on the door to OPEN.

He held the door wide. "What brings you here this morning, Riley?"

My words tumbled out. Dad wrapped his arms around me, led me to one of the chairs by the fireplace, and brewed a cup of my favorite Yorkshire black tea. I sipped the aromatic treat, letting the warm liquid soothe me as I sank into the comfort of the overstuffed chair.

"I heard the emergency vehicles," Dad said. "Poor woman, such an awful thing to happen on her wedding day. Dominic must be a wreck. Her kids must be a wreck."

Not really, I thought. Out loud I said, "Rob Wainwright took it hardest."

Dad's eyebrows flew up. "Well, he's always carried a torch for Diantha, ever since they were in high school."

The sound of the little bell over the door jangling as a customer entered prompted me to look at my watch.

I'd been so relaxed, I'd completely forgotten that I had to get to Udderly for my afternoon shift. I put down my mug and stood. "Sorry I have to run, Dad, see you tomorrow night."

Dad kissed my cheek. "With bells on."

All was quiet behind the Inn as I got in Sadie and took off. I threw a glance at the darkened windows of Rob's apartment as I wondered about his outburst—obviously he still had strong feelings for Diantha.

As I drove away from the green and turned onto

the road that led to Udderly, the shock and horror of finding Diantha's body fell away like the autumn leaves stirred by my tires. The unreality of finding a woman dressed as an evil queen in a tiny colonial bedroom, the Inn decorated with skeletons, the symbols of death she'd found so charming. All that remained was a feeling that I'd seen something important, something that was just out of reach.

Chapter 9

My tires rattled over the wooden planks of Peniman's red covered bridge onto curving Fairweather Road, a scenic two-mile stretch bordered by stone walls constructed hundreds of years earlier by the town's hardy founders.

I turned onto Farm Lane and then took a quick right into the parking lot of the Udderly Delicious Ice Cream Shop. The sight of the rustic building, painted purple with window boxes crowded with mums and marigolds, usually raised my spirits, but now I felt unsettled and impatient to know what happened to Diantha Collins.

A sturdy woman with pewter curls woven into a waist-length braid pushed open the shop's back door. She was dressed in the colors of fall: swirling orange paisley skirt, gold turtleneck, and a forest green sweater.

"Hi, Pru."

Prudence Brightwood and her husband, Darwin, ran Fairweather Farms, which comprised the rolling acres across Farm Lane from Udderly and the small Victorian farmhouse I shared with Caroline. Pru was a midwife, and when she wasn't caring for her patients or the farmhands who were part of the international organic farming program she and Darwin ran, she worked at the shop. I don't know when the woman slept.

"Riley." She rushed up to me and put a warm hand on my shoulder. "Diantha Collins died? You found the body?"

Penniman's gossip network had already begun to spread the news.

I filled her in as we went into Udderly's kitchen and she clucked with sympathy as she resumed stirring a bowl of pumpkin puree.

"It was awful, and I have a feeling . . ." My voice trailed off as I tied an apron around my waist.

Pru gave me a wry look as she finished my sentence. She knew about my earlier investigative exploits. "A feeling that there's something not quite right about Diantha's death."

"But, sometimes vibrant women die the night before their wedding," I said. "So what's going on here?"

She took a pan of brownies from the oven and set it to cool on the immaculate stainless-steel countertop by the shop's binder of recipes we all referred to as the *Book of Spells*.

"We have our own mystery." Pru led me to the freezer, opened the door, and pointed to two deep pans on the shelf where we kept test recipes. "Look." A lumpy white mixture filled one pan, and an ice cream in blotches of purple and blue the other.

"I closed last night and these weren't here then," she said.

I grabbed a tasting spoon and scooped a bit of the lumpy white ice cream.

"Don't eat it!" Pru exclaimed. "It might be some mischief-night prank."

"You're right." I focused on the curl of the mystery mixture on my spoon, then examined the purple and blue concoction. "The consistency's off. These are no-churn recipes." I'd experimented with some quick and easy recipes that didn't need to be made in an ice-cream chiller and could be whipped up with a hand mixer. The technique sacrificed the creamy texture of regular ice cream, but no-churn was fast, convenient, and could be delicious.

I closed the freezer door and said, "You're sure one of the interns didn't make these?" Sometimes the interns from the farm worked in the shop to earn extra cash.

Pru shook her head. "We were too busy last night to do anything other than scoop ice cream."

"Who was here?"

"Flo, Gerri, Caroline, and some interns," Pru said. "I called the farmhouse and asked. The interns all say they didn't make them, and I didn't see any lights here last night."

I went to the door and examined the lock, saw no scratches, no sign of a forced entry.

"The front doors and windows look okay too," Pru said. "Nothing's missing. The cash box was undisturbed."

"You, Caroline, Flo, and Gerri have keys." I hesitated. "The only other person with a key is Brandon, and I saw him leading the band on the green last night."

Pru said, "And Brandon had the high school lock-in after that."

I stepped outside and scanned the doorway. The previous night had been dry and cold, so the ground was too hard for an intruder to leave footprints. I circled to the back of the building, where the sound of a sharp *miaow* made me look up. An all-black cat with the tip of his left ear missing looked down at me, his tail swaying with indignation.

"Hello to you too, Rocky," I said. Rocky was a barn

cat I'd rescued a few months earlier. Battered and emaciated by his early life in the fields, he now lived with me and Caroline in the farmhouse, where he was the unlikely friend of imperious Sprinkles. He turned tail and disappeared over the rooftop. I followed in his direction, stopping as he meowed again from the roof above the dumpster where cardboard boxes and milk crates were stacked in a pyramid that gave Rocky an easy-to-climb ladder. He jumped down and I scooped him up and gave him a cuddle, but he wasn't having it and went boneless, slipping from my arms onto the chilly ground.

"Punishing me, huh? I get it, I wasn't here last night. So sue me," I said.

He sniffed at the bottom box of a stack, pawed at it, then darted away.

"What is it?" Seeing nothing on the box, I circled to the rear of the pyramid and noticed that three cartons had been flattened and tucked behind the stack. I slid one out, then the others. Strips of masking tape clung to all of them. One was larger than the others, and one had a tiny black smear on the bottom. I looked closer. A fingerprint. I tucked that box under my arm.

I circled back to the kitchen door as I considered the exterior of the shop. Facing Pru's farmhouse were two windows: one in the kitchen door and one large window over the sink. I circled to the back of the building; one smaller window faced the farmhouse up the road where I lived. None of the windows had curtains.

Across the lane, I waved to Pru's husband, Darwin, as he drove a tractor pulling a pallet of purple, yellow, and garnet mums to the farm stand in front of their sprawling colonial saltbox house. I turned back to Udderly. Three windows faced the farmhouses. There were three flattened cardboard boxes.

Three window coverings. Two very unusual ice-cream flavors. One employee who had made a name for himself creating unusual ice-cream flavors—and had a key.

I went inside and ran my fingers around the windows, pausing at a spot where the tiniest bit of stickiness remained. Disappointment and disbelief mingled in me as I told Pru what I was thinking. "I don't think Brandon went to the lock-in last night."

Chapter 10

I tried to sort my feelings. I didn't know for sure that Brandon had broken into the shop to make ice cream last night, and how could I call it "broken in" when I'd given him a key? I'd get his side of the story. I intended to ask Brandon what he'd been up to on Halloween night, but how could I be upset at him? He was experimenting with flavors. That was nothing new, he'd made a name for himself by making flavors that appealed to those with adventurous tastes. But sneaking into the shop? Why, when I'd let him make ice cream whenever he wanted to? Maybe that was it. Maybe he thought he could come here *any time he wanted* to make ice cream. But covering the windows, that indicated something else—that he'd sneaked out of the lock-in.

Caroline joined us, hanging up her coat and donning an apron. "What's up?"

"Someone made batches of ice cream last night," I said.

Caroline's forehead wrinkled. "Really? It was so busy, we didn't have time . . . I'm sure I would've noticed."

"No, I mean after the shop closed." Pru and I walked

Caroline to the freezer and showed her the pans of ice cream.

Her eyes widened. "Looks like one of Brandon's experiments. You're sure these weren't here when you left?"

"Positive," Pru said. "We had a run on pumpkin spice ice cream and I had to run back here to get more. These pans weren't here."

I closed the freezer door, then held the flattened cardboard up to the window—it covered it. "I think these were used for curtains, to shield the lighted windows."

Caroline bent close to the cardboard and pointed. "Look! There's a fingerprint! It might not've been Brandon. Maybe someone else came in and—"

"Made ice cream?" I leaned a hip on the counter and lifted the cardboard. I held my fingertip up to the print, which was smaller than mine. An idea began to form.

"This print's narrow, delicate. Would you say Brandon has delicate little fingers?"

Pru scoffed. "He's getting bigger and taller every day." They scrutinized the print, tiny Caroline lifting her tortoiseshell glasses and putting her finger next to it. "Maybe it's a partial?"

"Listen to us, like we're CSI. Maybe he had company," I said.

Caroline's jaw dropped. "A party?"

Pru's eyebrows raised. "A girlfriend?"

I set the cardboard against the wall. "If Brandon wanted to make ice cream, I'd let him in any time."

Pru shook her head. "But having parties in here . . . you know how one kid tells another, then you have a hundred kids in one spot?"

The sound of cars pulling into the parking lot made Caroline and Pru hurry to the front of the shop. I checked the schedule on the clipboard by the sink. Brandon was working Wednesday after school. I'd talk to him then.

I ruminated on Brandon as I munched on an oversized brownie and gathered ingredients for a test batch of my new gingerbread ice cream. Managing any business came with so many challenges, especially for someone like me who'd jumped into the deep end of running an ice-cream shop with no prior business experience. I'd worked at Udderly through high school and loved creating new flavors with ingredients from the local organic dairy and farm, especially when I could experiment with recipes I'd discovered on my travels and had written about in my food blog, Rhode Food. I'd been a librarian at the CIA, so I had good organizational skills, but because I'd been a librarian at the CIA— with occasional undercover missions—I had other skills that didn't transfer as well.

My biggest professional blessing at the shop had been the staff. I'd known the hardworking Brightwoods since childhood. The Spooner family had started Udderly and Caroline was my best friend ever since Buzzy Spooner had fostered her as an eight-year-old. The Brightwoods, their artistic daughter Willow, Caroline, Flo and Gerri, and the whole Penniman community had rallied to keep the shop open after Buzzy's passing. Staff had never been an issue.

Until now. Brandon Terwilliger had been an enigma to me, a good-natured teenage drummer with a flair for making off-the-wall flavors that were a hit with the less-refined palates of Penniman's teens. But he was a hard worker, reliable, and against stereotype of teenage males, exceptionally good at cleanup. Maybe he simply didn't realize coming in overnight wasn't cool, even if he did cover the windows so the light wouldn't bother

Caroline, the Brightwoods, and me. That was the most
logical explanation. After I poured the gingerbread ice-
cream mixture into the chiller, my mind returned to the
tragedy at the Inn. Diantha's body loomed in my mind.

One thing my work at the ice-cream shop didn't feed
was my curiosity. Sleuthing did.

Udderly closed at six in the fall, and usually shut
down for the year the day after Halloween, but a change
in weather had brought a later start to leaf-peeping season. I'd decided to keep the shop open to take advantage
of the crowds coming to our quiet corner of Connecticut
to enjoy the colorful foliage, fairs, and festivals. After
cleanup, I trudged up the hill in the gathering dark,
doubting my decision and aching for dinner and a hot
bath.

A Halloween tableau of mums and glowing pumpkins
on the front porch cheered me as I climbed the farmhouse steps. Caroline and I had carved our own, mine
a very amateur traditional grinning jack-o'-lantern and
Caroline's a skillful portrait of our fluffy queen, Sprinkles, etched into the flesh of one of the biggest pumpkins
Fairweather Farms had ever grown.

A faint scurrying sound made me turn my head, but
it was dry leaves skittering on the lane. Rocky materialized from the shadows of the porch, and I opened the
door to let him enter ahead of me.

Caroline stood at the kitchen table pouring a bag
of miniature candy bars into a large wooden bowl. She
looked up in surprise. "You've got a date tonight, don't
you? Isn't Liam taking you to dinner?"

"Oh, no! I completely forgot!" I rushed upstairs and
threw myself into the shower, then dashed into my bedroom, grateful that I'd given thought to the date earlier
in the week and had an outfit ready. I tugged on a brown
faux-suede shirt dress and accessorized it with a wide

brown belt and a vintage Vera scarf in shades of green I'd picked up at London's famous Portobello Road flea market. I jammed my feet into ankle boots as I ran a brush through my hair.

My phone buzzed from the bed where I'd tossed it. Rocky sidled in and leapt up next to it, giving the phone a curious nudge.

Caller ID read Liam Pryce. "Hi, Liam."

"Riley, how are you?" His voice was one of his best attributes, warm and deep, with that slight Jamaican accent.

At the sound of his voice, I felt myself relax. "Fine. How are you?"

"Bereft. I'm so sorry, but I can't go to dinner tonight. I have an emergency here at the clinic. Ms. Dippel's corgi got into her sock drawer and we're afraid she's eaten some."

"Oh, that's awful." My heart dropped. "I understand completely."

"Rain check?" he said.

"Of course. I hope Coco's better soon. Bye." I hung up and sank onto the bed.

Coco was a frequent flyer at the clinic, always into something. Did corgis have nine lives like cats did? If so, Coco had already run through quite a few of hers.

Rocky jumped to the floor and brushed against my ankles. I sighed. "Time for a costume change."

I kicked off my boots, hung up my dress, and put the scarf on the hanger where I kept the collection I'd picked up on my travels. My foot brushed the backpack in the corner of the closet, unused since I'd come back to Penniman. Next to it was a pair of hiking boots, also gathering dust. Running a business didn't leave much time for other pursuits.

I slipped into sweatpants and an oversized Washington

Capitals sweatshirt, a souvenir of my time living in D.C. Well-worn fuzzy pink slippers completed my ensemble.

Sprinkles padded into the room, settled next to the floor-length mirror, and regarded her reflection. After giving herself a soft purr of approval, her gold eyes flicked to me and she strutted out of the room, her fluffy tail waving in disdain. I could read her mind: *Loser.* I swear she knew Liam had canceled our date.

I turned off the light and headed downstairs, carefully skirting Sprinkles, who sat at the top of the stairs. Generally this was the place she'd launch her attack, tripping me as I approached the top step, but tonight it was evident she didn't think I was worth the trouble.

Caroline, also in sweats, sat at the kitchen table with her Kindle and the wooden bowl of candy. She blinked. "Well, that outfit'll turn heads at the restaurant."

"Liam can't go. He has an emergency." I smiled ruefully. "Ms. Dippel's corgi."

Caroline gave me a sympathetic smile and extended the bowl of candy.

"How about you?" Instead of taking one I went to the refrigerator and looked in the freezer. Caroline knew that I liked frozen Milky Way bars and had stashed some here. I took one out and unwrapped it.

"Jack's busy." Caroline avoided my eyes and unwrapped a bar.

"I'm sure it's a crazy night for him." I recalled Jack's evasiveness when I spoke to him at the Inn, so I changed the subject. "Do you think we'll get any trick-or-treaters?"

"Some farmhands came by, but you know we never do." She gave an exaggerated sigh. "We'll have to eat all this candy ourselves."

I laughed and bit into my slightly softened but still-chilled candy bar. Heaven.

Caroline went into the dining room and returned with a package wrapped with bright floral paper and a silky coral ribbon. "I know we're celebrating your birthday on Monday but I wanted to give this to you now." A glow of appreciation warmed me. I could always depend on kind-hearted Caroline to cheer me up.

I unwrapped the box to find a beautifully soft emerald-green cashmere cardigan.

"It's gorgeous! Thank you!" I held the meltingly soft fabric to my cheek then hugged Caroline.

"It looks great with your hair and green eyes," she said.

We tidied the kitchen and spent the night watching Halloween movies with the cats. Rocky stalked and pounced on the crumpled wrapping paper, while Sprinkles claimed the box and settled her considerable girth inside it.

Before I went to bed I jogged down to the shop to be certain no one had broken in, but all was quiet and dark. As I climbed the farmhouse porch steps again, the jack-o'-lantern's grin mocked me.

Why couldn't I shake the feeling of watching a storm approach after a distant rumble of thunder? Perhaps the feeling had been kindled by hearing Diantha's sons' less-than-loving conversation about her money, or seeing her dried-eye loved ones gathered in the lounge the way a detective gathered suspects in a British TV show. Diantha's murder seemed like the start of something rather than the end, the first chapter rather than the last.

Chapter 11

MONDAY

Eating multiple candy bars before bed is not a recipe for a good night's sleep.

My phone buzzed and I peeled open my eyes to squint at the screen. It was an unfamiliar number, one I'd probably let go to voice mail before I started running an ice-cream shop. But now I never knew if a call was something business related, so I groaned and picked it up.

"Hello?" I croaked.

"Um, Ms. Rhodes? It's Lucretia Adams."

Ruthie's granddaughter. There was a strain in her voice that made me sit up.

"Lucretia. Are you okay?"

Her words rushed. "My gran's in the hospital. She went in last night with chest pains."

Now I was fully awake. "I'm so sorry to hear that. How is she?"

"The doctor says she's okay now but she has to stay for observation," Lucretia said. "She was supposed to go to work at the Inn today. She says she knows you don't

open Udderly until one o'clock and wants to know if you
could do the rooms at the Inn this morning?"

I flopped back onto the bed, partly in relief that Ruthie
was okay, partly because I can't believe I'm now the go-
to sub for the maid staff at the Inn. It shouldn't even be
Ruthie's job to find a substitute. It's the owner's job—or
the manager's. Of course, the owner was dead, and who
knew where Rob was. Before I could say anything else,
Lucretia spoke. "Listen, I'd do it, but I have a calculus
test and Ruthie says I have to go to school."

"You have to go to school," I said. "I'll do it. Please
tell Ruthie I'm thinking of her and I'll come see her when
I'm done."

"'Kay."

I threw back the covers. This was an opportunity.
I wanted to get back to the Inn, see why there'd been
something bothering me since I'd seen Diantha's body,
something beyond the shock of seeing her dead. Unfortunately, it also meant I had to scrub bathrooms and
vacuum. Poirot never had this problem.

As I drove down Farm Lane, I had a flash of inspi-
ration and swung into Udderly's parking lot. I'd made
plenty of fudge swirl ice cream when I'd crafted Dominic and Diantha's cake. I ran inside to the freezer. Scoop-
ing up a pint of the luscious chocolaty treat, I recalled
the times my work at Udderly had eased my entry into
conversations that would've otherwise been impossible.
Ice cream opened doors.

I added one of the shop's decorative stickers to the
cardboard pint and headed out.

I swung past the town green, surprised to see the road in
front of the Inn closed off not only by police barriers
but by two semitrucks and several workers unloading

equipment. I'd forgotten about the film crew and *Bound for Love*. Were they really going to start filming the day after Diantha's death?

Just as I was about to turn into the parking lot behind the Inn, I had to slam on my brakes as a guy hurtled out on a skateboard and swooped down Long Meadow Road. When my heart rate returned to normal, I recognized the floppy dark hair, lanky frame, and overall skateboarder cool of Sam Collins, and I felt a grudging admiration for the graceful way he slalomed down the quiet, narrow road. It might not be what I'd do the day after a death in the family, but people mourned in different ways.

A beefy guy in a windbreaker with SECURITY printed across the chest pointed me down the road, where I parked on the shoulder and jogged back.

"Name," he said, brandishing a clipboard.

I told him and said I was working at the Inn. He called to check, then allowed me to enter.

"Marley, what's going on here?" I said as I hung up my jacket in the kitchen.

"Finally, someone shows up!" Marley whined. He was turned out in his pristine white chef's coat and toque, but a few wisps of auburn hair escaped his ponytail. "Mary Anne came in early and prepped a bunch of stuff but then took off without any explanation!"

"Was she okay?" I asked.

"She didn't talk to me." He continued his tirade as I put the ice cream in the freezer. I ignored him and texted Mary Anne, but she didn't answer.

"The cops and firefighters were here and they've halted renovations in the spa wing. They're shooting *Bound for Love* today. And my hollandaise . . ." he moaned.

"Firefighters?"

Marley sighed. "That big cop, Voelker, came back.

He's not saying anything, but they have the north wing taped off. They had the fire department here checking the boiler."

The furnace system? Had there been a malfunction? Carbon monoxide? Is that what happened to Diantha? I was in the room right next door to her . . . my stomach clenched. Had I come close to being poisoned? Were there smoke and CO detectors in the hallway? I didn't remember one in my room. Had Diantha neglected safety equipment in her Inn's rooms in the name of historical accuracy?

Marley's voice surfaced, an irritating high-pitched drone. "But they didn't find anything wrong with the heating system. You should've been here for the negotiations over who's in charge, you would've thought they were brokering a peace treaty. Construction stopped for now, that's the silver lining. Mary Anne's checked out, Ruthie's in the hospital, Rob's disappeared, probably getting his drink on. Cooper's bossing everyone around. Sam did the only sensible thing and took off. Some of the actresses were crying." Marley paused to gulp a breath.

I weighed Marley's words to separate useful information from complaints. Did the police think Diantha had suffered carbon monoxide poisoning? I hadn't seen her face clearly, but flushed skin was a sign, and her skin had been grayish, not red, and the furnace was fine. What were the police thinking?

One thing was clear: Marley was even more insufferable today.

"Dominic's here but he's in mourning," Marley said as his knife flew over carrots on a cutting board. "He sat in the hallway to Diantha's room all last night, but of course he couldn't be there now with the cops and firefighters. The cops parked him in the lounge."

How awful for Dominic. I slipped on my blue housekeeping smock and realized with a shock that I had no idea how to be a maid. I'd make the beds. That I could do.

Without looking up from his task, Marley said, "Be sure to tidy the lounge. Chip said the family and film crew were in there last night till the wee hours and it was open bar. I think they drank everything they could get their hands on."

"Marley, when did you go home?" I tried to keep my voice casual. "Where do you live?"

Marley waved his knife in the direction of the green. "I don't remember exactly when. Late. I have a room over Just The Thing."

Just The Thing was a gift shop on the first floor of a rambling Victorian house across the green from Dad's bookstore.

"Wait. Did you mean the night Diantha died?" He shrugged. "Midnight. Everyone cleared out and the family went to bed. Rob locked up."

My mind whirled. I knew taking Ruthie's place was a gift that could allow me to figure out what had been bothering me about Diantha's death. But if I had to play my part as a cleaner, I had to actually get cleaning and not draw the attention of any cops, especially the chief of police.

My past with the CIA had included very few undercover assignments—I hesitated to even describe them as such. Nothing flashy. Simple things. Delivering a letter to a tea house in Seoul. Shelving a particular book on a particular shelf in an old library in Dubrovnik. Wearing a particular-color shirt on a particular street at a particular time on a trip to Rome. I'd learned how to evade notice, that the cover story, blending in and being believable as who you say you are, is the most important element of undercover work. Not driving a car full of gadgets or dressing in sequins and slinking across the high-rollers' room of a casino like a James Bond girl, but those would've been fun too. No, real spy craft is subtle.

So I'd have to look the part. I had my invisibility cloak—my blue smock—but I also pulled a bandanna from my bag and pulled my hair back into a neat pony-tail.

"Enough chit chat." Marley made a shooing motion. "There are housekeeping closets on each floor. The key's on the board in the office. There's a laundry chute and a trash chute. Don't get them mixed up. Elevator's broken. They're filming in the grand parlor so you have to use the back stairs, take the door before the lounge." Marley moaned and rattled a frying pan. "How is a person sup-posed to work under these conditions!"

I left Marley to his meltdown and peeked into the din-ing room. Every bit of the gothic Halloween wedding décor was gone, replaced by techs with sound and light-ing equipment and a rack of costumes. When I returned to the kitchen, the sickly looking woman I'd served in the lounge yesterday stood at the butcher-block table. Emilia, Sam's wife.

"Could we please have some tea? I'm happy to bring a tray back with me." Emilia, wearing an oversized beige sweater over a white turtleneck and gray sweatpants, looked so thin and pale I didn't think she'd be capable of carrying the tea tray back to the lounge.

"I'll bring it to you," I said as Marley opened a box labeled LILY's, my favorite tea shop across the green, and the buttery scent of pastry wafted out.

"Thank you." She walked slowly from the room, running her hand on the wall for support.

I put a pot of tea, lemon, sugar, cream, and some tea-cups on a tray. She'd said "we." Here was my chance to learn more about the family's reaction to Diantha's death. As I hefted the tray, Marley raised an imperious hand and added the plate of Lily's miniature pastry—donuts, pumpkin muffins, currant scones, savory cheese and dill biscuits—each more delicious looking than the next.

"For the guests," he said.

Killjoy.

I carried the tray to the lounge and looked about for a clear space to put it, but beer bottles, empty wine glasses, and plates with half-eaten snacks littered the tabletops. Through the entrance to the lounge I could see into the lobby, where Cooper and Jenira faced off. Cooper wore a brown plaid Pendleton shirt open over slim jeans and a black T-shirt, with headphones looped around his neck. Jenira was dressed as a bride, and it took me a moment to shift gears and take in the lights and staff milling behind her. She looked fresh and lovely in a wedding gown with a sweetheart neckline, full skirt, and lace trim, but her face was red and the cords of her neck stood out as she waved her bouquet and shouted at Cooper.

"It's grotesque!" Jenira shouted as she pointed the bouquet into the grand parlor. "How can you do this? When it's your mother's wedding arch! And the groom's over there crying? You're heartless!"

Behind her, Chip raised his hand, met Cooper's eyes, and pointed to his wristwatch.

"Babe." Cooper took her arm but she wrenched it away, sending a shower of pink rose petals wafting to the floor. He stepped closer, speaking in a soft, deliberate tone, as if gentling a skittish horse. "Jenira. We talked about this. Moving forward's a way of paying tribute to Diantha. She was so pleased that we were going to use the backdrops from her wedding. She laughed about being a cheap old Yankee and how this would help the movie stay under budget. She gave the whole production her blessing. And"—he lowered his voice and lifted her chin delicately so she'd look at him—"she thought you were the perfect actress to play Jodi Hope."

The romantic gesture and gentleness in his voice made my knees go weak and I almost dropped my tea tray.

Jenira took a steadying breath and her shoulders relaxed. Cooper looped his arm into hers.

A guy leaning against the wainscoted wall of the lobby straightened. He had sandy brown curls, dark brown eyes, and the clean-cut square jaw of the typical Skylark hero, except his hair was a bit too long and fell over his eyes in an incredibly charming way. He wore a gray morning coat with a vest crafted of burgundy silk printed with antique books. Ah, an artsy type. He must be playing the bookseller. Spoiler alert. They fall in love and get married. I didn't mind—I loved a good Skylark movie.

"Can we get another bouquet for Jenira?" Cooper called.

Cooper led Jenira to the "groom" and put her hand in his, and the actor escorted Jenira back into the grand parlor.

Chip stepped close to Cooper, winked, and gave him a thumbs-up. "Good job, Coop. She's a tough one."

Cooper blew out a breath. "Every minute we're not filming is thousands of dollars down the tubes. Those flowers aren't going to last." They followed Jenira into the grand parlor.

The show must go on, I mused, but I had to agree with Jenira, it was pretty cold. Twenty-four hours hadn't passed since his mother's death.

I heard a stifled sob and turned back to the lounge.

Emilia sat at a table in a dark corner with Dominic. He bent over his cell phone, texting, oblivious to Jenira and Cooper's drama. I elbowed aside some beer bottles on the bar top and set down my tray. I caught Emilia's eye as I poured a cup, lifted the sugar bowl and creamer, and at Emilia's nod, added a spoonful of sugar and a splash of cream before I handed it to her. As I did, I could see the text Dominic was writing on his phone. ALL MY DREAMS ARE GONE. I retrieved the plate of pastries and set it on the table.

"Thank you," Emilia said.

"Would you like some tea?" I said to Dominic.

"No thanks, Riley," Dominic sniffled, "I'm too bereft."

"I understand," I said. "I brought you some ice cream, your favorite, fudge swirl. I put it in the freezer."

Dominic took my hand and stood. "So kind. Thank you. Excuse me, I need some air."

I could only imagine what Dominic felt, seeing the filming continue in the room where he was supposed to marry Diantha.

Emilia cleared her throat as Dominic left the lounge. "They're all so theatrical. Well, that was a dumb thing to say. Of course they are, they're all actors." Her pale lips curved in the barest hint of a smile. Her hair, styled in a smooth pageboy, was so glossy today compared to yesterday that I realized she was wearing a wig. "Poor Dominic's been on his phone for hours."

Out the window we watched Dominic sit at a black metal table on the small slate patio, his head in his hands, still bent over his cell phone.

"I'll bring him a cup of tea and those nice pastries in a bit," Emilia said. "Right now I'm a little tired." She gestured to the couch, a bright gold wedding band catching the light as she did. "Would you mind sitting with me for a minute? You're a friend of Ruthie's, right? Is she okay?"

She took a seat on the couch and adjusted a pillow behind her back with a sigh. I sat across from her as I introduced myself and relayed what Lucretia had told me.

Emilia sipped her tea then said, "I have to go visit her. She was so kind to me when Sam and I came here on our honeymoon." She coughed then leaned back against the cushions.

"Are you feeling okay?" Her skin was so pale I could see a tracery of blue veins at her temples.

She nodded and forced a smile. "Better than Saturday night; I was exhausted when we arrived. It was a long flight back from Johannesburg. Everyone must've thought I was rude, but I couldn't keep my eyes open and went to bed before the party." Her lips trembled. "Then early Sunday morning, I heard voices in the hallway outside our room, and well, it must've been when Ruthie found Diantha. I was still so groggy and jet-lagged."

The thought kindled: *She didn't know I'd been there.*

Emilia turned the wedding band on her finger as she continued, her voice growing soft. "After a bit, I woke fully and went into the hall and there were EMTs everywhere. The police made us all go to the lounge. When Sam came back from his run and heard the news he was"—she lowered her eyes to her lap—"flattened. Just went numb, I think."

A sympathetic silence grew between us until two techs came into the lounge and helped themselves to tea. "Sorry, I really should get back to work," I said.

"Sorry, I've kept you. I hope we can talk more later," Emilia said, rising. "I'm going to bring Dominic some tea. Thanks for chatting with me, Riley."

My phone vibrated in my pocket. Mary Anne texted.

DOMINIC WANTS TO CRY ON MY SHOULDER! HE SAYS HE NEEDS ME NOW THAT HIS DREAMS ARE GONE!

Was Dominic texting Mary Anne for support? That was incredible.

I texted. ARE YOU OK?

Mary Anne answered. LET'S TALK TOMORROW. LILY'S AT NOON?

Tuesday was my usual day off. SEE YOU THERE.

I didn't text the question that came to mind: *Have you spoken to the police?*

I slid my phone back into my pocket, gathered glassware, tossed trash, wiped down tables, popped into the office to get the keys to the housekeeping closets and rooms, then stopped in the kitchen to drop off the bus tray at the dishwashing station. Delicious aromas of rosemary, garlic, lemon, and roasting chicken filled the air, but Marley was nowhere to be seen. The way he'd been so eager to throw Mary Anne under the bus because of the cake still left a bad taste. Besides, she wasn't the only one upset about the wedding. Hadn't I seen Diantha and Rob in a heated argument? Was it possible he'd taken his feelings out on the cake? Or could Marley have done so in order to discredit Mary Anne?

Taking some gloves from a box by the stove I slid them on and hurried into the walk-in freezer. I lifted the lid of the wrecked wedding cake, an angry mess frozen in time. A glossy black hair I hadn't noticed earlier was frozen to the cake's surface. I closed the lid with a shock of dismay. *Mary Anne, what have you done?*

Chapter 12

If I ever decide to make another career change, it will not be to become a hotel housekeeper. I rejoiced when I saw the little LOVE-THE-PLANET-SAVE-WATER cardboard sign by the bed in Jenira's suite that announced that, unless requested, the sheets wouldn't be changed every day. I'd already made an executive decision that life was too short to change strangers' bed linen. I made the beds; picked up clothing from floors; emptied wastebaskets; wiped down showers, sinks, and toilets; polished mirrors; restocked fancy mini bottles of shampoo and conditioner; and set out clean towels, and I was ready to collapse after an hour—and I'd done only three rooms: Jenira's, Cooper's, and Evan Smith's, the handsome actor I'd seen downstairs, who must've come in late last night or early this morning. I turned over the tag on his unpretentious canvas duffel bag: EVAN SMITH. Even his name was bland. His bed was pristine, the silky blue duvet undisturbed, the chocolate skeletons intact, but he'd had time to use every towel and spill hair products all over the sink.

I skipped the Bluet suite, which had been turned into an office for the film, with computer screens, cables, and laptops crowding every surface except the bed. I did take a quick glance at some promotional materials for *Bound for Love*: "*Can a shy bookseller and feisty librarian find a happy ending to their love story? A bookseller falls in love with a librarian when he discovers a cache of letters to his great-grandmother from a mysterious 'M' and asks for her help in discovering the identity of the writer.*"

I'd learned little so far, except that Jenira traveled with three pink leather steamer trunks and a pink stuffed bunny, and had a stash of airplane-sized vodka bottles in an ice bucket in her bathroom. A pink swimsuit hung in the shower. A script was on her desk, but it wasn't *Bound for Love*. Instead, I flipped through *Meteor*, a dark tale of a movie star who loses it all to drugs. The star died on the last page, OD'ing in a gutter. Literally, in a gutter. Talk about a role against type.

I walked down the hall and turned. Facing me at the other end of the south wing was Diantha's massive suite. On my left were four doors: starting from Diantha's room, they were Jenira's, Cooper's, Evan Smith's, and the housekeeping closet. On the right, the room for gifts, the suite used as Cooper and Chip's office, and the broken elevator. It was sweet that Emilia and Sam had taken their honeymoon room instead of one of these for sentimental reasons. If my and Diantha's rooms were any indication, they'd turned down a luxurious king-sized space for a tiny closet.

I walked down the hall of the north wing, peeked into several empty rooms that were in various stages of re-decoration and renovation, and pushed open the door to Chip's room. The bed was made, not neatly, certainly not to Ruthie's standards, but I appreciated Chip's effort. I smoothed the silky duvet, my eye scanning the night-stands for anything interesting. With a shock I realized it hadn't taken long for me to lose any scruples I had about snooping in strangers' rooms, but the image of Diantha's body and the stabbed cake assuaged my guilt. Something was wrong here, I could feel it, and I was afraid for Mary Anne. I'd seen Jack's expression when Marley showed him the cake.

Marley. He'd been so eager, even gleeful, to show the cake to Jack. Why was he so set against Mary Anne?

Opening the heavy blue drapes, I craned out the window of Chip's room, orienting myself. I could see down into the dumpster of construction debris that was screened from street view by the white stockade fencing. This window was directly above Diantha's Little Room.

I left Chip's room, pushed open the emergency exit and descended to the second floor. Through a narrow window in the exit door, I saw an officer walking down the hall toward Diantha's room. I'd have to come back later. I continued down to the ground floor, pushed open a door labeled SPA and POOL, and crossed a pool deck and pool screened for privacy by a thick row of arbor vitae planted outside a wall of glass. Dodging more construction equipment and debris, I peeked into the spa, then stopped at a door that opened into the hallway leading to meeting rooms. It was empty.

I quietly retraced my steps, turning over the events of the previous night once again. All I had were new questions.

I thought of all the footsteps I'd heard the previous night, some overhead and some much closer. Who had I heard walking in the hall? Had Evan Smith arrived by then? Who had I seen at three a.m. in the mobcap running across the parking lot to the carriage house? The figure, little more than a shadow, I'd seen in the parking lot at midnight? Rob Wainwright had been outside then. I'd ask him, if I could find him.

Was there access to the Inn from the construction

entrance? I checked the pool doors. All were chained shut. There was one fire door and I noted a camera over it. So the police would soon know if anyone had entered or left the Inn from this door last night.

Rob must have access to the security system and could possibly be watching me right now. I bent my head and went upstairs to Diantha's suite.

Diantha's bed was smooth, but the bed pillow was still missing. *Strange.* Lucretia had been tasked with cleaning, but perhaps she'd skipped this room since Diantha had slept in the Little Room. The chocolates on her bedside table were undisturbed, the skeleton bride and groom now a mockery, as was Diantha's magnificent gown. I shut the door between the bedroom and the dressing room, unsettled by the sight of the headless mannequin, too much like a watchful specter.

The last time I'd seen Diantha she'd been holding court in the lounge, looking every bit the regal evil queen of Disney fame in her high-necked black gown and horns. People certainly did choose costumes based on their personalities; I'd always opted for something bookish from the time in eighth grade Caroline and I dressed like students at a well-known school of witchcraft and wizardry.

The room was as Ruthie and I had left it, except for Diantha's desk—it was a mess, with papers heaped into untidy stacks. Had the police searched this room? A strand of hair on top of one stack caught my eye and I held it up to the light from the window. It was dyed orange at the tip.

Lucretia. I took a deep breath. Had the desk been in this state when she arrived or did she search Diantha's desk? Why? Was she simply a curious person with few boundaries, like her grandmother and certain ice-cream shop managers? I let the hair fall and wondered if the cops had talked to her.

The only item on the desk that seemed undisturbed was a photo in a silver frame, an image of Diantha with two wriggling boys on her lap, her face raised to the camera with a serene smile. Undeniably beautiful in a summery dress and heels, she sat with her skirt arrayed around her on the lawn of a sprawling white clapboard house. I was certain there'd been a nanny off camera who took the boys as soon as the photographer finished.

I picked up a paper that had fallen to the floor: an oversized site plan from Penniman Construction.

A "before" rendering showed the Inn and property beyond the carriage house, which comprised a graveyard and plot with three buildings: the Collins Homestead and two small outbuildings. One of the outbuildings was labeled OCEANUS COLLINS.

I sifted through the papers and found another rendering. In this one, Ruthie's home and outbuildings were replaced by a clubhouse, an outdoor pool, and a huge parking lot. The cemetery remained, shielded behind rows of arbor vitae.

Humming the song about paradise and parking lots, I bypassed the staff stairs and ran down the main staircase to the lobby. When my foot touched the bottom step, I caught sight of the row of old-fashioned keys on the wall behind the reception desk. The key hanging from the hook on the far left had a white ribbon, not a blue one like all the others. *Why?* I wondered.

I stepped into the lounge and bit back a groan when I saw the platter Marley had heaped with delectable pastries sitting empty on a table littered with crumpled napkins and dirty glasses. I loaded all the plates, glasses, and mugs onto a tray as I listened to voices from the Grand Parlor.

Squaring my shoulders, I cleaned the lavatories—not as bad as I'd expected—finding only crumpled tissue and an empty bottle of Benadryl in the wastebasket. This was not how I envisioned spending the day after my birthday. Thank goodness I had the celebration tonight at Dad's to look forward to.

After a quick pass cleaning crumbs from the piano bench against the lounge's far wall, I cleared and wiped down the bar top. The whiskey bottle Chip had been helping himself to was now empty. I put it into the overflowing bin behind the bar. Lucretia hadn't taken out the trash or recyclables.

I fumed as I tied up the bags and hauled them out.

That left one room to tidy: the office. I moved down the back hallway, my feather duster at the ready, and ran into Marley.

"Hey, Riley." He blocked the doorway and pulled the door shut behind him, his abrupt movement kindling an instant certainty that he was up to no good. "Don't worry about the office. If you're done upstairs and in the lounge, you can go. Police said the second floor's off limits."

Movement and voices from outside drew me to the lounge windows, and Marley followed close behind. Several people in windbreakers emerged from a blue van parked in the lot. CSI. State Police Lab. My heart rate ticked up. Penniman was too small to have its own specialist homicide investigators, so in the case of serious crimes, towns used the resources of the state police.

"CSI!" Marley whispered, his hazel eyes glowing. "So Diantha was murdered!"

Chapter 13

Back at Udderly, I threw on my apron and blessed Pru, who had left a tray of roast beef sandwiches in the refrigerator. I dug in. The meat was topped with piquant provolone cheese and roasted sweet red peppers, tomatoes, and lettuce, and I washed it down with a chocolate milk shake. Normally I'd savor the sandwich's farm-grown vegetables and fresh-baked bread, but I hardly tasted anything as Marley's words echoed: *So Diantha was murdered.*

I knew the involvement of a CSI team wasn't confirmation of anything other than the police believed Diantha's death warranted investigation. But if it was murder, how had she been killed? Judging from the presence of the fire department and the construction stoppage, the police at first must've thought Diantha's death was due to accidental carbon monoxide poisoning. I looked up symptoms in my favorite online medical database: headache, dizziness—she might have attributed those to her drinking—rapid breathing and heart rate . . . confusion . . . seizure and coma . . . flushed skin . . .

I remembered the fireplace in Diantha's Little Room. Had there been a fire in it? Had the flue been closed?

The room didn't smell like smoke—the air was fresh and flowing in through the open window. I recalled what little I'd been able to see of Diantha's face—it hadn't looked flushed. A faulty heating system had been ruled out by the fire department. From previous research I'd learned that the purple color on the side of her face would be attributable to blood pooling due to gravity. So what were the police looking for?

Tourists crowded into the shop and we were much busier than I'd expected, temporarily driving thoughts of Diantha and murder from my mind.

At a lull, Flo and Gerri joined me at the dipping case. Flo whispered, "Did you hear any more about Diantha Collins?"

I nodded and filled them in with what I'd seen at the Inn.

"All this going on, plus a movie!" Flo exclaimed. "I'm going to go into town to see if I can catch sight of Evan Smith."

"The king of the Skylark movies," Gerri sighed.

I recalled the promo materials I'd seen. "In this one he plays a bookseller who falls in love with a librarian when he discovers a cache of letters to his great-grandmother from a mysterious writer known only as 'M.'"

"That reminds me." Gerri waved a scoop. "Don't forget the letters that need to be catalogued. I'll bring them over."

Dusty old papers when I had a mysterious death to think about. I hid my sigh.

Gerri and Flo shooed me out the door early when I told them I wanted to visit Ruthie before my birthday dinner at Dad and Paulette's.

At Eastern Hospital, I checked in at the desk and was

told that Ruthie was being discharged. When I arrived at her room, she was tying her sneakers and Lucretia was seated on the bed, scrolling on her phone.

"How do you feel, Ruthie?" I made my tone upbeat. I didn't want to be the one to break the news that the police were investigating Diantha's death to a woman who might've had a heart attack.

"You get to my age," Ruthie groused, "you get a little chest pain, they want to keep you all night. It was probably just indigestion."

"Stress, Gran." Lucretia looked up from her phone, her voice bored but her eyes warm with concern. "You've had a lot of stress lately and then you found Diantha's body. That's a shock, that's what the doctor said. Plus, now that they suspect she was murdered, it's even worse."

"Where did you hear that?" I asked, failing to keep the surprise out of my voice.

Lucretia waved her phone. "Some friends of mine were walking by the Inn and saw CSI vans. They texted me and I told Gran."

Ruthie's eyes welled. "I may have had mixed feelings about Diantha, but she and that place have been part of my life for years."

I handed Ruthie a box of tissues.

Without looking up from her phone, Lucretia said, "Plus we're related."

That was unexpected. "You are?"

"Way back, many-times-removed cousins. The Collins family was related to everyone." Ruthie dabbed her eyes. "We'll see what happens now, if Dominic'll stay with the Inn. Did everything go all right with the rooms? Of course Rob will pay you."

"Everything was fine." I didn't mention that Lucretia

hadn't done a great job cleaning, nor that I thought she'd gone through Diantha's desk. I had to be fair. Anyone could've gotten a pass key with all the chaos surrounding the discovery of Diantha's body, but the way Lucretia avoided my eyes reinforced my suspicion. *Pass key.* "Ruthie, do you think Diantha went to her suite for anything before she went to her Little Room?" At my words, Lucretia went still.

Ruthie shook her head and kept her head down. "No, I put her nightgown and spa robe and slippers in the closet and her makeup bag in the bathroom of the Little Room, her toothbrush in the holder. And her pillow. She always had her own pillow."

"I noticed a different key hanging behind the desk," I said. "The key to Diantha's Little Room had a white ribbon, not a blue one like the others."

"The keys on white ribbons are extras." Ruthie nodded to a nurse who handed her some paperwork.

My mind whirled. Why had that key been replaced? The space would've remained empty until Diantha returned her key in the morning, the key I'd seen clutched in her hand. Someone put that extra key there.

My heart started to pound. I didn't want to upset Ruthie with questions.

Still, as casually as I could, I asked, "It was fun to see those beautiful rooms. Lucretia, you cleaned yesterday. Did you see anything interesting?"

Lucretia muttered, "Too many wet towels."

As soon as I left I called Jack, but the message went to voice mail. "Jack, the key to Diantha's Little Room behind the reception desk. It's different. I think you should look at it. Maybe check it for—" At a look from a nurse, I choked back the word "fingerprints" and ended the call. Here I was telling a chief of police how to do his job. I winced and put the phone in my bag. If Jack didn't dump Caroline over her meddling friend it would be a miracle.

At seven o'clock, I made my way to Dad's house, taking the steps of the beautiful porch slowly as my back reminded me about all the cleaning I'd done. I'd taken a detour past the Inn where the film crew carried on, spotlights trained on the front door, as a large crowd dressed in warm jackets and knitted caps watched from a distance. The show must go on.

My heart warmed as I noted all the carved pumpkins and beautiful mums Paulette had used to decorate the porch. The pillows on the porch swing where I'd spent many a happy hour reading had been covered in autumn shades of red and bronze. Gold balloons, one in the shape of a 3 and one a 5, dangled from the railing. I wrenched them down and carried them into the house with me—maybe I did have mixed feelings about turning thirty-five. When I opened the door, a chorus of voices rang out, "Happy belated birthday!" and Dad, Paulette, Flo, Gerri, the Brightwoods, and Caroline surrounded me with hugs.

As a child, having an October 31st birthday was complicated. In my opinion, only kids who have birthdays on major winter holidays like Christmas and Hanukkah are cheated worse. Dad always made sure I had my favorite chocolate cupcakes with orange-colored frosting and sprinkles the day after Halloween because there was no way I would miss trick-or-treating on Halloween with my friends.

As Paulette took my coat, my phone buzzed with a text from Mary Anne. SORRY I CAN'T COME. SOMETHING CAME UP. I wondered if that something was a call from the police, but I forgot all about Mary Anne,

Diantha, and the Inn as Dad linked his arm in mine and swept me into the dining room, which was decorated with orange balloons and swags of orange and black crepe paper.

"We ordered in from that Indian place you like," Dad said. Paulette was a great cook, but I loved Indian food and dug in to spicy vindaloo, saag, and vegetable samosas with a sweet tamarind sauce. Everyone chatted at once. There was so much happening with the filming of *Bound for Love,* and Dad and Paulette were in the thick of it with scenes set at the bookstore.

Caroline checked her phone and gave me a wan smile as she tucked it back into her pocket. Jack had been invited but it was clear from her expression that he wasn't coming.

"Filming at the shop starts Wednesday," Dad said.

"And you'll never believe it, Riley," Paulette gushed as she handed me a mug of fragrant spiced cider. "Sprinkles will be in the movie!"

I could believe it—once Paulette got an idea there was no stopping her—but I couldn't help shaking my head.

Paulette continued, "Sprinkles' online presence and portfolio of calendar work helped seal the deal."

Caroline leaned close and whispered, "I couldn't say no. Sprinkles has been so bored since the Sprinkles All Year calendar project wrapped." A photographer friend had made Sprinkles the star of a fundraiser calendar, and since they'd wrapped up the project, Sprinkles had been out of sorts . . . well, more out of sorts than usual.

I put aside thoughts of Sprinkles as everyone serenaded me with an off-key but enthusiastic rendition of "Happy Birthday" and I opened presents.

Dad handed me a stack of envelopes. "Here are some cards, including a few letters that came to the shop."

"Thanks." I put them in my bag. When I left my apartment in Old Town Alexandria, Virginia, I'd made my forwarding address Dad's house. I had my room at Caroline's, but something didn't feel right about making it my official address, especially now that she was dating Jack. One day I could see them moving in together into her beloved childhood home. I kept thinking I'd find a place in town, perhaps an apartment over one of the shops on the green, like Marley's. No way I wanted to return to my childhood bedroom with Paulette living in the same house.

At end of the evening, Paulette gave me and Caroline hugs at the door and handed me a box with leftover cupcakes. "I'll be over to get Sprinkles in the morning. She needs to be on set at nine."

"About that," Caroline twisted her hands as she began. "I have to go back to Boston in the morning and—"

"No worries." Paulette waved it away with the assurance of one who didn't know what she was getting herself into. "She'll be perfectly well cared for. Skylark keeps a pet wrangler on staff to take care of the animals, a trained pet psychologist-slash-veterinarian."

Caroline and I exchanged a glance. We couldn't forget what happened the last time Sprinkles had seen a pet psychologist—she'd run him out of the house.

"Let us know what happens," I said, trying to keep the laughter out of my voice. I couldn't help it. Part of me was hoping for a full-on Sprinkles meltdown.

"I will!" Paulette practically sang the words.

"I'll see you two out." Dad walked me and Caroline to Sadie.

"Dad, you know this'll be a disaster," I whispered as we walked to the street.

He squeezed my shoulder and sighed. "Paulette really wanted to be an extra, but she didn't make the cut."

"No surprise there," Caroline said. "They want people who blend. Paulette's striking."

I had to admit Paulette was as lovely as any actress.

"This is her way of getting to be part of the excitement. Let's keep our fingers crossed," Dad said. "You know how Sprinkles loves to be admired. I imagine there'll be a lot of that on the film set."

I wondered. From what I'd seen at the Inn, it was a lot of hurry up and wait while lights were adjusted.

"Fingers crossed, Dad," I said.

Back at the farmhouse, Caroline and I enjoyed more cupcakes and tea at the kitchen table as Rocky lounged at my feet.

Caroline lay Sprinkles over her lap, stroking the cat's snowy fur as she smiled down at the fuzzy white monster. "Do you think this cat has any idea what's going to happen to her tomorrow?" Sprinkles' swanky carrier, an oversized purple metal cage with a jeweled crown attached over the door and stuffed with silky purple crate pads and lovies, stood ready by the door.

"Does Paulette?" I allowed myself a chuckle at a mental image of Paulette chasing Sprinkles all over the set.

Rocky stalked over and sniffed at Sprinkles' cat carrier. Both cats knew something was up, but probably assumed it was a trip to see Liam Pryce for a checkup. Since the man was part Dr. Dolittle and part St. Francis of Assisi, there wasn't any misbehavior. They loved the handsome vet like everyone else did. That would play in Paulette's favor until Sprinkles realized she wasn't going to see Liam.

Sprinkles leapt from Caroline's lap and headed into the powder room. "Any calls from Liam?" Caroline asked as she carried our empty mugs to the sink, then followed Sprinkles. I heard a flush. Sprinkles preferred to drink water from the toilet—quite an acrobatic trick for a cat of her majestic girth—and to my chagrin, she'd trained *me* to flush too.

"Nope." I wasn't disappointed; I didn't expect a call from the busy vet. A different emotion warmed me as I opened cards, most from friends back in D.C., all full of jokes about ticking biological clocks and wrinkles, with a few librarian jokes about being "overdue" thrown in for good measure. I missed my old life, especially the travel, and now I was feeling nostalgic.

The last item in the stack wasn't a card. I held a long, thin envelope to the light and felt a cold stab of dread as I recognized the handwriting. I'd seen it only once before, but it was burned into my memory—"Signorina Riley Rhodes" inscribed on an envelope with tickets to a film opening in Rome. Blood pounded in my ears as I stared at the address. This envelope was addressed "Riley Rhodes, c/o Penniless Reader Bookshop, Penniman, Connecticut." The postmark was Hartford and there was no return address.

"What is it?" Caroline said. "You look like you've seen a ghost."

I felt as if I had. "This is Paolo's handwriting."

Caroline fell into her seat and took the envelope from my hand. "He sent you a birthday card? He has some nerve."

My mind reeled as I took the envelope from Caroline's hands. Seeing his handwriting sent me back to Rome, to the horror and shame I'd felt when I realized he'd duped me as part of his plan to steal a small but very valuable statue from my office.

How did he find me? I threw my mind back to a dinner in a dimly lit trattoria on the Via dei Vascellari. As we sampled the café's delicious pasta, I'd mentioned growing up in a small town in Connecticut. I hadn't been specific, but I did mention that my dad had a book-shop. *Dumb mistake.* There were a few bookshops in this part of the state but I should've lied, come up with a different story . . . but I'd trusted him. I'd fallen for him. I'd felt safe talking about Connecticut since I lived in Virginia at the time. I never expected I'd be living in my hometown mere months after the disaster in Rome.

He'd found me. Why, after he'd burned my career to the ground and broken my heart, did he want to get in touch?

"Burn it." Caroline scooped up Sprinkles and gave me a level look.

"I should." *But . . . what did he want?*

Had he been watching as we went to Dad's house for the party? Had he followed us home? I jumped to my feet, pulled the yellow gingham curtains shut, and locked the front door.

"You don't think he wants to hurt you?" Caroline's soft voice wavered as she peered out the kitchen window with Sprinkles draped over her shoulder.

"No, no, I don't think so. Not physically anyway." I picked up the envelope again.

"Maybe he wants to make amends?"

I scoffed. That was impossible.

"I'm serious, get rid of it," Caroline said. "Whatever that jerk has to say, you don't want to hear it."

"You're right." Still, I jammed the letter in my pocket and swooped up Rocky, who gave a small *meow* of com-plaint but allowed me to hold him close. I wanted to curl up and disappear.

"I'm going to bed. See you in the morning." In my room, I made sure the blinds were tightly closed. Rocky curled up at the foot of my bed, grooming a paw, uncon-cerned.

"Some help you are." I took the letter from my pocket. Caroline was right. I should burn it but . . .

I'd never admit it to Caroline, but crazy as it was, I still felt something for Paolo. Some attraction, some dangerous attraction. He'd burned down my professional life but . . . I was curious. What *did* he have to say to me? I put the letter on my bedside table and threw myself back against my pillows, the abrupt movement jolting Rocky from his comfortable spot. He moved closer to me and cuddled against my side. I stroked his soft fur as I tried to calm myself to sleep.

Chapter 14

C ome on baby, time to shine," Paulette cooed as she
placed Sprinkles' oversized carrier into the back of
her Volvo wagon. "Mama's going to make you a star."

That's it, I thought, *Paulette had officially lost her
mind.* The curtain of Stepford perfection had been pulled
aside to reveal an inner stage mother I'd never suspected.

Rocky watched from the porch, his tail swishing.
He'd been on high alert since Paulette picked up Sprinkles, sensing, correctly, something very wrong about
Paulette's arrival. Sprinkles, however, didn't pick up on
anything, probably because Paulette radiated positive
getting-her-own-way energy in a way that short-circuited
Sprinkles' own.

Caroline waved from her car, practically vibrating
with anxiety. She hated driving in traffic and usually left
for Boston after rush hour had died away. Now she had
the added worry of Sprinkles going ballistic on the film
crew. Still, she managed to squeak, "Good luck, Paulette." We exchanged what I hoped was an encouraging
glance as she pulled out, the dust from her tires saying
clearly, *not my circus, not my clowns.*

"See, Riley, that wasn't so bad. She went right into the

car," Paulette said as she settled a blanket over Sprinkles' carrier. "Piece of cake."

"That's because Sprinkles thinks you're taking her to see Liam Pryce," I said.

"That reminds me." Paulette's eyes gleamed as she walked over to me, giving her beautifully manicured hands a carefree little dust off. "Didn't you tell me that he was taking you to a new Ethiopian restaurant? How did that go?"

I didn't want to talk about being stood up on my birthday. I cleared my throat. "He had an emergency. I got a rain check."

Paulette patted my arm. "I hope so, dear. As we age, we can't always attract them like we used to. Well, some of us. Better run!"

Paulette closed the hatch on the wagon and got in, giving me a cheery toot of the horn as she pulled away.

I exhaled. "How long do you give them till the explosion, Rocky?" I said, turning to the porch, but he was gone—even my cat had ditched me.

I tightened the laces on my running shoes and jogged up Farm Lane, adding annoyance with Paulette to my churning emotions about Diantha's death and Paolo's letter. A black Lincoln Continental roared down the narrow road and halted next to me.

Gerri leaned out the window, raised her oversized Jackie O sunglasses and parked them on her black bouffant. "Good morning, Riley. You keep forgetting to pick up the Collins family letters for cataloguing, so I brought them by." Gerri patted the box on the seat next to her. "I'll drop them on your porch. Since it's your day off, I figured you'd want to get cracking on them."

Cataloguing old papers for the historical society hadn't been on the to-do list for the day, but I didn't dare tell Gerri that I'd forgotten.

"I'll look at them as soon as I get back."

"Please do," Gerri said. "Since Diantha planned to tear down those historic buildings, it's imperative we know as much as possible before her estate takes over. There may be a history card to play to preserve it."

"You knew about Diantha's plans to expand the parking lot?" How ironic would it be if Diantha's bid to impress the historical society and the Colonial Dames ultimately undermined her plan to tear down the historic house Ruthie lived in.

Gerri's arched eyebrow and tilted head said, *Of course.* "Now that the sons inherit, my concern is that they'll want to continue with those plans, or sell the Inn, or do one of any number of things that could destroy a piece of Penniman history."

"They inherit." I thought out loud. "If she'd lived long enough to change her will, I imagine Dominic would've become her beneficiary?"

Gerri shrugged. "As far as I know, there wasn't a legal bond between Diantha and Dominic at the time of her death. Word is she purchased some property for his new experimental-cuisine restaurant and didn't put his name on the contract. I'm afraid poor Dominic's left in the lurch. See you later."

I hardly heard Gerri say goodbye. It occurred to me that if Mary Anne killed Diantha, it would hurt Dominic twice—taking away his bride, and potentially, leaving him without his dream restaurant. What would Diantha's sons do about Dominic? I doubted they felt any kinship with him, and I'd heard Sam and Cooper say they needed money.

I'd planned to run to burn off nervous energy kindled by Paolo's letter, but now my thoughts were filled with Diantha.

I took my usual route up Farm Lane, past the red Cape

Cod Fairweather Homestead Gerri and Flo shared.
The plain colonial façade had been brightened with orange mums, and a flock of miniature white tissue-paper
ghosts hung from the spreading branches of an old oak—
Flo's doing, I was sure. I crossed four-lane Town Road
to rarely traveled Woods Road, and as I rounded a curve
on the twisting lane a familiar red VW Beetle—Tillie
O'Malley's car—crept ahead.

She was moving so slowly I'd pass her at my present
pace. As I pulled even with the car, I saw the reason for
her speed—a woman in pink jogged twenty yards ahead,
her high dark ponytail swinging. Jenira Ford glanced
back and adjusted her ear buds, and at Tillie's wave,
turned back to her run.

Tillie stopped and rolled down the window, her face
partially obscured by a Red Sox baseball cap and oversized aviator sunglasses.

"Aren't you a little close to her?" I asked.

Tillie jutted her chin at Jenira and whispered, "She
had a run-in with her stalker yesterday."

"Stalker! What happened?" I scanned the roadside,
dense with trees and laurel bushes. If Jenira was being
followed, this was a terrible place to run. The twists and
turns of the isolated, little-traveled road provided opti-
mal hiding places for a stalker.

"I told her not to go out by herself." Tillie lowered
her glasses and rolled her eyes. "Yesterday, I had to
work at the station, and she went running alone on Long
Meadow Road, you know the section that goes from the
green out past the private school? That's where he approached her. Came up behind her, called her Carrie or
Cara or something like that, and then ran off when she
screamed at him."

"Carrie?" I said. "That's odd. Maybe that was the

name of a character she played? Did you get a description?"

Tillie handed me a sheet of paper. "Here. Male, mid-thirties, light brown hair, six feet, sunglasses, blue track suit. Skylark's security team should've taken her concerns more seriously."

I stuffed the paper in my pocket as Jenira turned, put her hands on her hips, and shouted, "I'm not paying you to chitchat!"

"See you later." I spun and headed back toward Town Road.

"Hey." Tillie leaned out the car window. "Are you doing lunch at Lily's? It's Tuesday, right? See you there later."

I nodded and waved, then turned east on Town Road, running two miles past the organic farm that supplied milk and cream for the shop, then looped back toward home, all the while musing on Jenira's stalker. Could there be a connection with Diantha's murder? It didn't seem possible that anyone could mistake one for the other. They were two very different women: Diantha a socialite in her sixties, honey blonde, statuesque, dressed—the night of the murder—as an evil queen. Jenira, medium height, slim-but-athletic build, dark brown hair, and if I remembered correctly, dressed on Halloween as a Dalmatian. If Jenira's stalker was the murderer, he must've been high to have mixed the women up.

It was remarkable how much drama Penniman had seen since the arrival of the Collins family. The excitement of the movie was a positive development, but then there was Diantha's murder, Jenira making her presence known at the Inn by getting two of the staff fired, and now dealing with a stalker. There was even Rob's fight with Diantha. What had he said to her? I searched my memory, something about her son.

At least Sam and Emilia seemed to have avoided the drama of the others, or perhaps their drama was of a different sort. Obviously Emilia was battling a serious illness and Sam—I remembered his graceful movement as he skateboarded away from the Inn. Perhaps that's how he coped with the rest of his family. He wasn't an actor, he was an athlete, an extreme-sports athlete and a philanthropist. He and Emilia made an odd pair.

I sprinted back to the house, hurried up the steps, and with a sigh picked up Gerri's carton of letters. Even if I lingered in the shower, I still had time to look through some of them before my lunch with Mary Anne. I set the box in the dining room, and when I lifted the lid the mold and dust of centuries made me sneeze. Still, it would be a welcome diversion if it helped me push thoughts of Paolo away.

After a shower, I slipped into a denim skirt and matching turtleneck. Because it was chilly, I reached for the beautiful cardigan Caroline had given me. I tugged on suede boots, combed my hair, and clipped it back into a ponytail, thinking once more how I had to make an appointment for a cut.

Back downstairs in the kitchen, I noticed that Rocky hadn't eaten much of his kibble. I checked his usual spots: the long rectangles of sunlight on the colorful rag rug that covered the parlor floor where he and Sprinkles lounged and the top of a table by the front door where he'd stand guard. He must've taken off on one of his hunting expeditions. I'd rescued him, but Rocky would never be a fully indoor cat.

Now that I was showered and dressed, I couldn't put off Gerri's papers any longer.

Caroline and I rarely used the dining room table, so

I removed the brass candlesticks and yellow plaid table runner and spread out the contents of the box to do an overview.

Some bundles of letters were tied together with ribbon so faded it was hard to tell what the original color had been. Underneath them all was a stack of thick paper that had been grayed by time, spotted with mold, and gnawed by insects and mice. Old rag paper. In colonial times, paper was made literally from rags, softened and spread on fine mesh, rolled thin and dried. Parchment, paper made from animal skins, was thicker and used for important documents. At the bottom of the box, I found several sheets of relatively unblemished parchment and marveled at its creamy smooth surface.

I'd have to develop a list of topics that I'd use to organize the letters and that meant reading every single one of the dusty old papers. My initial scan showed the handwriting was crabbed and the ink faded, something to be expected. Ink made in the colonial era used natural ingredients like herbs, tree bark, black walnuts, even powder made from burnt potatoes. Just thinking of the task before me made my eyes ache.

I heard a car go by and rose to look outside, expecting a chastened Paulette to return any minute with Sprinkles, but the car passed. Two hours had elapsed and she hadn't brought Sprinkles home with her tail between her legs. I texted Dad.

ANY WORD ON WHAT'S HAPPENING WITH SPRINKLES?

Dad replied. THEY'RE STILL SETTING UP LIGHTS. THE PET WRANGLER'S STUCK IN TRAFFIC. PAULETTE TOOK SPRINKLES HOME TO EAT AND WAIT.

I sent a thumbs-up emoji and wondered how Paulette's

furniture would survive a few hours of Hurricane Sprinkles.

I opened my laptop and entered each item in the box into an initial inventory, then reached for the first bundle, holding my breath as I unfolded the paper, excitement building as I mused that these words hadn't been read in over two hundred years After the first letter, a missive to John Collins from John (no last name) concerning the purchase of corn, I found myself struggling to keep my eyes open. A pot of Lily's good Earl Grey tea would revive me. I set the letters aside and headed out, giving the doorknob a good pull to make certain it locked.

Chapter 15

Lily's was one of my favorite spots in the entire world. Set in a pink and teal painted-lady Victorian, its walls papered in intricate William Morris designs, the tearoom had an air of cozy gossip. It was named for Coleman and Zara Hennessey's white Highland terrier, Lily, and my favorite decorative touch was the portrait of the pampered pooch that hung over the fireplace. Lily was the only creature in Penniman as spoiled as Sprinkles.

Coleman and Zara were also some of my favorite people. Transplants from London, the community-spirited couple and their elegant, classic British tea helped put Penniman on the map.

"Zara, how are you?" I hung up my coat on a stand in the entryway and gave her a hug.

As usual, Zara was impeccably turned out in a yellow shirt dress and her trademark pearl earrings, her hair worn in a short Afro that highlighted her high cheekbones. "We were sorry to miss your party, but they started filming last night and Coleman was an extra! We never thought we'd be picked, but then the director heard that Coleman plays the piano, and he asked him to

play in a scene where Jenira Ford and Evan Smith have
their first dance."

"It sounds wonderful," I sighed.

Zara led me to a table in a quiet nook by the fireplace.
"We're already planning a viewing party when the movie
premieres. You must come."

"I'll be there." I told her how Paulette maneuvered to
get Sprinkles in the movie.

Zara laughed. "That cat will steal every scene."

Mary Anne waved from the hostess stand, and as
she approached, Zara stiffened. My reaction was the
same; her appearance shocked me. Mary Anne's usually glossy hair was lank and her eyes dull. She generally opted for vibrant lip color but today she wore no
makeup, and her outfit was a baggy gray sweater over
faded yoga pants and scuffed clogs. She greeted Zara and
took the seat next to me. Zara threw me a worried look,
then bustled off to get our tea.

I leaned forward with concern. "Are you okay?"

Mary Anne rubbed her temples and winced. "I haven't
been able to sleep."

Zara set a tea tray with three layers of goodies before
us and then poured each of us a cup of strong Earl Grey.
Mary Anne forced a smile and said, "Thanks." Two
worry lines creased the space between Zara's eyebrows
and she started to say something to Mary Anne, but was
called away to the hostess stand.

"I know, I look like something the cat dragged in."
Mary Anne added a heaping spoonful of sugar and a generous splash of milk to her tea. She leaned her elbows on
the table. "I had to turn off my phone. Dominic keeps
calling me at all hours," she fumed, "for emotional support!" She turned her phone to me and showed me text
after text on some variation of CALL ME, LET'S TALK, or
I'M SORRY.

"After"—she caught sight of diners at a neighboring table looking over at us and lowered her voice—"what he put me through." She slurped her tea.

I slathered a scone with Devonshire cream, topped it with strawberry jam, and put it in front of her. She took a bite, moaned, then wolfed down the rest. "I don't know how Zara gets these so light." She smiled and I felt my shoulders relax a bit.

"I'm not going to bore you with a rehash of the whole story: Dominic meets Diantha, she promises him a new restaurant, he dumps me, you know all that. I'm over him, Riley. Truly. It's just that now he's stabbed me in the back again," her voice shrilled. "Dominic stole from me!"

Apprehension made me grip my teacup tighter. "Stole from you?" I whispered.

Mary Anne nodded. "When we were married, I used to take care of all our business stuff, correspondence, taxes. Dominic didn't understand that we had a shared email account. After I went home the night before Dominic and Diantha's wedding, I checked the email." She folded her arms. "A couple of years ago, Dominic and I played with the idea of doing a cookbook. I put some of my recipes together and we sent it to an agent but never heard back. Around that time, he got into this experimental gastronomy stuff and won that TV competition and got famous. That's when Dominic met Diantha and soon I was out of the picture. He told me that he'd shelved plans for our cookbook."

A bitter tone crept into her voice. "I guess the agent forgot to update Dominic's email, because last night that email address was copied on a note from the agent, a note asking if this was the final version of the cookbook because the book was going to auction and there are at least three publishers planning to bid. The agent said Dominic could expect a seven-figure deal."

Tears spattered her cheeks and she wiped them away. "The recipes were all mine, Riley. Every last one. So you see, I could've killed *him*. Not Diantha. Though, if I'm being honest, I blamed her, right? She offered him everything I couldn't give him. His own beautiful restaurants. So yeah, I guess maybe I could've killed her too."

A woman at the next table choked on a macaron, and her friend pounded her back.

My throat went dry and I poured myself another cup of tea, taking a sip of the too-hot liquid. She'd just admitted to two motives for Diantha's murder.

Mary Anne's cell rang, and she turned the screen so I could see the caller's name: PENNIMAN POLICE SERVICES.

My teacup rattled in the saucer as I set it down.

"Yes?" Mary Anne answered. I recognized the deep rumble of Jack's voice.

"I'll be right there."

Mary Anne hung up. "Well, at least it's convenient." The police services building was right around the corner from Lily's.

Mary Anne joked, but she grabbed a chocolate macaron from the top tier of the tray and instead of eating it, she crumbled it between her fingers. "Captain Voelker wants me to come in to answer a few questions. I have to go." Her lips trembled as she stood, dug in her pocket, and put some money on the table.

Mary Anne was such a wreck, so emotional and understandably angry I jumped up, gave her a hug, and whispered, "You'll be okay. Jack's a good person. And you're not guilty!"

She held on for a long moment, then pulled back

and gave me a rueful smile. "I'm going down, Riley. The cake. I did that. Even if I didn't kill Diantha, once people know I stabbed the cake, they'll think I killed Diantha too."

The women at the next table didn't even bother to pretend they weren't listening.

"Don't say that," I whispered fiercely, throwing a sour look at the neighboring table. "You weren't even at the Inn that night!"

"But I was, Riley. I went back at midnight." She hunched her shoulders and hurried out.

I dropped back into my seat. I'd figured she'd destroyed the wedding cake before she left for the day, then I remembered the figures I'd seen the night of Diantha's death: the woman in the mobcap I'd seen running through the parking lot at three a.m. and the shadowy caped figure I'd seen at midnight. Mary Anne admitted she'd been back at midnight. So who was the other woman? Or had Mary Anne stayed and tried to disguise herself when she left at three? Why?

I barely had a moment to catch my breath when Tillie power walked past the hostess stand and slid into Mary Anne's vacant seat, shrugging off a beige trench coat.

Zara hurried over and cleared Mary Anne's plate, silverware, and cup, giving me a worried look. I didn't know what to say but I knew that Mary Anne was her own worst enemy, and her deeply emotional state did nothing but make her look guilty. Maybe she *was* guilty. With a wince, I remembered the butchered cake, the dark hair in the ice cream.

"What kind of tea today, Tillie?" Zara said.

"I do like to change it up." Tillie's deep-set brown eyes glittered. She knew something. "A nice Darjeeling, please, with a splash of brandy to warm me up."

"Right away." The table next to us waved for their check, and Zara bustled off to get it.

Usually, Tillie favored bold colors and patterns, most often with a tropical theme and accessorized with neon-hued jewelry, but today, instead of her trademark headwrap, her mass of dark curls was tamed into a tortoiseshell clip, her stocky frame outfitted in subtle brown corduroy pants and a cream tunic top. I couldn't believe I was talking to Tillie.

"What is"—I waved at her outfit—"this?"

"I'm incognito for my protection work for Ms. Ford. Was that Mary Anne Dumas? The psycho who stabbed Diantha's wedding cake? Marley's been telling everyone that story."

I took a calming sip of my tea and changed the subject. "Did Jenira say which way the stalker went yesterday?"

Tillie tsked with a dismissive wave. "No presence of mind, that one. Totally went off screaming, eventually called nine-one-one, but the stalker disappeared into the woods near Magistrate's School. We sent a car over." She nodded thanks as Zara set a pot of tea in front of us and replaced the empty tiered tray with a full one.

"How are you managing both your job and, um, your protection work?" I asked.

Tillie rubbed her hands and selected several sandwiches and scones, glowing at my words. "Protection work, yeah. Sounds better than *security*. That sounds like a bouncer at some dive bar. Jenira's on set long hours, but she likes to run and that's when she needs me to look out for her."

I bit into a watercress and egg salad sandwich and chewed thoughtfully, remembering how Tillie had followed Jenira in her car. "She prefers running on pavement, not trails?"

"She's afraid of the woods, said her psycho stalker may be hiding there."

Something wasn't adding up and I finally realized what it was. "Wait a minute, Tillie. When we talked at the fall festival, you told me Jenira asked for private security before she got here."

She nodded. "Right. She reached out last week, Monday, and she got in town Saturday. So?" She took a delicate raspberry macaron from the top of the tray and popped it in her mouth.

"So this guy started stalking her before she got to Penniman?" I took another scone and slathered it with cream and jam. "She's sure this guy's the same one who was stalking her previously?"

Tillie licked her fingers, fished in her bag, and pulled out a file folder. "Her dossier," she said as she scanned a sheet of paper. "Jenira's been hopping from one film to another. She just wrapped *Furever Heart*—that's spelled F-U-R-ever. It's about a dog walker who also does pet portraits, and she and this guy meet cute when they discover their dogs were littermates—anyway, she was the dog walker. She said she was followed by the same car any time she went off set."

"Where did they film?"

"San Diego." Tillie set aside the folder.

I almost dropped my scone. "She thinks he followed her here to Connecticut from San Diego?"

Through a mouthful of scone, Tillie said, "Yep. White male, brown hair, and sunglasses driving a small white Ford."

"A white male with brown hair and sunglasses?" *Only a million of those.* "Did she get the plate?"

Tillie rolled her eyes in a way that said, *Do you think I'm an amateur?* "She didn't, otherwise I would've run it. It was a California plate."

Only millions of those too. "The man she claims was stalking her here was on foot. She's sure it was the same man she'd seen earlier in the car?"

Tillie shrugged, minus a bit of her usual bluster. "She says so."

I was starting to wonder if this stalker business wasn't some publicity stunt. "I'm sure Jenira feels better with you keeping an eye on her, and if she ever wants to run some trails, tell her I'll be happy to go with her."

"I'll let her know." Tillie patted her lips and gathered her things.

"Before you go"—I lowered my voice—"did Jack check any keys from the Inn?"

Shrugging on her trench coat, Tillie whispered, "Yeah, I saw one in an evidence bag. Had a white ribbon. No prints. Wiped clean."

That was certainly suspicious when everyone staying in the Inn was family. *Why would anyone with a right to be in the hotel wipe a key?* We shared a look.

"Sorry, gotta get to work at the daytime situation."

I blinked.

"My regular job," Tillie said.

"Wait. Anything else?" I waved her close. "Any word on the postmortem?" I whispered.

She cast a glance around the room and said even more quietly, "The bloodwork's being reviewed."

Bloodwork? Did that mean poisoning? The memory of Diantha raising her glass surfaced. I shook my head. She had the same drink everyone else did, the punch from the bowl on the bar. My heart plummeted when I remembered that Mary Anne had been in the kitchen preparing food for the celebration, but I considered, too, that no one else had been sickened.

"Can you let me know what you hear?" I hated to ask, but Tillie was my only source of police information.

Tillie popped the collar on her coat. "I'll be in touch."

She hustled out, conveniently forgetting to pay for her tea. While I waited for the check, I googled "Furever Heart" and scrolled through the credits. Jenira's character was named Madeline, not Carrie. Chip was listed as director and Cooper as assistant director.

It wasn't likely that Jenira's stalker would fly across the country to stalk her again. If so, that was one determined stalker with deep pockets, and Jenira would require more security than Tillie could provide.

Chapter 16

After I paid and said goodbye to Zara, I stepped into the cold, pulling the collar of my jacket tight as I waited for a break in a stream of window-shopping tourists.

Several cars with a variety of license plates were parked at the curb. I couldn't believe that Jenira's stalker had followed her to Penniman from the West Coast, but I didn't want to discount her concern either. Jenira was a beautiful woman, a popular actress in the public eye, and the news was full of too many instances of unhinged fans making the object of their obsession miserable. But it didn't square with someone on foot accosting her. Maybe her stalker had been an overzealous fan, or the encounter was a case of mistaken identity.

Whatever it was, it was more drama.

I cut across the green, throwing a glance over my shoulder at the police services building. Mary Anne's mental state and appearance weren't going to help her cause. Based on her actions and the crazy attack on the cake, I had to admit she looked pretty unstable. A week ago I would've completely dismissed the thought of

Mary Anne being involved in a murder, but now I was confused and heartsick for my friend.

I had to see what else I could find out about the night Diantha had died, dig deeper into my memory of what I'd seen and heard that night. I remembered Rob standing outside in the parking lot at midnight when I'd seen the first caped figure. I wondered what else he'd seen that night.

My phone buzzed with a text from Paulette as I crossed the green toward the Inn. CAN YOU COME TO THE SHOP NOW?

Ha! I knew it. Sprinkles was probably wreaking all kinds of havoc and Paulette wanted me to save the day. I sprinted past the war memorial toward a large crowd across the street from The Penniless Reader. Skylark's security team and sawhorses blocked off the street in front of Dad's shop and confined onlookers to the green.

"Hey, look up there." A man pointed at the roof of the shop as a little black shadow slipped over the top and disappeared onto the other side. Not a shadow. A cat.

Rocky! How did he get here? The Penniless Reader was two miles from home.

A slight man in a tweed suit and bow tie, his tortoiseshell glasses askew, stormed out the front door of Dad's shop, his face red and sweating. I recognized him—Dr. von Furstenburg, the pet psychologist Sprinkles had driven away months ago. He fumed as he pushed through the crew and practically ran down the street. I was relieved to note that unlike his last encounter with Sprinkles, his pants weren't torn and he appeared uninjured.

Three intimidating guys in Security jackets were doing a good job at crowd control, so I jogged around the block to the shop's back door where no guard stood. I used my key to get in and quietly shut the door behind

me, then I tiptoed through the storage room. Holding
my breath, I eased the door open and peeked out the
crack, but my view of the shop's interior was blocked by
the back of a burly crewmember. I grinned as I texted
Paulette. I'M IN THE STORAGE ROOM. I'm not proud
to admit it, but I couldn't wait to see what kind of disaster Sprinkles had caused.

Paulette opened the door, her eyes shining, not a hair
out of place. I cast a glance down to her spotless slacks,
where no tears were evident.

"You should see how marvelous Sprinkles is!" she
whispered.

"Wait, what? Sprinkles is marvelous?" I didn't expect
that. "I'm . . . so glad." She waved me into the shop and
I joined her and Dad behind the film crew and a phalanx
of lights, reflectors, and cameras.

"I saw Rocky on the roof," I whispered.

Paulette nodded. "When I unloaded Sprinkles from
the car, that little scamp darted out. He must've jumped
in and hidden when I picked up Sprinkles this morning."

Jenira and Evan sat in the overstuffed chairs by the
fireplace. To my surprise, Liam stood close by, just out
of camera range, a badge reading CREW clipped to a lanyard around his neck.

Paulette's tone was a bit too casual. "I thought you'd
like to know that the director called in Liam when the
pet psychologist was so late."

Translation: She was playing matchmaker. "I . . .
thank you."

"And then the other psychologist finally showed up
and turned tail when he saw Sprinkles. He actually ran
out the door!" Paulette tsked. "How unprofessional!"

Just prudent. He didn't want to ruin another pair of
pants.

Liam caught my eye and gave me a smile, and as I

returned it I felt a blush warm my cheeks. A real-life Skylark meet cute, engineered by Paulette.

Chip joined me and Paulette as Cooper conferred with the actors. "Hi, Chip. How is Sprinkles working out?" I said.

Chip grinned. "Sprinkles and Evan are magic together. Never seen a cat take to an actor like that. Don't tell Jenira, but that's our love story."

He caught Jenira's eye and she stuck her tongue out at him.

I couldn't argue. As Evan held Sprinkles on his lap, Sprinkles gazed at him with such adoration that I had to stifle a laugh. She was starstruck.

Jenira sat across from them, her knees almost touching Evan's, but Sprinkles ignored her. Jenira wore a blue shirt dress, suede boots, and a soft green cashmere cardigan no librarian could ever hope to afford, her hair pulled back into a high ponytail. Oversized tortoiseshell glasses perched on her pert nose, a style I thought of as "Hollywood librarian."

"Quiet on set." The shop fell silent and I marveled at Jenira's and Evan's ability to ignore the carnival of cameras, hot lights, techs, production assistants, and hangers-on mere inches away as they played their roles.

Cooper said, "Okay, Jenira. Here you are, cuddling your beloved pet Sprinkles as Evan reads you the letter he found in that dusty old book."

A woman I assumed was the pet wrangler took Sprinkles from Evan's arms and settled her on Jenira's lap. Sprinkles stiffened at first, but relaxed when she realized that she was still close to Evan. Laughing, Evan and Jenira made kissy noises at Sprinkles, and Jenira stroked her fur, but the besotted feline diva didn't take her eyes from Evan. She did, however, adjust her paws on Jenira's knees ever so slightly. Paulette's eyes shone as she watched and I could tell the bookshop crowd was charmed, but still the tiniest spark of apprehension kindled in me. Sprinkles was being good, too good.

"Okay." Cooper moved the camera close as Evan murmured his lines. Music may calm the savage breast, but Evan's mellow voice was a close second, and Sprinkles tilted her head and ad-libbed a soft, tender *meow*.

Cooper grinned and exchanged a pleased look with Chip, and kept the camera rolling.

Jenira leaned toward Evan as he finished reading the letter. "With love, your own Monty."

Jenira sighed, her lips curved in a sweet smile, her eyes shimmering with happy tears as she leaned past Sprinkles to share a chaste kiss with Evan.

Cooper raised a hand. "And cut. That was—"

Jenira shrieked and threw Sprinkles off her lap.

"This damn cat dug her nails into my leg!"

As Chip, Cooper, and the furious animal wrangler conferred, Evan, unconcerned, snuggled and baby-talked with Sprinkles. Jenira, fuming, stalked over to the travel section in front of me and Paulette as a makeup person tried to brush powder on her cheeks.

A few minutes later, peace brokered, Cooper walked over to Jenira and squeezed her arm, deploying his charming smile.

"We have what we need," he said. "I'll check the dailies, but Jenira, that scene was magic. Those tears . . ."

"You'd cry too if a cat was digging its claws in you." Jenira jabbed her finger at Sprinkles. "I'm not working with that devil cat again."

"No worries, no worries." Cooper's voice was soft.

"You might not need to. We can get what we need from Sprinkles without you sharing any more, ah, physical contact."

Jenira narrowed her eyes at Sprinkles, then strutted to the coffee maker. Evan didn't notice and Sprinkles didn't turn her head, though I was certain that under that fluffy exterior the little beast was gloating. Cooper rubbed his forehead and returned to his camera operator.

Liam wound his way past the mysteries into the travel section with Paulette and me.

"Riley, how are you?"

"Hi, Liam, fine. I didn't know you were in the movie business."

He leaned his broad-shouldered frame against a row of travel guides to Europe. "The psychologist Skylark hired is a colleague and he called me in when he realized the movie cat was Sprinkles. I guess they have a history." Liam was too much of a professional to laugh, but his dark eyes sparkled as we shared a smile.

I noticed Paulette hovering at my elbow and cleared my throat. "How's Mrs. Dippel's corgi?"

Paulette said, "Yes, how is the little dear?"

Liam flashed me an amused look, then smiled at Paulette. "Fine now, thank you."

Paulette said, "I heard that your date was canceled—"

My face burned as I felt myself blush again. *Oh, please don't, Paulette.*

"Oh yes, we must get to that Ethiopian restaurant," Liam said. "Are you free Thursday? Same time?"

I nodded, and despite Paulette's presence felt my knees go a bit weak.

"It's a date." The animal wrangler waved Liam over and he excused himself.

Paulette preened. "Oh, he's a catch, Riley. Every

woman in the village has set her cap for him, and he's taking you out."

Calling Penniman "the village" was another thing Paulette did that set my teeth on edge, but I couldn't be mad at her now.

"So why did you call me, Paulette?"

"Isn't it obvious?" She looked from Liam to me. "You're welcome."

"We need you at the costume truck now," a voice said as a tap on my shoulder made me turn to a woman flipping pages on a clipboard. She looked up at me and her eyes widened. "Oh, excuse me! I thought you were Jenira's stand in."

Paulette's head swiveled from me to Jenira. "I guess from the back you do look alike."

The costumer apologized and slipped through the crowd to Jenira.

I put my hand to my hair and watched Jenira. We did have similar builds, and with my too-long hair pulled into a ponytail, I guess you could mistake me for the star of Skylark movies.

The thought put a spring in my step as I left the shop. I cast a glance up at the roofline, but didn't see Rocky. I decided not to worry. He was probably enjoying himself watching the intriguing movie action and would return to the car when Paulette left with Sprinkles. But to be sure, I sent Paulette a text to watch out for him.

The afternoon sun's low angle spilled ethereal golden light like veils through the branches of the oaks lining the street as I walked toward the Inn. Where would Rob Wainwright be now? Swishing through several inches of fallen leaves, I cut through a yard into the parking lot of the Inn. Lights glowed in Rob's apartment over the carriage house, and the garage door was open to reveal a gold Jaguar. Rob was sitting in the driver's seat.

At my approach, he jumped out of the car. "Riley, hey, how are you?"

"Good. How are you?"

Rob looked haggard, his chin covered with stubble, as he shrugged into his blue blazer.

"Got a lot to do, what with the cops and Diantha"— he shut the door—"gone."

Sam skateboarded into the parking lot, flipping his board as he stopped at the kitchen stairs. Rob's words were clipped with anger. "The boys are carrying on. When the going gets tough, they go skateboarding and make movies."

I changed the subject. "It's a gorgeous car."

"I helped Diantha pick it out." He ran his fingers along the hood. "She said it was the same color as her hair."

"Can you talk for a minute?" I asked.

"Sure. Come on, I'll get you a drink. It's after five o'clock somewhere." Instead of going into his apartment, we climbed the back steps to the Inn's kitchen, where he pulled out a chair for me at the table in the alcove. "What can I get you from the bar? Glass of wine?"

"Pinot noir, please," I said.

He nodded and soon returned with a glass for me and a tumbler of whiskey for himself.

"To Diantha," he said.

I raised my glass.

He slid an envelope across the table. "Your pay for helping when Ruthie was in the hospital."

"Thanks." I'd completely forgotten about being paid to sub for the missing maids. I stuck the envelope in my bag and turned my attention to the wine. It was soft and rich, a drink to be savored, from a bottle that I was certain I couldn't afford to buy with the amount of money I'd earned.

"The maids you had to fire—were they from Penniman?" I asked.

He nodded. "High school kids. I have a list a mile long of people who applied for the job, but anyone I hire now only wants to be here because of the movie. Since it's family only staying here for now and Ruthie's back to work, we'll muddle through until the film wraps."

I heard footsteps in the kitchen, a low murmur of voices, followed by the rattling of pots and pans.

"Marley's carrying on," I said.

"Dominic's back too." Rob lowered his eyes and swirled his drink. "It helps him to be here, close to her, he says, instead of his place down by the lake. He's staying in Diantha's suite."

"How's the family?" I sipped.

He shrugged. "The cops say we can get back to normal as soon as they clear the Little Room. Should be tonight. Good thing. I've got a hotel to run."

"With the news, are people canceling?" I asked.

Rob met my eye and scoffed. "You kidding? We have more people who want to book than ever, but I have the family and movie taking all the suites upstairs. Maybe I can clear the gift room . . ."

We sipped our drinks and I wondered if the family knew that Rob carried a torch for Diantha. Gerri and Flo knew, and even my dad remembered Rob and Diantha dating in high school. That was a long time for an unrequited love, and Rob's pained expression made me hesitate to ask about his history with Diantha. I changed tack.

"Rob, is there security footage from . . . the night . . ."

"Yeah, well, about the security footage." He winced. "The cops asked too. There isn't any from the hotel. The only place I run footage is on the doorbell of my apartment and the garage. Diantha had some expensive vehicles."

So the police would be able to see if Rob left his apartment, I mused.

"But here in the hotel"—he straightened his back—"we pride ourselves on our discretion. Some of our guests are high profile and they appreciate not being photographed with people they shouldn't be with. But that night the doors were locked as usual. The only people staying were the family, and you. I have a key to the outside doors and so does Marley, Dominic, and Mary Anne."

He went silent, lowering his eyes and swirling the amber liquid in his glass. "And Diantha, of course."

My heart rate ticked up. "Did you see anyone go into the Inn the night of the murder?"

Rob knocked back the rest of his drink. "Sure you wanna know?" He jutted his chin toward the back door. "At midnight the night Diantha died, I saw Mary Anne go right inside that door."

Chapter 17

Mary Anne had told me she was at the Inn the night Diantha died, but hearing Rob confirm it was a blow. I'd been hoping that somehow Mary Anne could be ruled out as a suspect.

"You're sure it was midnight?" I asked.

Rob nodded.

"Were you awake later?"

"Couldn't sleep, got up a few times, but I'm not sure of the time."

I lowered my voice. "A noise woke me around three o'clock, and out my window I saw a woman in the parking lot. She was wearing a long colonial-style dress, a cape, and a white mobcap." I didn't say out loud that the costume reminded me of the one Mary Anne had worn earlier.

Rob rubbed his unshaven chin. "Maybe Mary Anne was in the Inn for three hours? I saw her go in but I never saw her come out."

My breath caught. "Did you watch the parking lot all night?"

Rob shrugged. "Can't say I did. But I saw her, I'm sure, at midnight. I saw her truck, the white pickup she uses to carry stuff from the farmer's market. She had a black cape with a hood. She could've had the what-chamacallit, mobcap on underneath."

This sounded even more damning for Mary Anne. How many women were running around the parking lot of the Inn at night? I took a big swig of my wine as soft classical piano music floated from the lounge.

"I meant to call you." Rob leaned forward. "You wanna come back for the morning shift? The movie people are up early. Until I can get some more help for Ruthie?"

Here I thought we were having a friendly chat, but he'd plied me with wine to loosen me up. *Well played, Rob.* The work was backbreaking, but I was free—Udderly didn't open until one. Perhaps I could check out the rooms I hadn't seen and return to Diantha's suite, perhaps find some evidence that would shift the spotlight of guilt from Mary Anne. "I'll be here."

A phone shrilled from the office down the hall and Rob excused himself to answer it.

I texted Mary Ann. DID YOU WEAR A WHITE MOB-CAP WITH YOUR HALLOWEEN OUTFIT? WHEN DID YOU LEAVE THE INN?

She texted back. WHAT'S A MOB CAP? I HAD A HOOD BUT NO HAT. I STAYED MAYBE FIVE MINUTES.

I followed the lush sound of the piano music, Beethoven's "Moonlight Sonata," famous enough that I recognized it, past the office door Rob had firmly shut behind him.

Table lamps glowed in the lounge as shadows length-ened outside. Emilia sat at the piano with Sam, his skate-board propped against the warm wood. There was a teacup and a first aid kit on a nearby side table.

Emilia's pale skin and wraithlike thinness spoke to her fragile health, but at the piano her posture was

145

upright, her elbows and arms at right angles, and she played with assurance. A lime-green ikat scarf tied on her hair added a vibrant touch to her outfit of a heavy gray cable-knit sweater over matching leggings.

I waited at the doorway as she concluded the music with a flourish and Sam clapped, the sound muffled by a bandage on his hand.

As I entered the room, Sam shook the hair from his face and I noticed another small bandage held in place on his brow with white tape. "Are you okay?" I asked.

Sam shrugged. "Trick didn't go as planned. One of my wheels came loose and I wiped out. Occupational hazard."

Emilia greeted me then took Sam's unbandaged hand. "Your hand this weekend, now your head, Sam. You know how it worries me when you hit your head."

"They're just scrapes. You worry too much." He gave her a crooked smile and I saw a trace of his brother Cooper's boyish charm. Sam shook his shaggy brown hair forward, hiding the bandage. "Out of sight, out of mind." He picked up the first aid kit, gave Emilia a kiss, tucked his board under his arm, and loped out of the room.

Emilia adjusted her sheet music and took a sip of tea. "His hand, now his head, and a few months ago he broke a collar bone. I can't tell you how many bones he's broken, just in the time since we've been married. I should've known. When we met, he was president of the San Diego College extreme sports club. Cooper was vice president."

"I didn't mean to interrupt your music," I said. "That was beautiful."

"Don't apologize, it's nice to talk to someone. Sam's been gone all day presenting skateboarding clinics at his old school and everyone else is either occupied with the movie, or they're the police." Her heavy sweater fell from her narrow shoulders as she turned on the bench to face me.

I took a seat opposite on a deeply cushioned leather chair and asked, "How long have you been married?"

Emilia glanced down at her delicate gold band. "Five years. We married right out of college. Sam swept me off my feet." When she looked up, her eyes were shining. "He was so cool, I couldn't believe he even noticed me. I first met his parents here at the Inn.

"Diantha and Darius, well, Darius was her husband then, Sam's stepdad. His father was Scott Collins, he owned a tech company. He died when Cooper and Sam were young. That's where the bulk of Diantha's money came from."

I wrinkled my brow. "I thought Collins was Diantha's family name."

"It is," Emilia laughed. "It was her maiden name *and* Scott's last name. Weird, huh? Her ancestors farmed here around the time of the Revolution and had this inn. Well, not this building—it burned down at one point and was rebuilt." She nodded to a secluded nook where a letter in a gilt frame hung on the wall over a love seat. I went to the dimly lit corner and read the brief message in ornate, spidery script thanking the innkeeper for his hospitality. I leaned close to read the signature and turned to her in surprise. "George Washington slept here?" This was news to me. I'd grown up in Penniman and had never heard this before.

"Didn't he sleep everywhere?" Emilia gave me a mischievous grin. "Diantha was thrilled to find that letter."

Emilia sipped her tea as I resumed my seat, then continued, "Well, Scott Collins was the father of Cooper and Sam, so she decided to keep Scott's name after she married the third time and the fourth and the fifth so she'd 'match' the boys. Plus, it was her maiden name, so it worked for her. Otherwise she'd be Diantha Collins Worth Collins Lopez Cameron Smalling." She hesitated, then said softly, "Dominello."

"Worth?" I said. "Isn't that Chip's last name?"

Emilia nodded. "Yes, Chip's dad was Diantha's first husband, but Diantha was Mr. Worth's second wife. His first wife, Chip's mother, died when Chip was four." Sadness softened her words. "Chip laughs about what he calls his nannies and boarding-school years. I get the impression Diantha wasn't the most attentive stepmother. Then Mr. Worth died, and Diantha married Mr. Collins. They had Cooper right away but Sam came years later, a surprise baby. So Chip and Cooper are closer, I think, plus they're both in the movie business. Though Sam's been getting into that too. He even had a bit part and taught Jenira how to skateboard for their last Skylark picture. I encourage it. I'm an only child, so I think it's good for them to be together."

I nodded. I was an only child too.

"Diantha keeps family albums in the office"—Emilia waved her teacup toward the hallway—"but I'm the only one who's looked through them in years, so I'm the unofficial family biographer and historian. The guys have no interest, I'm afraid."

My thoughts turned back to the framed letter. "Where did Diantha find the George Washington letter?"

"That was discovered recently, in a cache from her ancestor's house. She had the paper tested by an expert in old documents to authenticate its age, a Mr. Blood." Emilia smiled and headed toward the office, beckoning me to follow. "What a name, right? He's a teacher up at Magistrate's School. Cooper and Chip are shooting in their library on Thursday morning. Say, I heard you were a librarian. You should come watch the shoot. Here, I'll show you the five husbands of Diantha Collins."

As she rooted in a bookcase, I glanced at the top of the broad mahogany desk. Rob had one of those clutter-free desks, with only a computer monitor, keyboard, and an actual leather inbox. On top of the inbox I noticed a memo. One of my small talents is the ability to read upside-down text, and as Emilia gathered photo albums I scanned the top memo and picked out Ruthie's name.

"Per our conversation re: longtime employees. To be offered severance: Ruthie Adams. Please let her know ASAP and hire some younger faces. I've updated the Inn, time to update the staff too."

It was signed simply "D." *Diantha?*

My stomach dropped. Poor Ruthie. This was not only illegal, but cruel.

"Here it is." Emilia held an album to her chest and waited for me to leave the room first. I swallowed my dismay as we took seats next to each other on the couch and she paged through the heavy book on her lap.

"Look at this, Riley. All Diantha's wedding pics. It's a fashion show."

She paused at one of a small boy with oversized glasses holding a ring on a pillow. "That's Chip, ringbearer at the wedding of his dad, Mr. Worth, and Diantha."

As the pages turned the grooms grew progressively older, as did the brothers—Cooper, Sam, and now, I knew, Chip—standing in the background of each wedding party. But in each photo, Diantha gleamed with a polished, ageless beauty.

The last photo was a casual snap of Sam and Emilia, sitting at the head of the table in the Inn's dining room. "We had a small wedding in the Magistrate's School chapel, with only a few friends. Diantha threw a party for us back here . . ." Emilia's voice grew dreamy. "It was lovely. She said she'd been eager for one of her boys to get married. Well, Chip was married twice, but she called only Sam and Cooper her boys." Her smile faltered. "That was awful, really."

"How did you and Sam meet?" I couldn't imagine a less-suited couple—Sam cool, vibrant, and athletic, and Emilia sweet but even in her wedding photos, so wan and fragile.

"In chemistry class." Emilia's pale lips curved at the memory. "I traveled to Africa for a project my sophomore year and learned how many villages need clean water. I wanted to help. I'd been diagnosed with breast cancer that year and I was filled with a sense that I had to make the most of my time." My heart dropped at her words, but Emilia spoke without self-pity. "When my parents passed away, I came into some money. Then I had a relapse. Sam stood by me through all those tough times, helped me with everything, from homework to chemo to the charity work."

This selflessness was well hidden under Sam's cool exterior. I felt myself warming to him and wondered if Rob knew any of this story. Obviously not from his earlier assessment of Sam.

"More tea?" Marley joined us and refreshed Emilia's tea from a pretty antique porcelain pot. I was sure he came in to pick up more scoop on Diantha's death.

"Marley, you've been too kind," Emilia said. "How's Dominic?"

"So brave." Marley gave an exaggerated sigh. "I didn't know if you'd heard"—he gave me an accusing look—"that the cops took that ice-cream cake into custody."

I blinked. "Custody?"

"The wedding cake?" Emilia said.

A satisfied smile curled Marley's thin lips. "Yep, it's evidence. Mary Anne killed Diantha, mark my words. I heard the police hauled her in for questioning."

"I can't believe it," Emilia said.

I figured Emilia was the type who saw only the good in people, and couldn't see that Marley was spreading rumors founded on his own dislike of Mary Anne.

Dominic carried in a tray of bite-sized hors d'oeuvres. "Ladies," he said with exaggerated bonhomie, "I did some *amuse-bouches*, and I hope you'll do me the honor of trying a few of my humble offerings." He set the tray on the coffee table in front of me and Emilia, and my mouth watered as I inhaled the delicious aromas.

Upstaged, Marley held the teapot to his chest. "Dominic, when you have a minute, I want to go over the menus for tonight and tomorrow."

"That's right, family meeting tonight after they wrap," Dominic said, rubbing a hand over the heavy stubble covering his jawline. "Give me a few, okay, Marley?"

Marley harrumphed out as Dominic introduced us to his creations. "Scallops à la Dominic, vegetable frittata sprinkled with parmigiano and mushroom foam, and cranberry and Stilton tuiles. Just a few things I whipped up to keep my mind off things. And Riley," he said, his huge brown eyes bringing to mind a basset hound, "your fudge swirl ice cream?"

At my nod he said, "It was delicious. You must let me work with you on some flavors."

Dominic's words sent a flurry of emotions through me—pride at his compliment, loyalty to Mary Anne, sympathy for his pain, discomfort at my own digging for information. Still, I said, "I'd like that, thank you," and helped myself to a bourbon-glazed, bacon-wrapped scallop. I almost melted from the heavenly flavor.

Emilia beamed and helped herself to one of the tuiles. "I won't be able to eat dinner after this."

The murmur of voices and a tendril of chilly air reached the lounge as the front door of the Inn opened. My phone buzzed with a text from Paulette: I'M TAKING

THE CATS HOME. ROCKY WAS SITTING ON MY CAR WAITING FOR ME.

Several crew members in Skylark sweatshirts entered the lounge and beelined for the hors d'oeuvres. I stood. "I should go."

"Nice talking to you, Riley," Emilia said as chattering crew members joined her on the couch.

"Same here." I meant it. I liked Emilia.

"Riley, a moment please." Dominic took my arm. I'd only reconnected with Mary Anne a few months earlier and I'd never seen her with her ex-husband while they were married, so I was surprised when he leaned close and said, "I heard you saw Mary Anne today. Did she mention me? She won't take my phone calls."

I froze, my mind full of all the things I shouldn't say. I choked out, "We didn't have long to talk. Perhaps you could give her some space."

I hurried from the lounge, and when I got to my car I texted Mary Anne. HOW ARE YOU?

She didn't reply.

Chapter 18

I arrived back at the farmhouse as Paulette's Volvo pulled up. To my surprise, Caroline's car was parked next to the house and she was standing on the porch wringing her hands.

"I was so worried, I had to come back and see how Sprinkles did," she said.

Paulette hefted the carrier out of her car and I helped her carry it into the kitchen. "Sprinkles was good as gold! Not a thing to worry about, though that one"—Paulette pointed at Rocky—"what a Houdini! He was in my car when I got to the shop." She paused. "Here's the best news. Coop said—"

"Coop?" Caroline and I shared a look.

"Cooper's nickname," Paulette said breezily. "Coop told me I can be background in the library scene they're shooting Thursday! Have to get my hair done. Ta!" Paulette floated out the door.

Caroline raised an eyebrow. "Sprinkles, good as gold?"

"Let me fill you in on what really happened," I said as I let the two beasts out of the cage. Sprinkles staggered out and collapsed dramatically, knowing Caroline would swoop in to cuddle her. Caroline responded exactly as expected, draping Sprinkles over one shoulder. Rocky sprang from the carrier and sprinted down the hall, stalking a shadow only he could see.

Caroline and I had pizza and salad delivered from our favorite parlor, Supreme Pizza, and opened a bottle of red wine. She was alternately amused and horrified to hear of Sprinkles' antics on the set. "But that nice Evan Smith loves you," she baby-talked to Sprinkles. "Easy to see why."

I choked on my wine.

My phone buzzed with a message from Mary Anne. THE COPS LET ME GO. FOR NOW. TALK TO YOU LATER.

I sighed with relief, but I knew her reprieve would be short lived. When Jack talked to Rob, Mary Anne would be questioned again.

"Two cupcakes left." Caroline set them on two plates and put on the kettle.

There was a knock at the door. Through the window I could see Jack's SUV parked in front of the house, and Jack standing in the porchlight, still dressed in his uniform.

I tried to keep my voice light as I opened the door. "Hi, Jack, come in."

"Hey, Riley," he said. "I see Caroline's home . . ."

"Hi Jack!" Caroline couldn't suppress the happiness in her voice. "We have some pizza left over. Have you eaten?"

"Some pizza'd be great, thanks."

There are some moments when a person is sure she's a third wheel, and this was one of them. I grabbed onto the first thing I could use as an excuse to give them space.

"Hey, I really have to work on these letters for the

historical society." I stepped into the dining room and gathered a ribbon-tied stack. "I'll take them upstairs. See you later, Jack."

Jack settled at the table as Caroline reheated pizza. His broad frame and gun belt made the cozy kitchen seem small. Rocky leapt into my empty chair and let Jack gave him a chin rub while Sprinkles stalked by the powder room door, eyeing Jack through narrowed eyes. I hoped Jack would keep his wits about him.

"Riley." Jack's tone was even. "I'd appreciate it if you'd stop by the station tomorrow. Say around one? I want to clear up a few details."

Caroline caught my eye. "I'm working remotely for a few days. I can cover at the shop," she said.

"Okay. See you then." I climbed the stairs to my bedroom and set the stack of papers on my desk, wondering what Jack had to say to Caroline. My eyes fell on the letter from Paolo. I knew Gerri would be breathing down my neck about the Collins letters, but the letter on my nightstand sent a bigger rush of anxiety through me. I shoved it in the drawer. *Out of sight, out of mind*, I hoped.

Soft conversation rose from downstairs. Leaving my door slightly ajar so Rocky could join me if he chose, I put on noise-canceling headphones to give Jack and Caroline privacy. As I picked up the stack of letters, I remembered the Inn's thank-you missive from George Washington. I curled up on my bed and texted Flo.

DID YOU KNOW THAT GEORGE WASHINGTON SLEPT AT THE INN ON THE GREEN?

Flo answered with laughing emojis. THAT'S A STORY I'LL TELL YOU TOMORROW AT WORK.

I lay back on my pillows, wondering what Flo had to tell me. I carefully untied the silk ribbon and took the first letter off the stack. I'd be careful to keep them in order. Dated April 2, 1776, it contained flowery wishes for good health and a protracted discussion of—once again—corn prices. Several random letters and numbers were underlined, either a puzzling addition or a trick played by my tired eyes. I transcribed them on a notepad and laughed at myself when they spelled out nonsense L K 2 7 29. *Once in the CIA, always in the CIA.* The spidery words on the page faded as my head nodded to my chest and I fought to keep my eyes open.

From the corner of my eye, I saw Caroline pass my door on the way to her room. I jumped to the window in time to see the lights on Jack's SUV disappear down the lane.

I tossed aside my headphones and hurried to Caroline's room. She was seated before her easel, setting up a new canvas, a bad sign. Sprinkles lumbered in after me, pulled herself up the cat steps to the bed, and flopped on Caroline's pillow.

"How's Jack?" I kept my tone neutral.

"He's okay, I guess. The whole conversation was about how busy he is and how he won't get to see me much." She turned to face me. "I haven't dated much— well, at all. Is this the 'he's not that into you' talk?" Her voice trembled. "I feel like he's going to break up with me."

"I think he's truly busy." My heart squeezed at her worried expression. I did believe my words, but I also knew Caroline's kind nature made her very good at reading people.

"Well, he did stop by, and ate a piece of pizza, and Sprinkles didn't attack. Gotta be grateful for small favors." Caroline's generous mouth curled in a small, sad smile, and she turned back to her canvas.

I gave her a hug and left her to her painting.

I returned to my room, fuming. What was wrong with Jack? Sure he was busy with Diantha's death, but he did eat and run. I checked my watch—he was in and out in twenty minutes.

I flung myself onto my bed, pushing aside the papers, then chastised myself as I scrambled to straighten them. These were old, fragile, and perhaps valuable. I recalled the George Washington letter hanging in the Inn's lounge. Maybe there'd be more missives from colonial luminaries in these papers or, I sighed, more wrangling over corn.

Instead of resuming my work on the letters, I put on my pajamas, then sat cross-legged on my bed and opened my laptop. My gut told me Diantha had been murdered. I had to find out as much as I could about the players in Diantha's family circle, in order to remove the cloud of suspicion from Mary Anne. With the assistance of the state's CSI team, Jack would solve it himself—I'd seen him work before, and he was a smart and dogged investigator—but who knew how long it would take? What if he focused too hard on Mary Anne? What if he missed important clues because people wouldn't share things with him like they would with me? And what if he drifted so far apart from Caroline during the investigation that they couldn't find their way back to each other?

I turned to social media to get more intel on the people I considered suspects.

From Mary Anne's social-media posts, it was obvious that she and Dominic had run the restaurant at the Inn as a team—until last year when Diantha entered the picture.

Although she'd visit the Inn occasionally, Diantha's home base was Los Angeles. She'd returned to Penniman a year ago after her last husband's passing, renovating and moving into her suite, spending more and more time with Dominic. Diantha had promoted Mary Anne to head of the Inn's very lucrative catering operation. In hindsight, I wondered if Diantha had done so to keep Mary Anne out of the picture. Diantha had even encouraged Mary Anne to join the Women in Business Club where I'd reconnected with her, and now I suspected she'd filled Mary Anne's every free moment to keep her away from Dominic. Mary Anne must've realized this too. No wonder she was so devastated. She'd been betrayed by both of them.

What did I know about Diantha Collins? A beauty, she was chronicled in several pieces in fancy shelter magazines where wealthy people allowed a photographer inside to show off their homes. In one photo, Diantha stood on the front steps of the Inn, arms held wide in welcome, with Dominic and Mary Anne behind her in chef's whites. The caption read "Diantha Collins and her vibrant staff are bringing modern luxury to the venerable Inn on the Green."

I'd glean nothing from these polished puff pieces. I needed gossip and I knew where to get it. I'd talk with Flo and Gerri at the shop tomorrow.

I googled Emilia Collins and found a magazine piece on Hope + Hydro + Hugs, her charity that was bringing clean drinking water to villages in Africa. One photo showed Emilia and Sam in hard hats, working with a construction team; Sam's dynamic athlete's energy and colorful attire contrasted with Emilia's too-thin build and wan appearance.

Her parents, the owners of a Texas energy company, had been killed in a car accident while she was in college, and Emilia had inherited everything. I recalled she'd also battled breast cancer during those years. So much tragedy to handle, so young.

Sam Collins had a vibrant social-media presence, full of striking images of him base jumping, freediving, swimming with sharks, dirt biking, and skateboarding. He'd won several competitions, but what I'd overheard my first night at the Inn was evident: many younger skateboarders were nipping at his heels, and in his late twenties he was an elder statesman in a youth-oriented sport. He'd also had a wild side in his teens, including a stint in drug rehab and brushes with the law.

Cooper Collins. There were still thousands of fans who carried a torch for the former teen wizard. His shaggy blond curls, his broad grin, those sea blue eyes . . . I sighed. He was still handsome and retained the sweetness of his youthful character. If he'd had any scrapes with the law, they'd been buried. I was ready to close my laptop after what felt like the fiftieth puff piece about Cooper and some starlet when a headline made me sit up. *"Production company sued over actors' deaths."* There were several short, vague articles in movie industry news sites about a film Cooper had produced in Poland with a company called Mojo Productions. *"Actors drown in horror film accident."* The link went to a Polish newspaper. I copied the link into an email to a former colleague working in Krakow, asked for a translation, and hit send as I wondered what had happened. But I couldn't imagine a connection between these deaths and Diantha. The accident had happened two years earlier.

I moved on to Chip. Chip Worth had produced and directed several low-budget films but now had a string of hits with Skylark, and on the last few he'd worked in tandem with Cooper. Emilia had mentioned that Sam was starting to get into the film business too. One photo from a shoot in Florida from two summers earlier showed all three brothers on a dive boat, tanned arms draped around each other's shoulders. That meant they all got along, right?

I remembered the conversation I'd heard my first night in the Inn—Cooper and Sam, the two "bros" lamenting their mother's tight purse strings. I was certain I'd heard only two voices. Did Sam and Cooper truly consider Chip a brother, a part of the family?

And how exactly was Diantha killed? Tillie had talked about blood work. I remembered the fire department checking the heating system. They had reason to believe Diantha had been killed by carbon monoxide poisoning. I let this play out in my mind . . . But how? I'd have to see what information I could glean from Tillie about the cause of death.

My mind shifted to motive.

Dominic had no motive I could see to kill Diantha. If she lived, he'd get his own restaurant. He had the most to lose.

Mary Anne had too many motives. Diantha had taken her husband. She was angry and hurt, but would that fury drive her to murder Diantha when her husband was the one who had done her wrong? Was killing Diantha a way to hurt Dominic? Whew. That would be dark and at odds with the lively woman I knew, but I shifted uneasily as I recalled the woman I'd had tea with at Lily's. Mary Anne was an emotional, betrayed woman at the end of a frayed rope.

What about Diantha's will? Diantha planned to change her will after her marriage to benefit Dominic. Chip, Cooper, and Sam would be cut off. Emilia's words came back to me: "She called only Sam and Cooper her boys. That was awful, really." Had Diantha ever formally adopted Chip? Probably not. Money wouldn't be a motive for him to kill, but maybe years of emotional abuse were?

Who else had been at the Inn the night Diantha died?

Rob. I'd seen him arguing with Diantha early in the evening, seen him at midnight outside in the parking lot. It must've been difficult to stay at a party celebrating the marriage of his beloved to someone else. Talk about a complicated situation. He lived behind his workplace and he worked for Diantha. I wondered if he'd been happy with that arrangement, if working for her was as close as he could get as she married so many others.

He'd been furious that night. I had to talk to him again, but I wondered what kind of answers I'd get. I typed "Rob Wainwright" into my search engine, but he had no social-media presence. The few photos of Rob were group shots in various Penniman business and charity organizations.

Jenira Ford was the opposite. Her name brought up thousands of hits and dozens of advertisements. America's sweetheart. Queen of Skylark movies. Her association with Skylark had clearly been lucrative.

I typed in "Jenira Ford stalker," and discovered that she'd had several over the years. She'd been involved with several actors, and I stopped scrolling when I saw a photo of her with Cooper Collins at an awards show. *"Former child star escorts Queen of Skylark to premiere."* It was the only photo of the two of them together. Did one date mean anything? I recalled the communicating doors between their rooms, his lock open, hers closed.

The firehose of Jenira's social media, endorsements, and advertising made me log off and rub my eyes.

As I closed the laptop, I recalled the memo on Rob's desk that recommended firing Ruthie. Had Rob spoken to Ruthie about Diantha's wish to let her go? Had Ruthie seen that memo? Ruthie told me she needed her job, needed it so she could take care of Lucretia. Lucretia was in high school, looking at college. That would be a huge expense for someone like Ruthie living on a retirement and her salary from the Inn.

Diantha had one of Lucretia's pumpkins in her room. Did that mean anything? What was Lucretia's story? She was a talented artist, but didn't have the best social skills.

I opened my travel notebook and grabbed my preferred pencil, a Palomino Blackwing. Dad teased me about my love of what he called the "Cadillac of pencils," but he always splurged and put a box of the pricey pencils in my Christmas stocking. Writing things down, organizing them, looking for similarities helped calm my mind, especially when I wrote in a favorite notebook with the luxurious writing implement. I labeled a fresh page SUSPECTS.

COOPER—Handsome child star transitioning to directing sweet romance movies. Stood to be disinherited.

SAM—Wild-child skateboarder who'd turned a corner thanks to his saintly wife. Stood to be disinherited.

CHIP—The charming stepson and experienced filmmaker. Heavy drinker. Did he stand to be disinherited too?

In the margin by their names I noted: THREE BROTHERS. Did that matter?

JENIRA—America's sweetheart, dealing with a stalker. Wants to explore grittier movie roles. Seems to have no connection with Diantha.

EMILIA—Cancer survivor, charity founder. No motive I could see. Already an heiress.

DOMINIC—Jovial chef had everything to lose if Diantha died. No motive.

Like Rob, he'd seemed genuinely broken up by Diantha's death—though he'd immediately looked to his former wife for support.

I added MARLEY. I'd forgotten to google him. He had no social media. I couldn't imagine him doing anything other than sucking up to Diantha. He focused his spite on Mary Anne, always hammering on any perceived or imaginary misstep. What did he have against her? Was it jealousy? I recalled him behind the bar with Dominic the night of Diantha's murder. He and Dominic were clearly chummy. I couldn't see him doing anything to jeopardize that friendship—or did he want Dominic all to himself? Did he see partnership with Dominic as a shortcut to professional success? If Diantha were gone, did he think he and Dominic would be closer than ever? But with Diantha gone, there'd be no new restaurant for Dominic. With reluctance I wrote, NO MOTIVE.

ROB. He'd seemed so genuinely broken by her death, more than anyone else. But what about the argument I'd witnessed? He had history with Diantha, going back to Penniman High School. Had the torch he'd carried been extinguished by Diantha's cruel rejection? Motive? I wrote, IF I CAN'T HAVE HER, NO ONE CAN.

At the end, I put MARY ANNE—JEALOUS, EMOTIONALLY OVERWROUGHT, WRONGED EX-WIFE. Unfortunately, nothing I'd found took her off the list. I sighed and wrote, TOO MANY MOTIVES TO LIST.

I suddenly remembered the figure in the mobcap and cape I'd seen running behind the Inn. Mary Anne said she hadn't worn the colonial cap under her hooded cape, hadn't run through the parking lot at three a.m. From the angle this person took, she might've exited the fire door by the swimming pool and spa wing. Who was this? A party guest taking a shortcut home? A ghost? My short-lived stint in the army had taught me this: always consider the unknown. I wrote "X," my unknown.

The killer's motive could be unknown too, I realized, as I scanned the few I'd jotted down. I had more questions than answers. I turned off the light and soon slipped over the edge of sleep.

Chapter 19

WEDNESDAY

K nowing that I'd need to save my energy for my
shift at the Inn, I decided it was wise to skip my
morning run. After getting ready for the day, I peeked
into Caroline's room. We both slept with our doors ajar
so our feline overlords could slip in and out of our rooms
as they pleased. Through the narrow opening, I could
see Caroline's canvas—an abstract of confusing lines
and muddy colors. Her state of mind, I supposed, a bit
literal, very unlike her usual sun-washed landscapes.

Sprinkles didn't dart out at the top of the stairs in her
customary attempt to trip me. Instead, I found her in the
kitchen, sitting by her carrier on the worn yellow linoleum, grooming herself.

"You're up early." I made a quick breakfast of scrambled eggs and pumpkin spice bread toast and brewed a
pot of coffee. I poured kibble for Rocky and put out some
of Sprinkles' froufrou diet food, but she turned up her
nose, instead holding my eye with a baleful expression
and looking from me to the door. Her meaning was clear:
she wanted to go back to the movie set, back to Evan.

"You'll have to join his fan club like everyone else," I said.

Evan. How had I forgotten him? His bland, good-guy Skylark image had prevented my brain from connecting him to anything as dark as murder. Could he have anything to do with Diantha's death? I jogged upstairs and wrote EVAN? in my notebook then ran downstairs. "Thanks, Sprinkles," I called as I raced out the door to Sadie.

At the Inn, I hung up my coat and slipped on my housekeeping smock. No one was in the kitchen, though pans on the range, bowls on the counter, and baskets of pastries were evidence of a chef at work.

I held my breath and eased open the door to the butler's pantry, and through the crack saw Marley listening to a murmur of voices at the door to the dining room. I closed it and returned to the kitchen. Two could play that game.

I hurried to the housekeeping closet and pushed the cart through the back hallway to the lounge. The door to the office was closed. I parked my cart, took the feather duster, went to the lobby, and dusted the reception desk. There was a pumpkin cleverly carved with a design of bats in flight next to the computer, and though I recognized the work I turned it to see the artist's signature— LPP. Lucretia's Perfect Pumpkins.

The computer's screen saver showed a photo of the Inn, but I couldn't see any way to access it without a security passcode. My gaze fell to an old-fashioned guest book behind the desk, along with a fancy quill pen. I flipped through the book, my eyebrows raising at the luminaries who'd stayed here without my ever hearing about it on the Penniman gossip network. The Inn was discreet, good at keeping the secrets of its guests.

I dusted the dust-free credenza and glanced into the

dining room. The three brothers sat at a round table covered with the detritus of breakfast and cups of coffee.

"What's the lawyer say?" Chip asked.

"What we already knew. Sam and I inherit after it all goes through probate. Sorry, man." Cooper clapped a hand on Chip's shoulder.

Chip scoffed and wrapped his hands around his coffee cup. As he did, a red stone on his ring flashed, the same style as the ring on Sam's hand. "I didn't expect anything. Honest."

"What about Dominic?" Sam said.

Cooper pushed his plate away, light glinting on a similar ring. Did the three men wear the rings as a sign of fraternity? Were they family rings?

"No idea," Cooper said. "Rob was asking me what to do with the wedding gifts. They're Dominic's, right? Let him decide what to do with them."

Sam took a croissant from the basket and slathered it with jam. "Half Diantha's."

Chip raised a hand. "Leave them. Dominic's so emotional. I don't want to be anywhere around when he starts opening them and the waterworks turn on."

"Rob says he has a hotel to run," Cooper said, "and he needs to move them out of that guest room."

Sam licked crumbs from his fingers, stood, and stretched. "I don't care about that as long as we're in agreement on the big stuff."

"Yeah." Cooper rubbed his eyes. "I'm based in California now. I can't run an inn and a restaurant in Connecticut. We'll sell everything: restaurant, inn, carriage house, outbuildings. Rob recommended a real estate company."

My breath caught. *Outbuildings? Did that mean Ruthie's house?*

I heard footsteps and turned to see Evan descending

the stairs. He gave me a smile, dipping his chin shyly and pushing back his wave of sandy hair, and joined the men in the dining room. If this had been a Skylark movie, he would've tripped over the cord of my vacuum so we could meet cute. Alas, life's not a movie and he strode into the dining room without incident. Evan was greeted by the brothers and the conversation turned to the film. I returned to the butler's pantry and whispered behind Marley. "Do they come back for lunch?"

He jumped and pushed past me to the kitchen, his pasty face now scarlet. "No, they have a craft services team in that tractor trailer that cooks for the entire cast and crew. I make sure they have something in case they want to eat here. Emilia doesn't work on the shoot, nor Sam, so they need breakfast. Rob eats here too."

"I can't blame him." I gave him my most engaging smile. "Everything looks delicious."

Marley preened at the compliment but he didn't invite me to partake. "I guess you'd better get working."

Thanks a lot.

Rob entered the kitchen and beelined for the coffee maker, poured himself a cup, then loaded a plate he took to the table in the alcove. He drank deeply of his coffee, then gave me a smile that didn't reach his tired eyes. "Riley, good morning. The cops are done on the second floor, so you can get to those rooms first." He cleared his throat and looked down into this cup. "Don't bother with Diantha's Little Room. I'm going to see that it's renovated. Ruthie's coming back later today after her follow-up at the cardiologist this morning, and she'll do the third floor. They said we can pull down the police tape."

"Okay." Trying to hide my eagerness, I took the back stairs to the second floor.

Across the hall a Do Not Disturb tag hung on Sam and Emilia's doorknob, so I pulled down the police tape and opened the door to the Little Room as quietly as I could. Unlike the morning Ruthie found Diantha, today the room felt warm as I stepped into a patch of golden sunlight streaming through the narrow window. If there were ghosts haunting the Inn, had Diantha joined their ranks? Despite the warmth, the room had a strange, hushed feel.

The first thing I noticed was that the mattress had been removed from the bed and the fourposter stood with rails exposed. No guest would want to sleep on a mattress that had held a dead body. Black fingerprint powder had been swirled on the beige door and walls. I threw my mind back to Sunday morning. What was different? Obviously the mattress . . . but . . .

The room had been cold, the window open. Many people preferred a cold room for sleeping, but Saturday night and the following morning had been frigid. I remembered Marley's breath puffing as he stood unsteadily by the window, gulping fresh air. I stood at the window, careful not to touch the smears of black powder on the sill.

Had Diantha opened the window, or had her killer? Below me in the parking lot was the dumpster used by the renovation crew, filled with wood, construction debris, bags of trash, boxes, and a scrap of white fabric, no—I shifted my angle to see better—it was a towel with embroidery in the Inn's distinctive blue. Was it Diantha's missing towel?

Why had Diantha—or her killer—thrown her towel out the window? I dialed the police services building.

A familiar, musical voice answered. "Penniman Police Services."

"Tillie, it's Riley. Is Jack there?"

"Just left. He's on his way to the Inn." Her voice lowered. "What—"

"Thanks." I hung up and silenced the phone when she called me back. Instead, I turned back to the room, wishing it would give up its secrets. My eyes fell on the carved pumpkin by the fireplace, the skeleton bride and groom locked in a macabre dance.

I closed the door behind me and hurried to the lobby, arriving as Rob opened the door for Jack.

"Can I speak to you for a moment?" I asked.

If Jack was surprised, he didn't show it. He asked Rob to wait in the office then followed me to the Little Room. From there I led him out to the dumpster where he climbed on a box to see better where I had pointed out the towel. "One was missing from Diantha's room," I explained. Jack climbed down and made a phone call, and I took his place and peered over the dumpster's edge.

The towel partially covered a couple of Styrofoam and cardboard boxes. There was other trash, including some wadded-up balls of gift wrap and a pile of papers. They were out of reach, so I pulled out my phone, zoomed in, and snapped several photos. I'd seen a similar set of bound papers in Jenira's room and the office—it was a script.

"I'm not even going to ask why you're still here." Jack waved his hand at my smock as I jumped down from the box.

"I'm helping while Ruthie's at the cardiologist." I slid my phone into my pocket, glad my excuse sounded so virtuous. "Did you see that script in there?"

Jack ignored my question. "Don't forget we have an interview at one o'clock. You'd better get back to work"— he gave me a wry look—"cleaning."

Chapter 20

I sped through cleaning the room I'd stayed in but returned again and again to the window to watch Jack at the dumpster. He was on his phone the whole time. I checked the photo of the script I'd taken, enlarging it as much as possible, but could only make out one line: *"The severed head belonged to her ex-lover, the drug dealer, K-Low."* My eyebrows flew up—this was definitely not the script for a Skylark movie.

Why was a pristine-looking hotel towel in the dumpster? Did Diantha's killer need to clean something? I examined my photos. The towel in the dumpster seemed unsullied, but I couldn't tell for sure.

I cracked my window as Rob joined Jack at the dumpster, and listened to Rob trying to pump him for information, but Jack was a brick wall, a polite brick wall, but a brick wall all the same. The CSI van pulled up and Rob went back inside the Inn.

The CSI team outside conferred with Jack then got to work erecting a tent over the dumpster, blocking my view. *Drat.*

My shoulders slumped. I had to get back to work.

I heard a door open and close and footsteps fade down the hallway.

The Do Not Disturb tag was now gone from Sam and Emilia's doorknob. I read the brass plaque on their door (YARROW) as I used my access key and entered, expecting a cramped room like mine and Diantha's Little Room. Instead, it was a surprisingly comfortable size, two rooms knocked together to form a small suite. Again, Diantha's designers had retained the cozy feel of the colonial style with soft blue toile wallpaper and white wainscoting, but all modern amenities—flat screen TV, soaking tub, minifridge—were integrated in ways that were streamlined and elegant.

The strange intimacy of the housekeeper's work struck me again as I emptied trash and stripped sheets and towels. Emilia must've tidied, because the surfaces of the antique furniture were free of clutter. Inside the closet I saw suitcases with tagged airport codes from around the world: KRK, AUH; the newest was JNB, Johannesburg's Tambo Airport, which corroborated what I'd learned of their recent travels.

Sam's shiny silver titanium suitcases were covered with colorful stickers advertising skateboard swag, and a month's worth of athletic gear hung in the closet. Emilia's suitcases were scuffed and battered, the utilitarian dark navy blue fabric faded and worn. Her clothing was comprised of practical pants, wool sweaters, a green duffel coat, and sturdy boots.

On the bedside table by what I assumed was Emilia's side of the bed were a stack of spiritual books, sheet music, and a thick textbook on the history of South Africa. On Sam's side was a laptop, noise-canceling headphones, and several bottles of vitamins. There were protein powders in large canisters on the wet bar.

Swim trunks hung in the shower surround, and I

counted two extra towels. They were plain, without the Inn's distinctive blue embroidery. I recalled the spa's pool and a dressing room door leading off the pool deck. There must be spa towels in there for people who wanted to swim. On the bathroom sink's marble counter were almost a dozen pill bottles. I looked up the names on the labels, read the accompanying information . . . *"taking for 5 years lowers the chance of breast cancer recurrence and new breast cancers . . ."*

Poor Emilia.

I returned to Diantha's Little Room, but it had no more to tell me. I stepped out and let the door lock behind me. I was certain the towel in the dumpster must have come from Diantha's room, but the script? Had she been involved with the movie at all? I recalled the layout of the Inn. Chip's room was directly over Diantha's.

The investigators had tracked in leaf litter and dirt, and I vacuumed my way down the hallway. When I turned off the vacuum, I heard piano music from the lounge.

I stowed the vacuum and hurried down the stairs, slowing my steps as I watched Marley behind the reception desk, bent over the guest book. He stowed his phone in his pocket as he hurried into the dining room. *What was that about?*

Emilia turned from the piano as I entered the lounge. The room wasn't as messy as the day before, and I sighed with relief as I gathered a few glasses and wiped down the bar.

Emilia smiled. "Good morning."

"Hi."

Emilia gestured to a basket and tea tray on the coffee table. "Marley brought me too much food. Would you like some?"

Emilia was lonely, and I was starving. I washed my hands at the bar and joined her at the coffee table.

"Thanks."

She poured me a cup of tea as I heaped a plate with a light-as-air apple and pear strudel, pumpkin and chocolate chip muffins, a skewer of jewel-toned fruit, and a miniature quiche. I bit into the quiche, marveling at the gooey cheese, spinach, and mushrooms with a hint of tangy horseradish. Sneaky Marley and I would never be friends, but I had to admit he could cook.

"So, Dominic told me you run the ice-cream shop by Fairweather Farm," Emilia said. "Have you worked there long?"

"Since this summer," I said. "Before that, I was a librarian." I left out the part about working for the CIA.

"Bit of a change," Emilia said.

I laughed and thought, *You have no idea.*

"I told Sam we have to get over there before you close for the season. I adore pumpkin spice ice cream."

"Any time, and if Udderly's closed, just knock on the door of the farmhouse. Or I could bring you some," I said. That would give me another excuse to visit the Inn. I didn't know how long I'd be able to pull off the housekeeper ruse. "How long will you be here for the filming?"

"It was supposed to be a couple of weeks, but of course with Diantha's"—she swallowed hard—"passing, the schedule was upended. And the boys and Dominic, of course, will have to plan a memorial service, but that'll take place later."

Sharing a pot of tea always creates a cozy atmosphere, one perfect for sharing confidences. "Did you know Diantha well?"

She shook her head. "Not really. We didn't even meet before our wedding. To be honest, she and Sam weren't close. She wasn't close with any of the boys, well, maybe with Cooper. She managed his acting career when he was a boy and that gave them a bond."

Rob entered the lounge, hands pressed together in a supplicating gesture. "Emilia. Dominic asked me to, er, help him with a task." His deep inhale said *somebody's being dramatic.* "He wants to inventory the gifts, but, understandably, he doesn't feel up to it himself."

I remembered that Rob wanted to get the gift room emptied and wondered if he'd pushed Dominic on this score.

"Could you possibly help me with that?" Rob said. "I think it best if two of us tackle that task."

"I could help." The words were out before I thought. I wanted to poke around more, and my work downstairs was done.

"Riley would be a great help, Rob," Emilia said. "She used to be a librarian, so she'd be very organized."

"If you don't mind." Relief relaxed Rob's expression. It probably would've been painful for him to be surrounded by wedding gifts for a man marrying the woman he loved. I also saw the calculation in his eyes.

"I'm off the clock," I said. Besides, I'd seen a menu, and whatever he'd pay me wouldn't equal the cost of the pastries I'd eaten.

He handed Emilia a key on a blue ribbon. "Thanks."

Emilia and I took the stairs to the third floor, Emilia gripping the banister to pull herself up and placing each foot with care. We hesitated at the top so she could catch her breath, then we moved down the hall to the gift room. "I'm a bit slow these days," she said as she turned the old-fashioned key and I remembered that the keys hung behind the desk downstairs, where anyone could get them.

"The keys are a charming touch," I said.

Emilia turned to me with a sad smile. "Right? Diantha thought of everything."

Light streamed through the double windows onto

the wrapped boxes that covered the bed and tops of the desk, bureaus, chairs, and even the wing chair's ottoman. Cardboard shipping boxes were stacked in a corner by a tall grandfather clock. We discussed a system, and Rob had provided us with index cards where I determined we'd note the giver's name, gift, and contact information.

On the mahogany desk was a basket filled with greeting cards and a brass letter opener. I cleared the desktop, pulled out the chair for Emilia, and said, "Why don't you get started on the cards?" I started opening the heavier cardboard boxes with the boxcutter Rob had given me, stuffing the wrapping into a bag and flattening the boxes for recycling.

"It's so sad that all these gifts are a source of pain for Dominic," Emilia sighed as she opened cards. "People were so generous. Many remembered that Sam and I have a charity and made substantial donations in Dominic and Diantha's names."

"That's great," I said as I opened a box and lifted out a tacky gilt clock flanked by two crystal lovebirds. Emilia caught my eye and we shared a laugh. I set it down and wondered what on earth Dominic would do with it.

Next, I picked up a medium-sized gift wrapped in silver paper tied with a white bow. It was the same paper I'd seen crumpled in the trash in the dumpster beneath Diantha's window. My heart started an uneasy drumbeat as I opened the attached card. *With all our best wishes for happiness! With love, Sam and Emilia.*

Emilia's voice cut into my thoughts. "That's from me and Sam."

I swallowed and set it down unwrapped as Emilia spoke.

"It's a basket woven by some of the craftspeople in our village in Ghana. Getting it here was quite the adventure." Emilia sliced open an envelope as she spoke, oblivious to my silence. "You can't bring a wrapped gift through customs, so on the way here we stopped at that nice gift shop across the green. Well, I thought I left the wrap in the library, but when I went back it was gone and I couldn't find it anywhere! I was so jet-lagged, I couldn't remember where I put it. So I had to run across the green to get more."

"You have a green duffel coat," I said. Of course, I'd seen it in her closet.

She nodded, surprised.

"I saw you at the festival." I considered how quickly she'd moved that night on the green as I looked around for a place to put the gift. Jack needed to see this, but I didn't want to call Emilia's attention to it. Trash from the rooms was bagged and put in the Inn's dumpster, not tossed into the construction dumpster. How did that wrapping paper get into the dumpster? A thought dampened my excitement. Had Lucretia taken a shortcut in her cleaning and tossed the gift wrap without bagging it?

Emilia gave me a rueful smile. "Sorry, I was so tired and jet-lagged I didn't notice anyone. When I got back, Sam made me a smoothie and I went to sleep."

I set the gift on the floor next to the bed and checked my watch. I had five minutes to run across the green to the police station for my interview with Jack. "I'm sorry, I have to go now."

Emilia set down her pen and looked up at the grandfather clock in the corner. "I probably should get some rest. It's nice to have something to do, and someone to do it with."

I gave her a smile I hoped masked my uneasiness.

Wrapping paper in the trash. Was I seeing shadows where there were none? I'd tell Jack about it and let him decide.

Chapter 21

I dashed across the green and into the police services building at three minutes after one. Jack stood at the door of an interview room, frowning at his watch as I entered. Tillie was at her desk, studiously avoiding my eyes, which made me certain she had news to share. Jack made an "after you" gesture and I walked into the interview room ahead of him.

"I went over your statement from the morning of Diantha Collins' death." He opened his notebook. I glanced down at it, but Jack clicked open his pen and turned to a clean page before I could focus on his writing. I raised my eyes to his stony look. "You didn't mention seeing someone at three a.m. in the parking lot."

My mouth went dry. He'd talked to Rob.

I cleared my throat. "If I remember correctly you said, 'Save the cake story for later. Tell me what happened when you found Diantha Collins this morning.' You didn't ask me about the night before."

Jack took a deep breath.

"Sorry," I said. "You know I'd always tell you what I know. I didn't have a chance to process what I'd seen."

Jack blew out the breath and said, "Okay. Tell me what you saw the night before."

I composed my thoughts. I told him everything I could remember about the sounds I'd heard, doors closing, footsteps, seeing a cloaked figure at midnight and another, with a mobcap, at three a.m.

"Mobcap, I keep hearing that word. What is it?" Jack asked.

"It's a soft white cap that colonial women wore. Think of Betsy Ross," I said.

"Someone in costume." Jack tapped his pen on the empty page, his concession to the frustration that must be building. "You're sure you didn't recognize anyone?"

His look told me he was weighing my veracity and I tamped down an ember of anger. He thought I was protecting Mary Anne. I searched my feelings. I was certain I didn't know who the person in the mobcap was, and although I knew Rob said the person in the hood was Mary Anne, I hadn't seen her face. I wouldn't conjecture. "I couldn't see any faces because I was looking down from the second floor. One had a hood up and the other I saw running, from above. The figure I saw at three a.m. wore a black cape, a mobcap, but her hair was tucked into it, I think. I didn't see hair. I don't know for sure who *either* figure was."

I hesitated, then said slowly, "The more I think about it, the way the two figures moved was different. I've run with Mary Anne, and the second figure didn't move like her. I'd say the one in the mobcap was younger." *Younger. Mobcap. Black cape.* A picture formed, and I shifted uncomfortably as I considered who that figure could've been.

Silence settled in the stuffy room where everything from the carpet to the walls to the top of the table where we faced each other was beige, everything bland, except for the man sitting in front of me. His eyes were an unusual gray blue, the color of the ocean before a storm, and shone with a keen intelligence. It would make his life a lot easier if I could positively ID the second figure, but I couldn't do it, despite my suspicions.

"If you hear from Mary Anne Dumas, please let me know right away." He ran an impatient hand through his thick hair, pushing it back from his broad brow. The way Jack's hair swooped back from his forehead always made me think of paintings of embattled Greek heroes or stern-faced prophets I'd seen in museums.

"Is she okay?" I asked. "Is she missing?"

"She's not answering her phone." He didn't say that she wasn't at her home. I'm sure he'd checked.

"Jack, I have to tell you something." I filled him in on Emilia's gift, how I was sure it was the same wrapping paper I'd see in the dumpster. "Trash from the Inn would be bagged, not simply tossed into the dumpster. And Emilia said her first roll of wrap went missing. I think that's important."

He took a deep breath and wrote "wrapping paper" in his notebook.

"Her gift's in the gift room, well, the Lilac suite, on the floor by the grandfather clock," I said.

"Thanks." We rose and he held the door for me. I expected him to walk me out, but instead he went to his office. Tillie wasn't at her desk. I felt that I'd given Jack more pieces of the puzzle, but I needed more information. In the meantime, I needed to talk to Mary Anne. Where was she?

Mary Anne had hosted the Penniman Women in Business Club at her place at the Elms, a newer townhouse development on Long Meadow Road near Magistrate's School. I ran across the green and jumped into Sadie, then tried to stay under the speed limit as I drove there. Mary Anne's assigned parking spot in front of her brick townhouse was empty, so I pulled in. I rang the doorbell, then lifted the heavy brass door knocker and knocked several times. Heavy drapes were closed on the broad front window. I tried her phone and knocked again, but there was no response.

The lace curtains in the picture window next door twitched, then the front door opened and a woman with brassy red hair used a walker to inch out onto the stoop.

Mary Anne had told me about her nosy neighbor, eighty-year-old Mrs. Malatesta, a woman who longed for the excitement she saw in the true crime shows she watched every day and wasn't above exaggerating the truth to get attention.

Her sharp brown eyes narrowed as she adjusted her cat's eye glasses and scoffed. "No dice. She's not home. The cops were already here. She's done a runner, mark my words."

"Hi, Mrs. Malatesta. Did Mary Anne say anything to you about where she was going?"

She rolled her eyes with a twist of her lips that said she couldn't believe how dim I was. "*Nada.* All I know is she wasn't happy about that big wedding. She told me herself she could kill her ex." Mrs. Malatesta stabbed the air to make each point. "And burn down the Inn. And she wasn't keen on that Marley character either."

I cringed. *Yikes.* "A figure of speech, certainly. You didn't mention that to the cops, did you?"

Her eyes gleamed behind her glasses. "You bet I did. Told that hunky chief. Invited him in for coffee, but he was busy. Maybe he'll return when they need more info for the manhunt."

"Let's hope it doesn't come to that." I wondered how long Mary Anne planned to be gone. "By the way, did Mary Anne take a suitcase?"

"She did! Oh, I forgot to tell the chief that." Mrs. Malatesta turned around and headed back into the house. "I'd better go phone him right away."

"You do that."

A gust of cold air swirled dry leaves across the parking lot as I got back into Sadie. As I drove back to Udderly I searched my thoughts. Before I reconnected with Mary Anne, I hadn't seen her since our high school track meets. I remembered her crying after doing poorly in a race, but she'd cried not for herself, but because her loss meant the team hadn't gotten enough points to qualify for the state championship. What did I know about her now? She was a talented chef. She'd moved to this townhouse after her divorce. She liked to run. She wore her heart on her sleeve. There was no filter between her thoughts and her mouth. She told me and everyone else she could kill Dominic.

But no one ever said she'd threatened Diantha.

Chapter 22

I returned to Udderly, on autopilot as I put on my apron and washed my hands, still wondering where Mary Anne had gone.

Gerri called from the front of the shop, "Customers here to pick up their anniversary cake."

"Got it." I retrieved a boxed pumpkin spice cake with chocolate chips and chocolate ganache frosting from the walk-in freezer. My decision to add ice-cream cakes to our offerings had definitely helped Udderly's bottom line and had, I realized now, been the whole reason I'd become involved in the death at the Inn.

I recalled the framed letter in the lounge. After I handed the cake to my excited customers, I asked Flo, "Did George Washington really sleep at the Inn on the Green?"

Flo threw a wary look at Gerri.

Gerri folded her arms and rolled her eyes. "Oh, *that*."

Flo said carefully, "Yes, but . . ."

"The original Inn burned down"—Gerri enunciated every word—"*after* George Washington died in 1799. Therefore it's hardly accurate to suggest he slept in that building by displaying that letter," Gerri huffed. "Plus, there's always been talk that a member of the Collins family of that time was a Tory. A traitor."

Flo raised her hands. "But it was never proven."

Gerri tossed her scarf over her shoulder. "Where there's smoke . . ."

"It was a dangerous game to play," Flo said. "Land could be seized, and of course there was Newgate for those Tories who didn't recant."

"Newgate?" The name was familiar.

"You should've learned about it in history class," Gerri said, her tone suggesting a lamentable gap in my education.

"An awful prison where traitors were sent during the Revolutionary War. It was a mine originally, and they lowered prisoners down into it, into the dark." Flo turned to Gerri. "Not that any family's perfect—we had a couple of horse thieves mixed in with our honest farmers and millworkers and schoolmasters. Family, you know?"

Gerri lifted her chin and gave Flo an imperious look. "But we never had a traitor." She looked out the window toward the parking lot. "Brandon's here."

A beige minivan pulled in next to Sadie, and a blue sedan mottled with rust spots parked next to it. Gerri, Flo, and I gathered at the kitchen door as Brandon unfolded his lanky body from the van. He'd shot up a couple of inches since I'd met him in July and he still seemed to be figuring out how to move his newly lengthened body. His narrow shoulders were slumped, his head bowed, and my heart tugged for him already. Being the boss didn't come naturally to me, and I glanced at Flo and Gerri to gauge their emotions. Flo's soft blue eyes radiated concern and love; Gerri's lower lip protruded and her jaw tightened, a judge considering how hard to throw the book at a criminal.

To my surprise, Lucretia, dressed in black cargo pants

and jean jacket over a black tank top, got out of the sedan and tossed a defiant look toward us as she slammed the door. The orange dye had been washed from her hair; the dull, black-dyed lengths remained, and now I could see that her roots were a sunny golden color. She'd slicked her hair back and it curled in a pretty way around her ears.

She strode to Brandon with confidence—or was it bravado?—took Brandon's hand and whispered to him.

Flo and I exchanged a look as they entered the workroom.

"Riley, I've had a stomachache for days. I don't deserve to have a key. I'm sorry. I'll quit if you don't want me anymore." Brandon took the key from his pocket and held it out, glancing up at me through his shaggy brown hair. "I—"

Lucretia cut him off. "No, it was my fault. Brandon told me you'd given him the key. I asked Brandon to show me the shop and make me some ice cream."

Brandon shook his head. "No, Lu, it was my responsibility."

Gerri's voice boomed. "What about the lock-in?"

Lucretia's sullen expression flickered as she took a step back.

Brandon kept his head down. "We skipped it. When we finished here, I dropped Lu off and then I went home."

Gerri turned to me. Brandon's transgression was now greater than making ice cream after hours at the shop. He'd skipped the lock-in, a school function.

"My parents already grounded me," he said. "Except for school, band, and work."

Gerri exhaled, a little puff of air that said *that was a start.*

I decided the lock-in was none of my business. The shop was. "Brandon, I don't think I was clear when I gave you the key. I do think you are responsible enough to open and close the shop, but if you want to use the shop after hours you must ask first."

Brandon raised his head.

"And"—I walked to the freezer and took out the trays of ice cream—"we don't do no-churn recipes. That's for emergencies, okay? Our customers expect the creamiest, richest ice cream we can give them. We churn."

"Okay," he whispered.

"But still, let's taste these." I handed everyone tasting spoons and slid the tray of beige ice cream toward them. "Brandon, you and Lucretia first."

Brandon's shoulders straightened. "I call this Bone Fracture." He and Lucretia dug in with enthusiasm and took hearty bites. They didn't fall over, so I took a spoonful, then Flo, then—skepticism oozing from every pore—Gerri.

Brandon savored his spoonful. "I used coconut and vanilla for the base and white chocolate–covered pretzels for the bones."

It didn't taste bad, but the texture and name made it hard to swallow. I nodded, trying to keep my expression neutral. Flo gave him an encouraging smile and said, "I like it!"

"Now this one." I pushed forward the purple-splotched ice cream.

Brandon held up a finger and got a scoop. He drew it across the top of the ice cream, and as the ice cream curled into a ball, it made a tie-dyed effect that was so pretty Flo clapped her hands and jumped in delight. Gerri struggled to maintain her cold demeanor, but I could tell she was intrigued.

"See how it makes that pattern?" Lucretia pointed, and I wondered if this had been her idea all along. "Brandon calls it unicorn ice cream."

We all took a taste. The unicorn ice cream was a delicious mix of blueberry, raspberry, and blackberry flavors. "Not bad," I said, "but it might benefit from a touch of citrus or lavender to cut the sweetness."

Gerri set down her spoon, folded her arms, and gave me an expectant look.

I cleared my throat. "But the punishment must fit the crime," I said.

"Brandon, you'll show us all how to make this." I tapped the tray with his unicorn flavor, then I considered Bone Fracture. I'd learned that there was a market for Brandon's crazier flavors, especially when he gave them unappetizing names. "I'll put it in the case, but I think it'll be better if you find a way to fine tune the sweetness in future batches."

Gerri raised an eyebrow so I added, "And you'll be on cleanup for the rest of the week."

She harrumphed with annoyance and spun on her heel, heading into the front of the shop. Flo gave Brandon a hug and threw me a smile. "I'll talk down the hanging judge."

Brandon's shoulders sagged with relief as he cleared his trays and returned them to the freezer. Lucretia pulled out her phone.

"Lucretia, did you carve the pumpkins for the Inn?"

She flicked me a wary look. "Yes."

"They're beautiful," I said, hoping the compliment would relax her enough to talk freely. "Did Diantha Collins ask you for the one with the skeleton bride and groom?"

She shook her head. "No, she asked for a dozen Halloween-themed pumpkins; you know, bats, monsters, cats. I delivered them earlier in the day."

"Who asked for the one with the bride and groom?"

Lucretia shrugged. "Some lady. We brought it to the

Inn pretty late after I closed my booth. Some guy took delivery and said he'd give it to her."

Some lady. Some guy. Her vague answers were testing my patience. "Do you remember what he looked like?"

She shrugged, "Some older white guy?"

She knew Rob and Marley, so it wasn't them. One of the brothers? "Good looking?"

She rolled her eyes and I felt my age. Even handsome Cooper Collins would be an old guy to her.

"The porch lights were off and they had the smoke machine on, so I didn't see. I wanted to get going." She crossed her arms.

I knew I wouldn't get much more out of her, so I switched gears. "How's Ruthie?"

"Fine. I have to go help her at the Inn. Please don't tell her about this, you know, lock-in thing "—she threw a look at Brandon and lowered her voice—"Please. I'm not allowed to date."

She hadn't told Ruthie about Brandon or the lock-in. Teenagers. "Okay."

Lucretia bid us goodbye and made the "phone me" gesture to Brandon as she backed out the door.

"Lucretia's an interesting person," I said.

A vivid blush crept up his cheeks. "Yeah. And nice. She's always trying to help her grandma. She wants her gran to be able to buy her house instead of paying rent. That's why she started selling the carved pumpkins and other stuff."

"Other stuff?" I knew he'd be more comfortable talking while he worked, so I handed him a sponge and he wiped down the worktable as I pretended to check the schedule.

"She does calligraphy for wedding invitations and inspirational signs people hang in their houses and stuff like that." Brandon scrubbed the table and moved on to the counters. "She even asked me to bring her some feathers from the farm to make quills to do some fancy writing."

"Sounds like she barely has time for school."

"She wanted to quit school to help, but Ruthie forbade it."

"What about her parents?"

"Her mom took off when she was young, went to Korea or someplace to become a Buddhist nun." Brandon shrugged. "She never mentions her dad."

Chapter 23

The cooler weather kept customers home, giving Gerri, Flo, and me plenty of time to talk as I mixed up batches of fudge swirl and pumpkin spice ice creams. Bringing another gift of ice cream would be an excuse to visit the Inn and ask more questions. Brandon tried to do everything at once, and it was almost a relief when closing time came and I could tell him to go home.

My phone rang as I turned off the shop lights and waved Gerri and Flo out the door.

Mary Anne's voice, slurred and too loud, made me wince and hold my phone away from my ear. "Riley, can you talk? I mean, come over and talk."

I closed the door behind me. "I'll come over now."

"I'm not at my townhouse." She gave me an address. "I'm at the lake, on the end near the scout camp."

I knew I should call Jack, but I wanted to talk to her first. I smothered an ember of guilt, promising myself I'd call him right after I spoke to her.

The road to the lake led past the green and I slowed to admire the magical scene created by the film crew at the

Inn. Through a thicket of booms and lights I could see a horse and carriage draw up to the Inn's porch where even more glittering twinkle lights had been strung.

I continued past the Inn parking lot, following the twists of Long Meadow Road. Headlights behind me, high and following too close, glared in my rearview mirror. The skin on the back of my neck prickled. I continued the half mile to the SIGN for Penniman Lake, a community where many of my friends' families had summer cottages. This time of year, most of the houses were dark and unoccupied, and the truck following me was setting off alarm bells. I decided to see if it was truly following me or was just tailgating.

At the next stop sign, I turned left, away from the address Mary Anne had given me. As I turned, I could see the vehicle behind me was a hulking pickup truck, but in the dark I couldn't make out the driver, only a figure with a baseball cap pulled low over their eyes.

I zigzagged through the narrow lanes, considering what to do. I remembered a friend's house, set on a curving road whose driveway led to a large barn.

I stomped Sadie's accelerator and tore through a stop sign, then turned the wheel sharply and cut the wrong way down a narrow, one-way street. In my rearview I saw the truck slam its brakes and back up to follow me. Sadie's tires screeching in complaint, I cut sharply into my friend's gravel driveway and swerved behind the barn. I cut my engine and lights and held my breath. Moments later, I heard the roar of the truck as it speed by.

A tail, and an obvious one. *Who on earth was it?* I let out my breath, eased Sadie from behind the barn, and checked the road but didn't see any lights. I backtracked to the address Mary Anne had given me and pulled into a driveway tucked in a thicket of pine trees, glad they'd shield the car from the road. At the end of the driveway, the view opened up to the dark lake and a small, raised ranch with a deck overlooking the water. Mary Anne stepped under a security light on the deck and waved what looked like a glass of wine.

I climbed the stairs to the deck, my knees still shaking from the pursuit.

"Hi, Riley." Mary Anne poured me a glass, sloshing some of the wine onto a table littered with pine needles and an empty ice-cream carton. Her hair was pulled into an untidy ponytail and she still wore the same sloppy outfit she'd worn at Lily's. "Let's go inside. It's chilly." We went into a kitchen gleaming with professional-grade stainless-steel appliances.

"Are you renting this place?" I asked as I took the glass.

"No. It's mine." She avoided my eyes then shrugged. "Well, sort of mine."

I narrowed my eyes.

"Riley, this was my home too. For seven years. I still have the key." She picked a key up from the butcher-block table and waved it. "When Dominic and I 'consciously uncoupled'"—her words slurred as she made air quotes—"Dominic said he'd buy me out when he sold it. But he still hasn't sold it. He said I could keep the key."

I decided the legality of the situation wasn't my business. "Why did you come here?" I asked.

She leaned against the breakfast bar and put her head in her hands. "I can't lie. I'm tired of talking to the cops. I don't want to be found. I heard that Dominic was staying in Diantha's suite at the Inn, so I thought it'd be a good change for me to stay here."

"Mary Anne," I said, "Everything you're doing makes you look guilty."

"Riley. I know I look guilty," she moaned. "Marley texted me to crow that Rob told the cops this story about me going into the Inn at midnight and staying for three hours the night Diantha died."

My stomach churning. I set down my wineglass as she continued.

"It's true I went at midnight. But I didn't stay long. I just—" She sighed and met my eyes, her expression contrite. "I'm so sorry I messed with your cake, but I don't know where Rob got the idea that I stayed for three hours and dressed up like Betsy Ross, then ran around in the parking lot."

I looked away so she wouldn't see my eyes.

Mary Anne stalked around the room, waving her arms. "I took a cape from the Inn and I put that on because I knew there was a chance Rob would see me. He stands outside smoking in the parking lot all the time." She stopped abruptly and set down her wineglass with a self-conscious smile. "You know who's loving this? Marley. He's always wanted me out so he could move up at the Inn, and he was positively drooling to be part of Dominic's new restaurant." She laughed, a bitter bark. "That's probably not going to happen now. Diantha didn't get rich by sharing anything with her husbands. I don't know if she ever intended to give Dominic even an interest in the restaurant. She was going to call it Diantha's Table, and I'll bet Dominic's name is nowhere on that contract. Now her kids'll get everything and they're not gonna share with him."

Blue and red police lights swirled in the broad bay windows. Mary Anne ran to the window and moaned, "Did you tell them I was here? Did they follow you?"

"Of course not." I joined her at the window. "But a big pickup truck did."

Mary Anne's eyes blazed as she spat, "Marley!"

Marley, I mused as I drove home, must've seen me as I passed by the Inn. Sadie, burnt orange, vintage, and a bit worn around the edges, was a distinctive vehicle. He'd figured (correctly) that I was going to see Mary Anne and wanted to make sure the police found her. *That rat*.

Back at the house, Caroline had made grilled cheese sandwiches, a salad, and a pot of tea. I devoured mine while telling her everything that had happened, including the look Jack had given me when I emerged from the lake house with Mary Anne. I tried to explain, but he'd walked past me, his expression stony. There wouldn't be any friendly visit to the farmhouse in the future. I feared I'd driven the final nail into his relationship with Caroline. I confessed it all to her, but she waved it off. "My relationship's with Jack," she said. "He has to decide what he wants."

Caroline sipped her tea. "Mary Anne does act so guilty, but she doesn't benefit from Diantha's death, right? Aside from ruining Dominic. Would she kill Diantha to hurt Dominic?"

I shook my head as we cleaned up, our conversation turning to Brandon and Lucretia, and then to Flo's news about a traitor in Diantha's family.

I needed something to settle my nerves. "I'm going to go through those papers from the Collins house. If anything, they'll put me to sleep."

"The corn letters?" Caroline laughed. "I'm sleepy simply thinking about them." She threw a longing glance toward the door, but didn't say anything. Instead, she scooped up Sprinkles and headed to the parlor. "I'm going to watch a Skylark movie."

Back in my room, I scanned each of the old letters. They contained perfectly innocuous news about farming, so innocuous my suspicion grew that there was more to them. After all, paper was precious at the time these messages were written. Why send such nothing-burger messages using such an expensive medium, especially when the letters were vaguely addressed to "John" and signed by "John." I carefully copied the underlined letters and numbers and read the first few out loud, hoping the sound would give me additional clues.

"L K 2 7 24."

Those combinations, patterns, of letters and numbers. Where had I seen them before?

A memory rose from long-ago Sunday School classes. LK. An abbreviation for "Luke"? Did these letters point to Bible verses? Could these underlined letters be a message? A cipher?

I dashed into Buzzy's room. We'd left the room untouched since she passed, and Buzzy's well-worn Bible was still on her bedside table. I curled up on her wedding-ring-pattered quilt, searched for the verses in my list, and noted the words they indicated. After a few minutes, I rubbed my eyes and set aside the book with only a list of disconnected words for my trouble: "of," "to," "city."

Rocky jumped onto the bed and curled into my side.

"None of this makes sense." I rearranged the words, but no discernible message emerged. If this was a code, it was tougher than me. I flopped onto my back, and my tired eyes fell on a Penniman Savings Bank calendar that was still tacked to the wall, still turned to July, when Buzzy passed away.

Out of date, I thought, then sat up so quickly Rocky leapt away with a yowl. Buzzy's Bible was a modern edition. The writer and recipient of these letters would've used a Bible from the 1700s. I wondered if Lucretia and Ruthie had found a Bible with these letters, or if they had a family Bible from the time of the Revolution. There were some online, but I suspected that messages might have been hidden in a Bible that belonged to the recipient. What secret had been passed with these letters? I returned to my room, my mind sparking with determination to solve this puzzle.

Caroline called good night through my door and Rocky ambled in. I readied for bed, unable to shake the memory of Jack's stony expression. After an hour of tossing and turning and soul searching, I decided I still would've visited Mary Anne before calling Jack. Rocky, irritated by my movement, leapt to the floor and vanished through the doorway as I drifted to sleep.

A buzzing woke me. A text flashed on my screen as well as the time: 1:00. Curse different time zones. My colleague in Krakow had emailed a short message and translation of the article I'd sent. As I read the article, a sense of dread grew in me, and when I finished I closed my eyes. The Styrofoam boxes, the towel, the open window, the gift wrap. They all pointed to a well-plotted and executed murder.

A faint light showed under my door—Caroline was still up painting. I got up and knocked softly as I went into her room. "I know how Diantha was killed."

Chapter 24

he fumes from dry ice killed her by taking all
the oxygen from the room?" Caroline pushed her
glasses up her nose, speaking quietly so as not to wake
Sprinkles sleeping on her bed. "Like these poor people in
Poland?" She jutted her chin to my phone, where she'd
read the translation of the article.

*KRAKOW—Two people died and several more are
in intensive care after a film set special effect went
wrong.*

*The company, Mojo Productions, was filming a hor-
ror movie called* Voices from the Ice *when the props
master added several hundred kilos of dry ice to a
swimming pool to produce a fog effect. The props master and an actor already in the pool died and several on
the pool deck were rendered unconscious by the fumes
in the air.*

I remembered the rest of the article mentioned a case
where a man had died while transporting ice cream that
was kept cold with dry ice. His car windows were closed
and fumes from an improperly secured container had
leaked. "That's why dry ice always carries a warning
about not using it in enclosed spaces. Dry ice can give

off fumes that can render you unconscious if it builds up in an unventilated space."

"And if enough builds up, it can kill you"—Caroline clutched her throat—"like in that Little Room. You said it was barely bigger than the bed."

I nodded. "I think the killer used a towel to block the draft from the window and closed the drapes to make the room more airtight. I'm pretty sure the bathroom door was closed when Ruthie went in the next morning."

"So how did the dry ice get in there?" Caroline asked. "Diantha didn't see it?"

I considered what I'd seen at the Inn. There had been several Styrofoam containers of dry ice by the back door. "There was a fog machine—Rob set it up. I saw Dominic and Marley making cocktails with it." At Caroline's shocked look, I said, "It's safe if done properly. The dry ice sinks to the bottom of the glass but makes a cool fog effect. You're fine as long as it doesn't touch your lips, and it's usually gone by the time you finish the drink."

"It can burn," she said. "I remember that from science class."

"Strange that something so cold could burn." *Burns. Someone had a burn, I remembered, someone at the Inn. Who?* "And it's also used in special effects in movies," I said, nodding to the phone. I googled "Mojo Productions," but there were no articles following the accident in Krakow; evidently the company went belly up following the outcry from the deaths.

Caroline put down her brush and started to pace. "So anyone around movies would know that it's dangerous."

"I hate to tell you who the producer of the movie was," I said.

Caroline lowered herself to the edge of the bed.

"Cooper Collins."

She hugged a pillow. "No!"

We sat in silence for a moment, then Caroline said, "No, I can't believe he'd kill his own mother. Think about it. Anyone who heard about that disaster would know dry ice is dangerous. Cooper would be a fool to use it, since it's already connected to him. That would be like a big flashing light saying, 'I did it.'"

"You still love Cooper Collins," I said in a singsong voice.

Caroline hit me with the pillow.

I sat down on Caroline's chair, careful not to touch the fresh paint on her canvas. "Either through movies or food service safety training, almost everyone at the Inn knew the dangers of dry ice."

"But how did they get that stuff in her room? You'd need quite a bit I'd imagine."

"A couple of coolers could've fit under her bed," I mused. I had suspicions but I couldn't see how to prove it. "She had some other health issues. I think she was overcome as soon as she went into the room because she didn't even change." I remembered the carved pumpkin by her fireplace. *Had the last thing she'd seen been the skeleton bride and groom?*

We sat quietly for a moment and despite this shocking development, I couldn't suppress a yawn.

"Better get to sleep," Caroline said. "I forgot to tell you. Paulette told me a production assistant called her. They need to do promo shots for the movie and Evan Smith insisted that he do some with Sprinkles."

At Evan's name, Sprinkles jolted awake so quickly Caroline and I laughed.

"Tomorrow morning at Magistrate's School at nine o'clock. Paulette has to be there at seven with the other extras, so she asked me to bring Her Majesty over."

"I think Sprinkles will need her staff to accompany her. I'm coming too."

Chapter 25

THURSDAY

Rocky's tail batted my nose as I struggled to wake. Caroline and I had talked past two, and thinking of how Diantha'd been murdered made it difficult to settle down to sleep.

My eyes alighted on the stack of old letters. I remembered Ruthie saying that she got up with the larks, so I sent her a text asking if she'd found a Bible along with the old papers.

She called me back. "I'll never get the hang of this infernal texting. Yes, we did find one. I kept it in the dining room because it didn't seem right to leave it in that cardboard box. Come over and look whenever you like. The back door's always unlocked."

I cast a longing glance at my running shoes. I needed to run, needed to think to make sense of all the muddled impressions and conversations I'd had with the inhabitants of the Inn since Diantha's death, but exercise would have to wait. Hollywood called.

Sprinkles was already inside her carrier as Caroline and I grabbed a quick breakfast.

"She's looking extra pretty this morning," I said as I poured some of my favorite high-test Yorkshire tea into two insulated bottles. Despite the bright blue sky, the temperature gauge outside the window read 48 degrees.

"I gave her a good brushing." Caroline added a few of Sprinkles' toys and a package of treats to her shoulder bag. "Better be ready for anything."

"Wait till you see her on set," I said. "She'll be more than fine with Evan."

Again, at Evan's name, Sprinkles' head jerked around.

I laughed. "Every moment between the two of them was a total love fest." I didn't know what would happen when Sprinkles' five minutes of fame were over, but for now I'd enjoy the new and improved attitude of lovestruck Sprinkles.

Rocky lay in a patch of pale sunlight on the floor, tail flicking as we stepped over him as we readied for the shoot.

"Do you think Rocky wants to come with us?" Caroline said as we hurried out the door.

I shrugged, remembering how the little ninja had secreted himself in Paulette's station wagon. "If he did, he would."

We drove past the Inn and followed winding Long Meadow Road two miles out of Penniman to Magistrate's School. The private school, sheltered behind iron gates and tall granite walls on the outskirts of town, was its own world. Occasionally kids in its garnet and gray uniforms would shop in town or come to Udderly for an ice-cream cone, but the school didn't play a role in the life of Penniman. Two miles may well have been two hundred.

A security guard stopped us at the gate. "Name."

Caroline leaned across me. "Caroline Spooner."

The guard shook his head.

Caroline shot me a concerned look and I said, "Riley Rhodes?"

The guard shook his head again.

"Paulette Rhodes?"

He tapped his clipboard and gave us a look that said he was ready to escort us off the property. "Already checked in."

I sighed. "Sprinkles."

He checked his list. "Ah, Sprinkles and support crew." He peeked in the car, then handed us badges on long yellow lanyards. "Go straight, then take a right at the quad and park next to the gym." He waved us through.

"This badge actually says Sprinkles Support Staff!" Caroline and I broke into gales of laughter. "Support staff! That's not too humiliating."

We followed the road past a magnificent quadrangle of brick buildings, the largest with a cupola topped by a gold pelican weathervane that glittered in the sun. At a stop sign, a woman in a Security sweatshirt held up her hand. "Badge."

We handed her our badges, she scanned them, spoke into her squawking handheld radio, then pointed us to a modern brick building fronted by bicycle racks where another crewmember waved us into a space. My jaw dropped as I nosed Sadie in—there was an orange traffic cone with a sign attached that read SPRINKLES.

I burst out laughing. "Sprinkles has her own parking space!"

I snapped a photo to share with Flo, Gerri, and Pru. After Caroline and I composed ourselves, we got out of the car and hefted Sprinkles' carrier from the hatch.

The crewmember oohed over Sprinkles and pointed to a magnificent oak tree by the quad. "That's the tree where they're doing the promo shots. You'll have to check in with our Animal Welfare Team here in the gym and then wait inside here until you're called." She checked her watch. "They're behind schedule, though, still shooting in front of the library—probably take about another hour."

"Is it okay if we take a quick look at the filming?" I asked.

"Okay, but watch the time."

Hefting the carrier between us, Caroline and I hurried to join the crowd of spectators lined up behind sawhorses. When I saw Chip and Cooper talking with the camera crew, I shot her a wary look.

"Anyone who read that newspaper article would know," she whispered.

I pressed my lips together. Maybe she was right—killing Diantha with dry ice after that awful accident would be like signing a confession. I took in the blue sky, the glowing autumn leaves, and the beautiful campus and determined to put aside thoughts of murder and enjoy watching the shoot, at least for a while.

"Look!" Caroline nudged me and jutted her chin. Jenira and Evan stood on marble steps that led to the heavily carved oak doors of the library. A bas relief of a pelican surrounded by a circle of ivy was carved in marble over the door. A bucket truck was positioned out of camera range high above them.

"Riley," a soft voice called. Emilia beckoned from a blue plaid picnic blanket on the grass just inside the sawhorses. "Come sit with me." She spoke to a security guard who nodded to us, and we joined her.

"Emilia Collins, this is my friend Caroline Spooner."

"Nice to meet you. And this must be Sprinkles!" Emillia gushed. "Evan will not stop talking about this cat!"

I set Sprinkles' carrier next to the blanket.

"How's the shoot going?" I said as we settled next to Emilia.

Emilia wore her green duffel coat with a wooly white scarf around her neck and black leather gloves. Caroline took Sprinkles out of the carrier, and the furry beast immediately went to Emilia, rubbing long white hairs all over her coat.

Unconcerned, Emilia gave Sprinkles an appreciative cuddle. Caroline and I shared a look of relief—you never knew with Sprinkles.

"With filming, it's always hurry up and wait," Emilia said. "The poor extras, they have to stand around until the main characters get blocking hammered out."

"Blocking?" Caroline asked.

"Where everyone goes and stands in their places," Emilia said.

I shaded my eyes and caught sight of Paulette at the other end of the quad. She and another woman wore light sweaters, jean skirts, and thin plaid scarves. Again, Hollywood's idea of how to dress on a fall day in New England. I pulled my parka tighter as Caroline pulled gloves from the pockets of her wool navy peacoat.

"So what's happening in this scene?" I asked.

Emilia stroked Sprinkles. "Evan and Jenira are walking down the steps, then they stop for a chat."

"That's it?" Caroline said.

"It can take hours to film a minute of a story." Emilia pointed up at the bucket truck. "Cooper wants just the right amount of leaves falling for a romantic effect." An admiring and indulgent smile warmed her pale features, and I wondered if she'd married the right Collins brother.

Cooper shouted up at the guy in the bucket truck, "Not a rain of leaves, not a deluge. A sprinkle."

Sprinkles' head swiveled toward the director, and we stifled our laughter.

Cooper and Chip had several assistants, each with

their own mission—wrangling the actors and extras, hefting a large mike on a boom, directing the lighting crew, plus the leaf guy in the bucket truck, to make the shot work. It was a tightly choreographed multi-ring circus, making sure each player was in the right spot at the right time, with the right light and the right sprinkle of autumn leaves.

"Too many yellow leaves. We want a mix," Chip called.

Leaf Guy gave a thumbs-up.

Jenira and Evan descended the stairs several times, leaves fluttering down, as Paulette and another woman walked behind them. Paulette, of course, did her walk perfectly, timed, I realized, to be moving out of range at the moment Jenira and Evan started speaking.

I was amazed at the way Jenira and Evan were able to radiate such chemistry, over and over, when the camera was on. When the camera was off, she stepped away, stretching or scrolling on her phone, as the prop leaves were swept out of the shot. Evan returned each time to his hovering makeup team to have his hair mussed to perfection.

Cooper called everyone to places. "Action."

Finally, just the right amount of colorful leaves fell from above, Evan and Jenira radiated the right amount of charm, and Paulette walked the right distance off camera.

"And cut!" Cooper high-fived Chip.

I looked down the line of spectators and caught sight of a beige trench coat. Tillie. She gave me a slow nod but didn't join us. Caroline chatted easily with Emilia, and both looked cheerful and relaxed. I resolved to sleuth without the police and give Tillie and Jack a wide berth. I was dying to find out what had happened after I left

Mary Anne, but I couldn't chance upsetting Jack more than I already had.

"We'd better get Sprinkles checked in with the Animal Welfare Team," I said. "See you later, Emilia."

"Be sure you go inside the old library, especially you, Riley. They wrapped shooting in there earlier. It's beautiful." Emilia gave Sprinkles a last snuggle, then handed her to Caroline. She pulled the neck of her coat close, the vibrant green contrasting with her pale lips and cheeks.

"I will. Thanks. Do you need a ride back to the Inn?"

Emilia shook her head. "No, I'm going to have lunch at craft services. Sam's doing a skateboard demo at Penniman High School. I think Cooper's doing a presentation to the film classes there too. When Sam's done he'll bring me back to the Inn. I don't mind the fresh air."

"See you later."

"Nice to meet you, Caroline, Sprinkles."

As Caroline started to put Sprinkles in her carrier, the spoiled beast dug her claws into the blanket. Her yowls of protest drew concerned looks from the other spectators.

"She thinks we're taking her away from her beloved E-V-A-N," I said.

Caroline managed to get Sprinkles in her carrier with only a minor tear to the cuff of her coat. "She's not usually like this," Caroline said, her face crimson.

I restrained myself from an eyeroll.

We lugged Sprinkles' carrier to the Animal Welfare table in the gym and I was disappointed to see that Liam wasn't working with the team. "Is Doctor Pryce here today?"

"We all wish he was," the woman at check-in said. "No, he was nice enough to cover the other day. Today it's little old me and Doc Ross." She pointed to a woman sitting by a vending machine, doing a crossword puzzle.

"Why don't you go look at the library?" Caroline said. "You know you want to. We may be waiting awhile."

Caroline didn't have to suggest twice.

I ran up the marble steps of the library building and paused inside the threshold. The two-story lobby opened to a magnificent staircase flanked by two wide door-ways. Above the doorway of the room on the left was a sign that read DIANTHA AND SCOTT COLLINS INFORMA-TION COMMONS. I peeked inside the sleek space where students studied at modern computer workstations and wooden sound-recording booths lined one wall.

Stepping across the lobby to the right, I entered the wonderful hush of the original library. Here shelves of books on two levels, oriental carpets, an old-world globe, and overstuffed brown leather chairs welcomed the reader. Most of the chairs were taken by students, who, despite headphones and laptops, seemed to be enjoying the relaxed atmosphere of the venerable space.

A librarian looked up from the desk. Straight out of central casting, she wore a white button-down shirt, gar-net cardigan, and tortoiseshell reading glasses. Her hair in neat cornrows was short and touched with gray, her makeup subtle. The nameplate on her desk even seemed appropriate: MRS. PATRICIA SARGEANT. But instead of shushing me, she smiled warmly and whispered a greet-ing. "May I help you? Are you here for the film?" She nodded at my badge.

"My cat is." I wondered how Sprinkles was faring, forced to wait for her closeup with Evan. I hoped she wasn't tearing the gym apart.

Mrs. Sargeant pointed to a group of students hud-dled on a window seat, watching something on a tablet. "That fluffy white Persian? The students were watching from the window. I think she already has fans." As she gestured, I noticed her ring, gold with a garnet stone, the same style worn by Chip, Cooper, and Sam.

"What a beautiful stone," I said. "Is that the school ring?"

She looked surprised. "Sometimes I forget I have it on. Yes. Magistrate's school color is garnet, so it's a garnet stone."

I introduced myself and said, "Is it okay if I look around? I used to be a librarian, and this place is so beautiful."

"Please do." She handed me a brochure. "Here's a short history of the school and the new addition across the hallway."

I whispered my thanks and drifted into the stacks, breathing in the scent of soft paper and leather bindings. Passing portraits and marble busts of former headmasters, I entered a study room with floor-to-ceiling windows. Kids gathered around long oak tables working on group projects, and I quietly found what I was looking for: a wall of yearbooks. I checked the brochure for the date of the donation to build the new Information Commons, pulled the corresponding yearbook from the shelf, and flipped through the pages until I came to a full-page spread.

Diantha had been Hollywood all the way, so the gift of a library seemed odd to me. I wondered about the boys' history at the school. Why make such a generous gift of a library?

There was a photo of Diantha cutting a ribbon at the door of the new Information Commons, flanked by people I assumed were the headmaster and several teachers. I scanned the text: "Given in recognition of the excellent education received by our sons, so their beloved alma mater can continue its mission into the future."

I recalled Diantha had had her George Washington letter tested by a teacher at Magistrate's. I searched my memory for his name, remembered Emilia laughing. Mr. Blood. I flipped through the pages to the faculty listing.

Mr. Blood was a Doctor Blood with PhDs in history and chemistry. His background seemed like a good bet for expertise dating an old letter—he'd know where to send it for authentication. I paged through several yearbooks, learning that Dr. Blood started as a housemaster, living in the dorms with the boys. Each year group had their house listed, just like in Harry Potter books. Chip Worth had been in Weathers House. Cooper and Sam had been in Everly. Dr. Blood had been head of house in Everly while the two younger Collins boys were in attendance. That must be how Diantha met him.

I tucked the yearbooks away, but before I did, I flipped to the Theater Arts page. *Oklahoma* had been performed when Cooper was in attendance, and he'd played Will Parker, the male lead.

An idea was taking shape, but its outline was blurry, out of reach.

I returned to Mrs. Sargeant's desk and asked, "Can you tell me how to find Dr. Blood?"

"He was here a few minutes ago, watching the shoot. I think he went to the café." The librarian pointed into the lobby. "Take a right and it's in the back of the building."

I thanked Ms. Sargeant and found my way to a small café behind the building. Since everyone else had class or had found a way to watch the shoot, the white-haired man sitting by the window was easy to spot.

"Dr. Blood?" He nodded, jumped to his feet, and, holding my chair, signaled the waitress for another cup of coffee.

A more quintessential professor would be hard to find, but there was something glossy about him too. Unlike the stereotype of an ink-stained professor in a corduroy jacket with worn leather elbow patches, Dr. Blood's jacket was a rich-looking Harris tweed, his Magistrate's tie tucked into a garnet sweater so silky it had to be cashmere. Not a hair of his full white mane was out of place and his school ring flashed on manicured hands.

"How may I help you?" His sharp brown eyes twinkled. "Ms. . . . ?"

"Riley Rhodes. I was at the Inn the other day and saw the letter from George Washington." I barely got the words out when Dr. Blood raised a hand and launched into lecture mode.

"A very exiting find! I had the paper authenticated, you know. Now back then, inns weren't like they are now. You couldn't call ahead to make a reservation," he chuckled. "So George would stay where he could, wherever he happened to be. He had many friends and grandees who were more than happy to host him. So it's entirely possible he stayed at the Inn on the Green, and we do know that he was in this part of the world during the time frame on the letter, April 1776, so it's entirely possible the letter's authentic."

I jumped on the word "possible." "You're not one hundred percent sure the letter's authentic?"

"As a historian, one must always be careful. But that was enough for the owner, my friend Diantha. You knew her, of course?" Dr. Blood didn't wait for my reply. "She was a woman who knew her own mind. And, you know, testing's expensive. So when she heard the paper was dated to the correct era, she framed it and hung it up. Good enough for her. I'd like to get more testing, but Diantha, she did her own thing."

"You knew her a long time," I said.

His lips turned down and he sighed. "Wonderful woman. Wonderful boys. Such a loss. We grew quite close over the years."

"She was generous to the school." I gestured in the direction of the Information Commons as the waitress set a cup of coffee in front of me and refilled Dr. Blood's.

Something flashed in his eyes, a wariness that he extinguished as he held out his cup. He murmured, "Yes, indeed. Diantha was very pleased with the education the Collins boys received."

The waitress laughed. "The Collins boys. Oh, those were crazy days. Remember when Cooper was here, Dr. Blood?" The waitress leaned toward me. "Girls would climb the walls, I tell you!"

Dr. Blood threw the waitress a patient look. "This is Sherry, she's been with us, oh, how long?"

"Since the last Ice Age!" she chuckled. "I started here Cooper's first year. Don't get me wrong, Cooper was a nice boy, but it got so crazy with the girls, his mother had a security guard following him, didn't she, Dr. Blood? Didn't want him in trouble or bringing home the wrong sort of girl. But he didn't stay long, went back to California part way through junior year. Broke a lot of hearts."

A throng of chattering students entered the café, and Sherry bustled back to the counter to wait on them.

Dr. Blood looked at his watch. "You'll have to excuse me. I have a meeting."

I thanked him and turned over what I'd heard as I headed to the gym. There was something about the Collins boys that Dr. Blood didn't want to talk about. What was it?

I rejoined Caroline and Sprinkles as the wrangler called, "Show time." Caroline, cuddling Sprinkles, jumped to her feet, her smile wide and excited. Sprinkles craned over Caroline's shoulder, no doubt looking for Evan. I checked my watch—the morning was flying by.

"Riley, I know you wanted to get to Ruthie's," she said. "You don't have to stay, we'll be fine, won't we, Sprinkles?"

"Okay, shouldn't take long. I'll come back to get you when I'm done."

"Sounds good." Caroline's eyes were shining. "This is so exciting!"

It was so good to see Caroline cheerful, I even gave Sprinkles a pat. "Break a leg, Sprinkles."

Chapter 26

I followed the road back to Penniman, thinking about the complex work that went into making movies, of the timing necessary to make all the parts of a scene come together. *Blocking. Timing. Choreography.*

That last word kept replaying in my mind: choreography.

Diantha's murder had been choreographed. The large boxes of dry ice had to be delivered to her room without raising suspicion, hidden under her bed, opened so fumes could build. I was sure the bath towel had been used to block any incursion of fresh air from the window, the bathroom door closed to make the small space airtight, so the oxygen levels could fall more quickly to dangerous levels, especially for someone who'd been drinking, someone with Diantha's health issues. Then the evidence had to be removed before housekeeping came in the morning.

When Ruthie opened the door to Diantha's Little Room, the window was open and no dangerous dry ice fumes remained.

Dry ice evaporated—no, the word from the article came back to me: "sublimated." It changed from a solid to a vapor without passing through a liquid stage. There'd be no dampness left behind, no trace—except a dead body with no signs of violence. It was a brilliant plan.

But dry ice could burn when it came into contact with bare skin, so it had to be transported inside something, and in sufficient quantity to do harm. The dry ice I ordered for the shop came in plastic bags inside a Styrofoam box. There had been two Styrofoam boxes mixed with construction debris in the dumpster beneath the window of Diantha's room. Someone must've gone into Diantha's room between the time she died and when Ruthie found her just after eight a.m. to open the window and toss the evidence into the dumpster.

Could Ruthie have tossed the boxes when she brought Diantha her coffee? Could Ruthie be the killer? Or could she be covering for the killer?

Memories of Ruthie leading us in songs around the fire at Girl Scout camp made me snort. I couldn't see Ruthie killing anyone.

I turned my thoughts back to the choreography of the murder. After Diantha was dead, the killer had to dispose of any evidence—get rid of the boxes and the towel, and air out the room. It would be dangerous to enter the room when it was filled with fumes. The killer had to wait for them to dissipate, but still the killer took a chance. That showed confidence. Or overconfidence. Or desperation.

How much time would the killer have to wait? Would three hours do it? The time that passed between Mary Anne going in the kitchen door of the Inn and the time I'd seen the woman with the mobcap running across the Inn parking lot?

Frustration and remorse surged, and I banged my fist against the steering wheel. No wonder Jack had zeroed in on Mary Anne. I'd pointed him to her.

I slowed to turn into Ruthie's driveway but changed my mind and instead drove down the road and into the parking lot of the Inn. I wanted to recreate the path that the woman in the mobcap had taken, see if it gave me any insights into what had happened the night of Diantha's death.

There were no longer any police vehicles behind the Inn and the dumpster with the construction debris was gone, along with any SIGN the CSI team had been here.

I parked and skirted the spa wing, peering around the outside wall of the Inn to a narrow alley of uneven, moss-covered bricks that led to the street. On one side of the alley, arbor vitae was planted along the foundation of the Inn. On the other, the bare branches of oak trees that had lost their leaves lined the gray cedar-shingled walls of Jenn's Yarn Shop. The walls formed a tunnel through which I could see the war memorial on the green.

I could also see Marley, his back to me, as he shouted on his cell phone.

I reared back so he wouldn't see me, but I could hear his words.

"These are even better than the last ones I sent," he said. "I want more money . . ."

His voice faded and I chanced another peek onto the path. Marley stalked away from me, his phone to his ear. *What was that about? What were the last ones he sent?* I doubted it was recipes. *What was his game?* Why make a phone call here, when he could go into the office in the Inn? I shook myself. I had enough mysteries to deal with, but Marley was up to something. Besides, was there any confirmation that he'd left the Inn the night of Diantha's murder as he'd told me?

I took a deep breath and looked at my phone, itching to call Tillie. *No,* I thought, *I'd check his story myself.*

I returned to the back entrance to the spa and looked up. The window of my room was clearly visible from here, as was the window to Diantha's room. I jogged diagonally across the parking lot, recreating the route I'd seen the woman in the mobcap take. She'd passed the steps to Rob's apartment and continued around the carriage house along a line of bushes. I followed a well-worn dirt path and pushed through a stand of laurel to an opening in a tumbledown stone wall. I climbed uneven granite-slab steps into the graveyard I'd seen on the map in Diantha's suite. Even though I knew they were there, walking past the winged death's heads on the worn slate headstones made me shiver.

There were signs the graveyard was well tended: leaves had been raked into a pile at the far end and two of the graves were marked by American flags and metal medallions inscribed SAR, Sons of the American Revolution. I scanned the names as I passed. John Collins and his wife, Jerusha. Abiel and his wife, Silence. I recalled the sampler in my room with the message "Silence Makes a Man's Heart Glad" in tiny stitches, and wondered if that sampler hadn't had a different meaning for Abiel. Behind the graveyard was a tumbledown building, four crumbling walls enclosing pieces of a collapsed slate roof, choked and covered with vines.

I followed the hardpacked dirt path that led through the weathered gray stones to a gate in a chain-link fence enclosing the backyard of Ruthie's house, the old Collins Homestead. Thirty yards behind Ruthie's house was another tumbledown stone building not much larger than a garden shed. I remembered seeing it on Diantha's construction plans. Oceanus Collins' house.

Ruthie's house was a tiny wood-sided Cape Cod with the steep sloped roof and narrow windows that declared its colonial pedigree. A satellite dish clung weakly to the chimney. The house had black shutters at the windows and needed a fresh coat of yellow paint, but two brilliant purple mums flanked the back door.

I closed the chain-link fence behind me, climbed the back steps, and raised my hand to knock at the back door.

"Riley," Ruthie called behind me, waving as she cut through the graveyard. "I finished work early. The film crew got going at six today so I was able to start work earlier." She opened her door and led me inside the house where three cute mutts whined and barked for her attention. "I was already at the Inn when you called this morning. Time for a break so I can let the dogs out and stream my soaps."

The pups tarried for a quick rub behind their ears, then scampered past us into the backyard.

Ruthie led me through the kitchen, a pristine time capsule. The dull green linoleum floor, maple cupboards, and Hoosier cabinet were relics from earlier decades, as was the spectacularly large hearth and fireplace, which had a colonial-era beehive bread oven. Tiny Ruthie could easily stand inside the fireplace. Over the wooden mantel were pewter plates, tankards, and an antique wooden mortar and pestle, in contrast to the microwave and coffee maker on the yellow Formica counter.

"That fireplace is incredible!" I said.

Ruthie hung up her coat and brushed dog hairs from her pants leg. "This is the second oldest house in Penniman, even older than the Inn."

I remembered how her house would be on the chopping block, and how that gave her a motive for murder. I couldn't believe this petite older lady could hurt anyone, but previous experiences had taught me that the least likely people were capable of desperate acts when their backs were to the wall. I'd tread carefully.

"How long have you lived here?" I asked.

"Oh, fifteen years." Ruthie measured coffee and switched on the coffee maker. "Did I hear that you went to see the movie shoot?"

I nodded.

"I heard them all talking. 'Every minute we're not filming is a thousand dollars.'" Ruthie pushed her graying hair from her forehead with a gnarled hand. "You'd think they'd be more concerned about burying their mother."

"Ruthie, when you went into Diantha's Little Room, did you see anything out of the ordinary?" So much for treading carefully. "That shouldn't've been there?"

She shook her head. "No space for anything in that room except for what little furniture there is. Well, as far as noticing anything, honestly I opened the door and saw Diantha, and then I . . ." Her voice trailed as she took a mug from a cabinet. "Want a cup of coffee?"

"No, thanks."

"Rob says he's going to renovate that room, but I don't know that he has any say. Mark my words, the brothers are going to clear out and sell everything, lock, stock, and barrel."

I recalled the conversation I'd overheard yesterday and had to agree. "How well do you know the brothers?"

Ruthie poured herself a cup and added a packet of artificial sweetener. "I'd see them a few times a year when they were kids. They'd come sometimes in the summer, or holidays. Diantha boarded them at Magistrate's School and she'd visit the Inn when she dropped them off and picked them up. The boys loved to run around the Inn; Chip was particularly good at finding hiding places for hide-and-seek."

"Chip?" I said. "The stepbrother."

The lines of Ruthie's face softened. "He was older, and good to his brothers, I'll say that. Sam was a wild one. Always in scrapes. No fear. No wonder he does extreme sports. And Cooper, well"—she smiled—"what a charmer. But he was only here a couple of summers. He worked all the time when he was a kid, till the show ended."

I followed Ruthie through a dining room with broad wooden plank floors into a snug living room. This room had been updated with a leather recliner and a large-screen TV in a corner by the fireplace. On the mantel I noticed a wedding photo in a silver frame.

"My Matthew." Ruthie set her coffee down and held the photo so I could see it. A wiry man with a crew cut in a white dinner jacket smiled at the younger Ruthie I remembered from my camp days. "He passed a few months after Lucretia was born. Oh, how he doted on her!"

I stepped close to admire two large school photos hung over the fireplace: one, a young woman with long straight chestnut brown hair parted in the middle. The other was Lucretia before she dyed her hair, with honey gold tresses that waved about her shoulders. Both faces had Ruthie's wide-set blue eyes, and their serious, unsmiling expressions were similar, but the dark-haired girl was a beauty with sculpted cheekbones and fuller lips. Still, I blinked. Except for the hair color and these differences, they could be sisters.

"Jamie, my daughter." Ruthie didn't say any more as she waved me to a chair. "And Lucretia you've met, her daughter."

"Strong resemblance," I said.

"Both musical and artistic." Ruthie sat in the recliner and put her feet up with a sigh. "Lucretia worries about me too much. She doesn't think I know that she's trying to make money to buy this house for me. I don't think the girl sleeps. That's why I was glad she went to the lock-in and had some fun with her friends."

I swallowed hard, remembering my promise to Lucretia. I managed to say, "She's very talented."

I had a quick vision of Lucretia in her authentic colonial costume at the Fall Festival. It was so authentic I was sure she must've also had a mobcap to complete her look. With difficulty, I pulled my mind back to what Ruthie was saying.

"All her moneymaking schemes started after Rob told me that Diantha wanted to tear down the house to make more parking. Well, when it became clear Diantha wouldn't change her mind"—Ruthie shrugged—"I decided I had to accept the inevitable. I started clearing out the stuff stored in the attic and the cellar. We found the papers I gave to Diantha, and Rob passed to Gerri." She gave me a smile. "And passed to you, I heard. Yesterday, I found some more. You're not allergic to dust, are you? Could you take them to Gerri for me? Diantha lost interest, she was always like that, a butterfly, going from one thing to another, and I asked the boys if they want anything else we find, but they said they're not interested either."

She pushed herself out of her chair and I followed her back to the kitchen, where she opened the door to the cellar. My skin prickled at the sight of the narrow, steep stairs descending into the dark. The rich smell of a dirt floor rose as we descended, a graveyard smell, and I suddenly thought what a good suspect Ruthie was, of Ruthie's strong hands, of the desperation of someone about to lose their home, that she could move anywhere at the Inn with her pass key. When we reached the bottom and Ruthie pulled a string that lit a bare bulb overhead. I almost gasped in relief.

"Ruthie, I was wondering," I said. "Do you have a key to the Inn? Not the pass key for the rooms, but to the doors."

"Now why would I want that?" Ruthie scoffed. "Then they'd expect me over there at all hours. No thank you."

We passed a washer and dryer to a long rough wooden work bench topped with rusting tools and cardboard cartons.

"Never throw anything away, us old Yankees. Never know when you might need something or what you might find. How Diantha crowed when Lucretia found that letter from George Washington and gave it to her! But did she give Lucretia anything for finding it? A lousy fifty bucks. 'Finder's fee,' she said." Disgust twisted Ruthie's face. "That letter would've been worth a lot more than that if Lucretia sold it on eBay! I bet Diantha paid the science teacher up at Magistrate's more than that for testing the paper."

"Did you find the George Washington letter in the box you sent to Gerri?" I asked.

"Yes. Lucretia said it was valuable, so I told her to take it to Diantha straightaway. Here's more of the old papers."

I reached for the closest box.

"No, the other one," Ruthie said. "That box has Jamie's school things." Ruthie showed me CDs, vinyl records, and sheet music for the score of *Oklahoma*. "I thought it would be nice for Lucretia to go through it, maybe feel closer to her mother. She didn't want it so I'll toss it. Seems I can't do anything right, these days."

I squeezed her arm. "Teenage girls are complicated." What I didn't say out loud was that Lucretia struck me as more complicated than the average teenager. I glanced into the box. "You might not want to toss those vinyl records. A lot of people collect them."

"I'll have a big tag sale when I have to move out," Ruthie said.

I noticed a stamp on the sheet music, a design of ivy encircling a pelican. I'd seen the same symbol over the library door at Magistrate's School. "You said Jamie was musical? Did she go to Magistrate's?"

"We could never afford private school, but Jamie was so talented she took private violin lessons with one of Magistrate's teachers, down at her house by the lake." Ruthie shook her head. "Lucretia refers to her as Jamie, not even mom. Well, she didn't know her or her father either." Ruthie's lips formed a firm line, sealing off that topic. "Oh, listen to me go on. You came over for the Bible, let me get it for you."

Ruthie turned to climb the stairs, and I reached for the string of the overhead light as my eyes fell on the Magistrate's School seal once more. I hefted the small box of old papers onto my hip, put out the light, and followed Ruthie upstairs.

"Was the stuff in this box similar to the stuff you sent to Diantha?"

"Yes," Ruthie said as I followed her into the dining room. "Lots of old papers. Oceanus Collins had a printing shop here at one time. My old eyes can't make heads or tails of it, especially with that faded ink and the way they wrote those S's that look like F's."

She took a very small book from a shelf in a corner cupboard. "So why do you want this Bible?"

"I think there's a code in those old letters," I said, hoping I didn't sound too nutty, "and I think the Bible may hold some clues."

"Now that is exciting." Ruthie's cheeks pinked as she

handed me the book. "Be sure to tell me when you figure it out. I do love a secret. And let me know if the Bible's worth anything."

I carefully placed the Bible on top of the papers. "I'll have Dad look at it."

Ruthie's dogs whined and scratched at the door and she hurried to let them in.

As I passed the coat rack by the kitchen door I noticed a long fall of black fabric next to Ruthie's navy blue peacoat. A cape. A scrap of white fabric peeked out from under it. I lifted the cape to reveal a poufy white cap rimmed with lace.

"Lucretia's costume." Ruthie tsked as the dogs surged inside. "I told that girl to put it away."

Chapter 27

Now I knew for sure who the girl in the mobcap was: Lucretia.

I also understood why Lucretia was forbidden to date. Had Jamie secretly dated the guy who'd left her alone with a baby? That would explain Ruthie's reluctance to talk about her daughter, and Brandon's comment that Lucretia didn't talk about her mother or father. Ruthie'd go through the roof if she knew that not only did Lucretia have a boyfriend, she hadn't gone to the lock-in, and she'd lied about it.

My mind churned as I closed Ruthie's gate behind me. When Brandon brought Lucretia home, he couldn't drop her at her front door. Lucretia had him drop her off in front of the Inn, and she'd come home through the Inn parking lot. She'd worn the mobcap to hide the distinctive orange streaks in her hair in case anyone saw her.

I'd talk to Brandon to verify this theory. The kid was incapable of lying without turning the color of a ripe tomato. Lucretia, however, I was sure was made of tougher stuff.

Learning about Ruthie's daughter, Jamie, and cross-ing the graveyard put me in a pensive mood as I tried to sort everything I'd learned.

A text stopped me on the path to the parking lot.

ALL DONE AT PHOTO SHOOT BUT THEY NEED SPRINKLES FOR ANOTHER SCENE. PAULETTE WILL DROP ME AT HOME. I MET EVAN SMITH!

Caroline's text included a photo of Evan, Sprinkles, Paulette, and herself under the oak with the library in the background. Caroline's grin was broad and more than a bit starstruck, but Paulette, Evan, and Sprinkles looked perfectly posed. In the background I saw two figures. I enlarged the photo.

Jenira and Chip. Her head was thrown back, laughing.

My phone dinged with another text from Caroline.

EMILIA TOLD ME THAT THE COPS ARE GOING TO QUESTION EVERYONE AT THE INN AGAIN TONIGHT 8 PM.

My heart jumped. That must mean that Jack wasn't one hundred percent ready to arrest Mary Anne—or at least, that he was open to looking for other suspects. I had to tell him about Lucretia . . . actually I had to get Lucretia to tell Jack the truth. It would necessitate an uncomfortable conversation with her grandmother, but it had to be done. Lucretia running through the park-ing lot at three a.m. didn't clear Mary Ann completely, but it did upend some assumptions. Nothing would clear Mary Anne completely until the real murderer was re-vealed.

I wanted to show Dad the Bible before I went to Ud-derly for my afternoon shift. Brandon was working after school and would be able to put me in touch with Lucre-tia. I needed her to talk to Jack. As I rushed through the graveyard, I heard raised voices. I shifted the box on my hip and hurried past the carriage house to the Inn's parking lot where Mary Anne and Marley faced off at the base of the back stairs. I stopped short.

"You sneaky little viper!" she yelled. "You brought the cops to my house last night!"

Marley smirked. "It's not your house, is it? It's Dominic's!"

"It's still half mine!" she shouted.

Rob descended the stairs from the Inn, his hands raised. "Let's keep it down, okay?"

"Stay away from me, you punk!" Mary Anne got back in her truck and slammed her door. I stepped out of sight as she spun the truck into a U-turn, tires screeching as it barely missed a parked car and rocketed out of the parking lot.

Marley put his hands on his hips and watched her go. The satisfied grin on his face made me seethe.

Rob wheeled on him. "What was that about?"

Marley snorted. "Someone has her knickers in a twist, that's all. The cops'll arrest her soon, and then we won't have to worry about her tantrums."

Rob folded his arms, his face hard. "She's been here longer than you, Marley, and she's a great chef."

"Is that a threat?" Though he barely came to Rob's chest, Marley raised his chin. "Well, go ahead and threaten. Dominic and I have plans, and they may not include you or the Inn." Marley ran up the kitchen steps as Rob swore, kicked a stack of empty liquor boxes, and sagged onto a step, his head in his hands. I hesitated, then walked out from behind the carriage house. Marley's eyes met mine, but he didn't say anything as he jerked open the door and went inside. The fight was upsetting, but I was relieved. Mary Anne hadn't been arrested or put in jail.

Rob raised his head and tried to joke. "Chefs. They're the ultimate drama queens."

I set Ruthie's box inside my car then went to him. "Are you okay?"

Rob's bulldog face crumpled. "I feel like a rat. I told the cops about seeing Mary Anne and I mentioned the woman in the parking lot you told me about. After what Mary Anne did to the cake, I jumped to conclusions. I've always known she's emotional. You know how I know Mary Anne didn't kill Diantha? She didn't admit it. She admitted wrecking the cake. She owns what she does, not like some people," he muttered.

"What do you mean?"

Rob lowered his head and I felt he was talking more to himself than me. "Mary Anne told me about Dominic taking all her recipes for his cookbook. I believe her. I mean he's the famous one, but that's because he does all that fancy foam and smoking stuff; she's the one who makes food people actually want to eat. Marley and Dominic are talking about their own restaurant. Good riddance. I don't want them here."

Now that I knew Lucretia was the woman in the mob-cap, not Mary Anne, I needed to start considering other suspects, including Rob. I hated myself, but he looked vulnerable enough to answer my questions.

"Rob, the night Diantha died, I saw you two arguing."

His head jerked up so quickly I had to resist the urge to flinch. But instead of anger, I saw something more painful: regret. "I was a fool, Riley. I was trying anything to stop her from marrying Dominic. I'm tired of secrets. Yes, I carried a torch for her. And like a love-struck fool, I did anything she asked. For years, Diantha had me hire private detectives to follow the women that Cooper and Sam hooked up with. She was afraid they'd marry someone who just wanted their money."

That would explain Jenira's "stalker." "Jenira too?"

He snorted. "Diantha really didn't like her. Jenira and Cooper dated briefly, and Diantha said she had higher hopes for Cooper, always hoped he'd meet someone classy like Emilia. Emilia was a surprise, especially for Sam. To put it mildly, he wasn't very particular about some of his girlfriends."

I changed the subject. "Rob, the night Diantha died, who was at the party in the bar?"

He took a deep breath. "A few of Dominic and Diantha's friends, but they left early. At the end of the night it was family, except for Emilia—she begged off early because of jet lag. Dominic left before midnight because the boys were teasing him about seeing the bride before the wedding."

Rob's forehead wrinkled. "Jenira and Chip left, actually he left and she followed him upstairs, said she wanted to talk to him then take a swim, but Chip came back just a few minutes later. A while later, Sam left to check on Emilia but came back, and he and Cooper sat in a corner with a nice bottle of tequila. Marley cleaned up and took off around twelve thirty."

I snorted, remembering the mess in the lounge the next day. "How about Diantha?"

His voice softened. "She was glowing, having a marvelous time. She didn't want to go to sleep, but the boys finally persuaded her. I mean she was hitting the drinks pretty hard, but that was Diantha."

I imagined it was another reason he loved her, she wouldn't judge his drinking. I remembered Dominic and Marley serving drinks from a punch bowl.

"Did she drink the punch?"

Rob nodded. "She loved it, loved the whole spooky vibe with the fog effect."

"Do you remember Lucretia delivering a pumpkin?" I asked.

"We took delivery of Lucretia's pumpkins earlier in the day. I remember her hair was orange," he said.

"No, later that night," I said, recalling that Lucretia told me a man had taken the pumpkin at the front door of the Inn when she closed up her booth for the night.

Ron shook his head. "If she went to the front door, it could've been anyone from the party who happened to pass by. They'd just have to undo the deadbolt."

"Rob, who do you think killed Diantha?"

He gave me a pained smile. "I don't know. All that matters to me is she's gone. For years I thought maybe I'd have a chance, but she was never gonna go for a regular Joe like me." He glanced at his watch. "Gotta get back to work."

I crossed the parking lot and retrieved the Bible from Sadie as Rob climbed the steps to the Inn. His slow steps and bent shoulders drew my sympathy, but could I trust Rob's recollection of events? Rob had been hitting the booze pretty hard himself, and in that party atmosphere, could he have kept track of everyone?

Choreography, I thought as I took the brick path to the green.

Rob remembered Jenira, Chip, and Sam leaving the party; Chip and Sam came back. Jenira had gone for a swim. I remembered seeing her swimsuit in her bathroom. Diantha's Little Room was right by the stairs that led to the pool. It was possible she could've taken the key to the Little Room, ducked in, and readied the dry ice. But why would Jenira want to kill Diantha? Had she discovered that Diantha had sicced private investigators on her? No. From what Tillie had told me, Jenira was convinced her tail was a stalker.

But, I mused, *she was an actress. Could anything she said be trusted?*

I decided to run in to Just the Thing on the way to

Dad's shop to check Emilia's and Marley's stories. I remembered Marley rented a room over the charming gift shop.

The owner, a longtime friend of Dad's, had already changed her shop's window decor from fall to Christmas, and was busy stringing tinsel onto a miniature artificial Scotch Pine tree as I entered.

After chatting for a bit, she answered my questions.

Yes, Marley lived upstairs and the police had already been by to check his alibi. She'd seen Marley coming home at around 12:30 the night of the murder. Unfortunately this cleared Marley.

"The woman in the green duffel coat who bought the wrapping paper? Oh yes, I remember her. She said she was a guest at the Inn. Had to come back twice, poor thing. She told me she put her wrap and bow down in the library and someone took it. She had to run back here to get more, and had to settle for a different-color bow, a white one, I think. Poor thing looked ill. I hope she's okay."

My mind whirled as I walked across the green.

An expensive-looking motorcycle and truck, the phone call with the demand for more money . . . Marley was up to something, but it wasn't murder.

I recalled the white bow on Emilia's gift.

That was how the killer disguised the boxes of dry ice. Carrying Styrofoam boxes through the Inn would call attention, but carrying a prettily wrapped box on the eve of a wedding, especially one where gifts were pouring in, would hardly be noticed.

I called Jack. His phone went to voicemail and a disturbing thought made me hang up.

Was Emilia the killer? Or had she helped the killer? She was right across the hall from Diantha's Little Room. Could she lift the heavy boxes of dry ice? Could she carry them from the back of the Inn all the way to Diantha's room and hide them under the bed?

I'd seen her walking across the green. Maybe she'd faked being tired so she could move the dry ice into Diantha's room. I didn't think she was faking the extent of her illness; if she was, it was masterfully done, right down to the detail of her medicine bottles.

What if she and Sam did it together? He'd inherit and then give her the money for her charity.

None of this felt right. She was the one with money. I'd heard Cooper and Sam discuss her inheritance the first day I worked at the Inn.

Would Emilia kill for her charity? Would she kill for Sam?

I liked Emilia. Was I blinding myself to a killer because I liked her?

I had so many questions and theories to share with Jack. I didn't want to meddle, but this was important. I called Jack again and left a message, telling him about Cooper and Mojo Productions. "And I think you should talk to Lucretia Adams. I'm pretty sure she was the girl in the mobcap running across the Inn parking lot."

I hung up and waited a few moments, hoping Jack would return the call, and that Lucretia and Caroline would forgive me.

Jack didn't reply.

Chapter 28

The cheerful jingle of the bell lifted my dark mood as I entered Dad's bookshop.

He broke into a grin and nodded toward the front of my coat. With a shock, I realized I was still wearing the badge that said SPRINKLES' SUPPORT STAFF.

He chuckled. "This whole family's gone Hollywood. Were you an extra too?"

With a shake of my head, I took off the badge and stuffed it in my jacket pocket. "Get this, Dad, Sprinkles had her own reserved parking spot."

He laughed. "Don't tell Paulette! She'll be envious."

"I saw Paulette's scene. She looked great." I wondered how much screen time Paulette would actually get, or if she'd end up on the cutting-room floor.

"She was floating this morning," Dad said, "and the movie has been a shot in the arm for Penniman. I was talking to a friend in Mystic. Skylark shoots movies there all the time, and every time the movies show on TV they're flooded with tourists. But you didn't come here to hear me talk about that."

Dad lifted the tea kettle, but I waved it off and placed the Bible onto the checkout counter. "Sorry, I don't have

much time. Dad, can you take a look at this old Bible?
Ruthie found it in a box of old papers."

"Happy to, but old Bibles are a specialty field." He set
his glasses on top of his head and put on the readers he
wore on a lanyard around his neck. "Bibles were hard to
get in the colonial era. By royal decree, they could only
be printed by British publishers and they weren't im-
ported during the war, so they were precious commodi-
ties." He lifted the cover and carefully turned to the
first page where a family tree was inscribed in a faded,
spidery hand. I could only imagine what people named
Silence, Increase, and Solomon would think of Diantha
and her sons.

"A Collins family Bible." He turned the pages with a
gentle touch. "They must be thrilled to have found this."

I shrugged. "Ruthie said Diantha and her sons weren't
interested."

Dad's eyebrows shot up over the rims of his glasses.
"That's odd. This is in good condition and would fetch a
very pretty penny from a collector."

"I'll let Gerri know about the situation when I'm done
with it."

"What made you interested in this Bible?" Dad said.

As I told him about the letters and what I believed to
be a cipher, his eyes glowed. "The Case of the Colonial
Cipher! What fun! Bring it over and we'll work on it
together, now that you'll have some downtime with the
shop closing for the winter."

I hadn't told Dad I'd been accepted into the gelato
class and I still wasn't sure I'd do it, or to be more specific, where I'd do it. Instead I said, "I'll have time to help
you with the holiday rush."

Dad gave me a skeptical look. "You sure? I figured
you'd be off on an adventure. I set this aside for you."
He handed me a copy of *Blue Highways* by William

Least Heat-Moon. I'd read the book in high school, and the author's memoir of his travels across America on little-traveled byways, which were printed in blue ink on old maps, had ignited my own love of travel. "And it's signed."

I wrapped my arms around Dad with a delighted whoop. "You know me so well." As I hugged him, I noticed a box of decorations behind the counter. "Christmas already?"

"Paulette wants to get the Christmas decorations up right away," Dad said, "but I think we'll wait a bit. I've always liked fall."

Chapter 29

To ease my churning mind, I threw myself into making ice cream. Though the shop doors would be closed for the winter, I had plans that would keep the kitchen at Udderly busy through the cold months. After all, New Englanders eat ice cream all year long.

I'd forged partnerships with some local restaurants, and I gathered ingredients for a recipe I'd developed for the upcoming Thanksgiving holiday, a Thanksgiving cranberry sorbet. I set my mind to cooking down the cranberries with different sweeteners and spices to determine the best flavor profile.

Flo stepped into the workroom to get more whipped cream but stopped to sniff the air. "Smells like Thanksgiving in here." I gave her a taste of the beautiful red base and she gave me a thumbs-up before returning to the front of the shop.

I poured the base into the chiller and washed my pots, watching the garnet color dissipate and fade in the soapy water, the same color as the stone in the Magistrate's school ring.

I glanced up as Brandon slouched in the door and

hung his green Penniman High School Band jacket on a peg.

He said, "Hey, Riley," in such a melancholy tone I regretted that I wanted to grill him about Lucretia.

"Brandon. How are you?"

He mumbled something that sounded like "fine."

I put on a fresh apron. "How was school?"

"'Kay."

I continued, "How's Lucretia?"

His shrugged as he washed his hands, put on his apron, and started making fresh waffle cones. "She said she had some stuff to do after school. She hasn't talked to me since last night."

His downcast expression tugged at my heart. They'd seemed fine when she left the shop; she'd even given him that "call me" gesture. But I remembered being a teen, and at that age a few hours of silence could feel like an eternity.

I threw a glance toward the front of the shop, making sure Pru and Flo were busy and we were alone. "Brandon, this is important. What time did you take Lucretia home after you left here Saturday night? You drove, right?"

He kept his eyes on the waffle-cone maker, but still managed to burn his finger. "Argh!" He rushed to the sink and ran it under cold water.

I knew why he was so jumpy. "You dropped her off, right?"

He grimaced and waved his hand, and I handed him a clean towel. "Yeah, around three, but not at her house. She told me to drop her in front of the Inn, then she'd cut through the parking lot and graveyard. The lock-in ran until eight a.m. She didn't want her gran to know when she came home."

I held up a hand. "Brandon, don't worry, I'm not going to tell Ruthie anything."

The wariness in his eyes made me feel that I owed him an explanation. "I stayed at the Inn the night Diantha was killed. I saw Lucretia crossing the parking lot at three a.m. She was wearing her cap, right?"

Brandon nodded. "She said Mr. Wainwright's up all hours with insomnia and she didn't want him to recognize her going home, so she put on her cap to cover her hair. Her costume cape doesn't have a hood."

I smiled. "She not the first girl who ever snuck back home after a date."

He returned to the waffle maker and kept his eyes on his work but a trace of a smile curved his lips.

There was something else he wasn't telling me. "What is it, Brandon? Did she see anyone when she ran through the lot?"

He shook his head. "No, she didn't mention anyone, and she's been fine, less worried actually." He slid his phone from his pocket and checked the screen. "She hasn't answered my texts. Maybe her gran found out she skipped the lock-in and grounded her or took away her phone."

I gave him a pat on the shoulder and prayed that Jack wouldn't mention my name when he went to question Lucretia. Brandon was a terrific worker and I had a very soft spot for him.

A wave of conversation and laughter flowed from the front of the shop. I glanced into the parking lot as I went to join Pru and Flo at the counter and saw two long fifteen-person vans parked by Tillie's red VW bug. Tillie stood by her car, hands in the pockets of her coat, her head swiveling at passing traffic.

"All hands on deck," I called to Brandon.

Film crew wearing badges from the shoot at Magistrate's School crowded the dipping cases. Jenira turned on her megawatt smile as she stepped inside. "I have an hour off and I had to sample the finest ice cream in Connecticut," she announced. "I heard you'd brought some ice cream to the Inn, but Dominic and Marley ate it all."

"The finest ice cream in New England." Flo waved a scoop. "What can I get you?"

The shop filled with excited chatter as the crew pressed against the dipping cases.

"Ooh, a triple scoop of mocha marshmallow swirl in a waffle cone for me!"

"I'll have a banana split with the works."

"That salted caramel with praline crumble looks divine."

We hustled to fill the orders, and a warm sense of pride filled me as the crew snapped selfies with Flo and praised their treats. Pru gave me an amused look and pointed her scoop at the empty pan of Brandon's unicorn ice cream.

Jenira took a single scoop of pumpkin spice ice cream to a café table for two by the window, narrowed her beautiful ebony eyes, and waved her spoon at me. "You were at the shoot with Sprinkles this morning."

"Guilty," I said.

"Come sit for a minute."

Pru waved me off saying, "We've got this," so I took a seat with Jenira.

"That demon cat stole every scene." Jenira rolled her eyes. "What's the saying, never work with kids or animals? Too true. Especially in Skylark movies. My next project won't have any animals or kids, I guarantee it."

I remembered the script for *Meteor* in her room, but I didn't dare mention I'd seen it there. so I said, "Your next project's not a Skylark movie?"

"Nothing official yet, but I'm going in a different direction," Jenira said. "I've done so many Skylarks, I want to get back to doing something more serious and challenging."

"Different genre?"

"I started out doing horror, believe it or not." She wrinkled her nose. "You'll take any work, anywhere when you're starting out."

Voices from the Ice had been a horror movie. "Have you worked overseas?"

"Not really, just some TV work in Canada and stuff." She took a big bite of ice cream, then looked away and smoothed her hair.

And stuff? I decided not to push her on this evasive answer. There was more I wanted to ask her and I didn't want to alienate her.

"This ice cream's so good," she licked her spoon and moaned. "I miss carbs. I try not to eat them, but sometimes I can't help it. If I fall off the wagon I make myself run ten miles to make up for it. Oh wait, I saw you running the other day. You're everywhere."

The only place she hadn't recognized me from was the Inn—the power of the housekeeper's invisibility smock.

Jenira pointed out the window at Tillie. "You know my protection detail."

I smothered a grin. "Protection detail" sounded like serious agents in black suits guarding the president's motorcade, not Tillie in a red VW bug.

"Yes, I know Tillie." I didn't add, *Everyone in Penniman knows Tillie.* "Has everything been all right? I hope you haven't seen that stalker again."

She snorted and waved a dismissive hand. "I scared him off when we had our confrontation, scared the daylights out of him," she crowed. "He took off running when he saw how serious I was."

"Good."

Jenira continued, "Yeah, he was probably some psycho. Called out 'Cara,' as if he knew me. Cara Mia. There's some chick out there named Cara Mia who's glad he's after me and not her."

She kept talking but I wasn't hearing her words. *Cara mia.* "My dear," in Italian. It was what Paolo called me.

My heart pounding, I recalled the wardrobe assistant on set at The Penniless Reader who mistook me for Jenira. Paulette's comment, *From the back you look like Jenira.*

"What did he look like?" I touched my high ponytail, just like Jenira's, and tried to remember Tillie's sketchy description of the stalker.

Jenira licked her spoon and considered. "Six foot, light brown hair, slight curl, you know long enough to be in style but not too long, designer sunglasses, so I couldn't see his eyes, but square jaw, not bad looking as stalkers go. He had a nice matching jogging outfit, designer, looked expensive for a stalker, probably Armani."

An Italian designer. Paolo did have good taste in clothes.

"Thanks." I managed to stand and not knock over my chair.

She scraped her cup to get the last bit of ice cream. "Yeah, keep an eye out. This guy could mean trouble."

She had no idea. In a daze I walked back into the kitchen and started wiping counters.

"I already cleaned that," Brandon said.

I parted the beaded-curtain door of the office and dropped into the desk chair. I'd imagined Paolo on a yacht somewhere, enjoying the ill-gotten gains from his theft. But he'd come to Penniman. Was he still here? I recalled his letter. Maybe I should've read it, to be better prepared in case he popped up. I dropped my head into my hands.

Paolo was a complication and distraction I didn't want and didn't need. The film crew was due to leave as soon as they finished shooting and I was sure the killer was one of the people who'd stayed the night at the Inn. I had to talk to Diantha's family one more time, clear Mary Anne once and for all, and pray that Jenira really had scared Paolo away from Penniman.

Chapter 30

Jenira's evasiveness when I asked her about shooting overseas made me open the shop laptop and search her bio on a movie database page. She'd appeared in seven Skylark movies, five as the lead. Before that she worked in some low-budget horror flicks, but *Voices in the Ice* wasn't on the list, probably because it had never been released, never completed after the horrific accident. She had worked overseas, done two films and some television shows in Canada and Croatia. I checked the dates—she'd been in Croatia the same year *Voices in the Ice* filmed, but that wasn't proof she'd been in that film.

It was almost closing time and I had two hours until Jack started questioning everyone at the Inn. I knew I should leave the investigation to Jack, but I was certain I could help. How to get myself welcomed at the Inn? I could bring over some of Dominic's favorite fudge swirl ice cream—ice cream did open doors. I could put on a smock and pretend to be housekeeping.

Plus, I didn't want to go home or near Dad's shop, anywhere Paolo could find me. I considered next steps, but all I saw in my mind's eye was the box of Jamie's papers in Ruthie's cellar and the sheet music with the crest from Magistrate's School.

There was a sudden silence as I realized the last of the film crew must've left the shop. After closing, I thought, running the trails around the lake would be a good way to burn off the nervous energy that coursed through my veins. I clicked on the Penniman Trails website and scanned the map of Penniman Lake. As I did, I noted that Magistrate's School property was even more extensive than I'd realized, extending from the main campus across Long Meadow Road to Penniman Lake, and encircling the Girl Scout camp and boat launch area. I typed in "Magistrate's School," clicked on the Diantha and Scott Collins wing of the library and whistled when I saw that their gift had been two million dollars, made when Sam was a student. I checked a list of other donations; there was a smaller, though still-generous, gift at the time of Cooper's matriculation, endowing a black box theater.

I recalled Ruthie's comment about Diantha's renovation of the Inn and the restaurant she was going to bankroll for Dominic. There was a lot of money at stake here.

Everyone needed money, right? With Diantha's death, Dominic was the biggest loser, losing both his bride and major funding for his new restaurant.

Marley and Dominic had hit it off. Did Marley view Diantha as a distraction for Dominic? With her out of the way, he could have Dominic all to himself? I scoffed. That was a lot of scheming in the short time he'd worked at the Inn. It'd make more sense for him to let Diantha continue with her plan to bankroll Dominic's new restaurant and then he could move there from his job at the Inn. It wouldn't be in Marley's interest to murder Diantha, but there was something so wormy about Marley that the thought of him behind bars delighted me. He was up to something shady, I was sure of it, but what I'd learned from the owner of Just The Thing made me reluctantly cross him off my list of suspects.

I'd overheard Cooper ask Sam for money. Wouldn't he have money from his acting career? I searched again and Diantha had acted as his agent, but from the photos online, he'd enjoyed a lavish lifestyle with expensive toys like sailboats and exotic sports cars. Location scouts and assistant directors probably didn't make much money in the Hollywood scheme of things.

I wondered if Chip was in the same boat. I googled him—he had a list of movies to his credit, all made in the US and Canada, and he was doing another Skylark right after *Bound for Love* wrapped. Though he was one of Skylark's favorite directors, his own romantic life was less sunny. He had two ex-wives—glossy, expensive-looking women. Alimony was probably killing him. He'd been left out of the will, but did he know that before Diantha's death? Could he have killed Diantha for spite, for years of treating him as less than her biological sons?

Cooper needed money. Chip needed money. I couldn't see the sunny wizard boy nor the cheerful barfly killing, but they both would benefit from an inheritance.

Jenira. She wanted to make a switch to a different kind of movie. Would she have to bankroll her own film to have the freedom to try different roles? But she wasn't connected to any of Diantha's sons. As a matter of fact, she'd broken up with Cooper, and I remembered that she'd locked the deadbolt on her side of their rooms' connecting doors. He'd left his open. Had he hoped for a reconciliation she wanted no part of? I couldn't see Jenira having a motive for Diantha's murder.

Sam. Emilia said he'd grown more interested in

working with his brothers. He'd lose his lucrative representation deals as he aged out of the skateboard world, but his own wife had been an heiress . . . who was spending all her money on her charity. Did he need to inherit to fund his lifestyle? I remembered his expensive suitcases and her practical, well-worn luggage. Had he realized his marriage to Emilia would involve a complete change in lifestyle, from international partying to backbreaking charity work? If anything, judging from Emilia's fragile state, he'd be inheriting from her sooner rather than later.

Ruthie. She had a lot to lose. Her home, paved over to make a parking lot. Her job. Still, could she kill? I couldn't square this with my image of salt-of-the-earth Ruthie, who'd taught me and generations of Penniman Girl Scouts how to canoe and sail on Penniman Lake.

Rob. Of all of the people staying on the Inn property that night, he had the most extreme reaction to Diantha's death. Would he kill her to stop the wedding? He'd admitted that he was desperate enough to blackmail Diantha. No one would question him carrying packages or opening any door. He had free reign throughout the Inn.

So did Ruthie.

So did Mary Anne.

With room keys hanging behind the reception desk, so did anyone else.

A banging door and a commotion roused me from my reverie. I closed the laptop and dashed through the beaded curtain as Ruthie burst into the kitchen.

Ruthie grabbed Brandon's arm as Pru and Flo ran from the front of the shop.

"Brandon, where's Lucretia?"

Chapter 31

W hat's going on?" I pried Ruthie's hand off Brandon's arm and led her to a chair, but she shook
me off, instead pacing and wringing her hands.

"Lucretia didn't come home after school." Worry and
exasperation mingled in Ruthie's voice. "We had a fight
last night after I found out she didn't go to the lock-in,
and I told her she was grounded and had to come home
straight after History Club."

Ruthie's reaction struck me as extreme until I recalled that Ruthie's daughter had left her and never returned. Pru and Flo exchanged a sympathetic look that
made me realize they knew about Jamie too. Brandon
cowered by the sink.

"She hasn't come home from school. Her car's gone."
Ruthie took a long shuddering breath. "I called her friends
and they said maybe she was here with you, Brandon."

Brandon shook his head and stammered, "I, no, she
hasn't answered my texts either."

"Do you think she went to a friend's house?" Pru said,
gently but firmly leading Ruthie back to the chair.

Ruthie shook her head. "I talked to her friends.
They said she'd been in a great mood in school but she

skipped her History Club meeting. I don't know what to do." Ruthie collapsed into the chair and Pru rubbed her back.

That was odd wasn't it? I thought. *Lucretia was grounded but in a good mood? Something must've happened to put her in a good mood. Why skip her club meeting? Where was she?*

Flo went to the shop phone. "I'll call the police."

"Do you think that's necessary?" Pru held up a hand, her voice soothing. "Teenagers do things like this all the time. It's only been a few hours. Maybe she had to settle down after your disagreement."

Brandon shook his head. "She never skips History Club."

I took a deep breath. "I think we should call them. Jack was going to talk to her about the night of Diantha's murder."

"Diantha's murder!" Ruthie blanched.

I couldn't bring myself to say that I'd told Jack about seeing Lucretia in the Inn parking lot the night of the murder, but Brandon made the leap.

"Maybe she saw the killer!" Brandon said, putting my fears into words. "Maybe he wants her silenced."

After a moment of shocked silence, everyone started talking at once.

I held up my hands, trying to project a calm I didn't feel. "Let's not get dramatic. Maybe she's simply gone to talk to Jack."

"If she's talking to the police, well, she couldn't get any safer, could she?" Flo turned on the kettle. "I'll make you some tea, Ruthie."

Brandon hunched over his cell phone. I was certain he was texting Lucretia and I prayed she'd respond. My mind was spinning. *What if Lucretia had seen the killer?* I could picture her running through the parking lot, looking up at the sound of the boxes being tossed into the dumpster from Diantha's window. The timing was right. There was security lighting in the parking lot; the killer would see her clearly. What if she knew the killer? If she'd seen them, they'd seen her.

She'd been worried but now her friends said she was in a great mood.

A thought chilled me. What if she'd seen a way to get some money for her grandmother through a little blackmail? Had the killer promised that they wouldn't sell the house and Ruthie could stay? It would have to be someone who had authority to do that, someone who'd inherit Diantha's estate.

Cooper or Sam.

Jack probably wouldn't pick up if he knew the call was from me. "I'll call the nonemergency number." I willed my hands to remain steady as I dialed. Instead of Tillie's voice, a man answered.

"Penniman Police Services. How may I be of assistance?"

After I explained the situation, the voice on the phone replied in a calm tone, "Teenagers do this sort of thing all the time, but I'll send an officer."

As we spoke, Pru stood by Ruthie as Flo encouraged her to sip some tea. Brandon stood by the window looking out into the dark, his phone clutched in his hand.

"She may have had an appointment to speak to the chief," I said. "Can you check with him?"

"I'll check." After a few minutes, he returned to the phone. I listened and then hung up, turning slowly. "Jack hasn't spoken with Lucretia. He's coming right over."

Chapter 32

The ten minutes it took for Jack to arrive felt an eternity.

After listening to Ruthie, he said, "At this point, I can't do much more than put out an alert. What kind of car does she drive?"

"A 2010 blue Ford Taurus."

Jack made a note then put a hand on Ruthie's shoulder. "Best you go home, Ruthie, in case she shows up there. Maybe her phone battery's out of power. Everyone else can get back to work." His stolid presence and no-nonsense manner had a calming effect. Pru and Flo threw me looks that said they were still concerned, but they went to the front of the shop without saying more.

"Riley." Jack nodded his head toward the parking lot and I followed him outside into the gathering dusk. "It's a little too coincidental, Lucretia going missing after you tell me to talk to her. What's up?"

I could hear his breath quicken as I explained my fear that Lucretia recognized and could be blackmailing Diantha's murderer, but his voice was steady when he replied, "I'll put out that alert. We'll check all the places kids go—the road behind the artists' colony, the usual hangouts." He looked up the hill past the warm lights burning in the farmhouse. "The pond off Woods Road. I'll drive there now."

He got into his SUV as I went back into the shop.

Ruthie slumped in her chair. "I'm too shaky to drive home."

"I'll drive your car for you, Ruthie, and get a ride home from your place later." I intended to be at the Inn when Jack interrogated the family.

"I'll drive my car over and stay with you," Flo said as she pulled on her coat.

Ruthie's voice was small. "Thank you, Riley. Thank you, Flo."

"Can I come too?" Brandon was already taking off his apron.

"I'll do cleanup." Pru shooed us all out the door. "Call me when you know something."

I drove Ruthie's car to her house and parked in her driveway. Flo and Brandon parked next to me. Any hope we'd had that Lucretia'd returned home was extinguished at the sight of the empty driveway and dark house.

Sensing Ruthie's return, her dogs kicked up a racket as we entered through the backyard gate. Motion-sensor security lights came on and illuminated the backyard and small, tumbledown shed by the cemetery wall.

"Did you check the outbuildings?" I asked.

"First place I looked," Ruthie said tiredly as we all climbed the steps to her kitchen door. She jutted her chin at the one behind the house. "She spends all her time there, it's her art studio and workshop."

"I'll check it again." My cell phone buzzed as I hurried to the outbuilding as Flo and Brandon followed Ruthie inside. As I approached, I could see the outbuilding was just this side of a ruin. Its wooden door hung crookedly in its crumbling frame and rasped against the dank dirt floor as I pushed it open.

"Lucretia?" I felt along the wall, but there was no light switch. I turned on my cell phone flashlight and played the beam around a single room furnished with two discarded wooden doors on sawhorses, two plastic lawn chairs, and a mattress covered with a sleeping bag on the floor. That explained how Lucretia could hide that she didn't go to the lock-in. She'd stayed here Saturday night.

The tops of the improvised worktables were cluttered. The first was piled with art supplies. I played my beam on a sketchbook and flipped through pages of pumpkin designs. I blinked as my flashlight illuminated my own face sketched next to the rendering of the pumpkin she'd made for the shop.

My beam shone on the cord of a kettle plugged into an overloaded power strip and bare lightbulbs with pull chains over the worktables. I moved to the next worktable, covered with a perplexing assortment of dried plants, amber-colored stones, a mortar and pestle stained with a brown residue, iron nails, and walnut shells.

My beam found another power strip. I followed the cord to a battered kitchen chair and an old-fashioned washstand, the kind that has a large bowl and pitcher, set in the center of the room.

Curious, I examined it. The bowl and pitcher had been removed, and all that remained was the wooden stand. The round hole in the middle had been topped by a sheet of glass and a light was rigged beneath it. I flicked it on. The parchment paper on top of the glass had several names written in script numerous times.

One name jumped out: G. Washington, the G and W linked in flowing calligraphy, written over and over, the G followed by tiny e's and o's. George Washington.

No, the signatures weren't written, they were *practiced*. Now it made sense. Brandon had told me Lucretia did calligraphy, but this wasn't calligraphy. My disbelief turned to dismay. This was forgery.

Oh, Lucretia.

The odd collection of herbs and elements on the worktable came into focus; they were used to make inks in the colonial era. The goose feathers she'd asked Brandon to bring from the farm were to make quills for writing on the parchment paper she'd found in the cellar, left behind by the Collins ancestor who'd been a printer. If the paper alone was tested, it would pass muster easily since it was authentic. Testing inks was more difficult and costly, unlikely to be done by anyone outside of a museum. Lucretia knew what she was doing.

She'd created that George Washington letter, probably hoping to get a big payday from Diantha, but Diantha had stymied her plan by offering the paltry finder's fee.

What did Lucretia want? Money to buy her grandmother's house. Perhaps she'd tried the forgery in an attempt to increase the historical value of the property, to ensure it wouldn't fall under Diantha's wrecking ball. Lucretia's naivete was sad but endearing; she could never earn enough to buy a house by selling her craft projects, but historic documents could bring a big payday with a collector.

So could blackmail.

I remembered her vague answers when I'd asked her who ordered the pumpkin for Diantha's room. That vague response was a red flag I'd missed. She was an artist, and artists notice things.

Lucretia was bold, but was she bold enough to blackmail the killer? How would she reach them? I thought of everyone who'd stayed at the Inn. She wouldn't know phone numbers unless she accessed the Inn's computer.

I wouldn't put accessing the Inn's computer past Lucretia but looking around, I didn't see a laptop, though she probably had one in the house.

I trailed my fingers along the smooth surface of a sheet of parchment. No, Lucretia was a paper person. She'd probably written a note to the killer, asking for a meeting. She could've easily walked into the Inn and slid a note under a door, assuming she knew which room the killer was staying in.

Or . . . she'd seen the killer somewhere else. Ruthie said Lucretia'd gone to school this morning. I recalled something Emilia had said about Cooper and Sam.

I checked Penniman High School's calendar of events on my phone.

Both Cooper and Sam Collins had done appearances at Penniman High School today.

Was one a killer? Both?

Chapter 33

I checked in with Ruthie, Flo, and Brandon, but they had no news of Lucretia. Ruthie's dogs, sensing her stress, whined and huddled at her knees. I left everyone sitting at Ruthie's kitchen table, each bent over their cell phone with an untouched cup of tea.

I dashed through the graveyard and met Rob as I hurried up the back stairs of the Inn.

He held up his hands. "Whoa, what's the rush?"

I tried to steady my breath. "Have you seen Lucretia?"

Rob's brow furrowed. "She still hasn't shown up? Ruthie came running over here a little while ago and told me she hadn't come home from school."

"Did Ruthie ask—" I hesitated. I was about to say *Cooper or Sam*, but amended my words. I didn't want Rob saying anything to tip off the brothers so I went with, "the guests if they'd seen Lucretia?"

Rob's puzzled expression told me he couldn't imagine why Ruthie would do such a thing. "No, they all came back a few minutes ago. Wrapped up shooting early. I'd rather not upset them now. They're put off enough by Jack wanting to question them again tonight. Besides, I can't imagine any of them keeping tabs on Lucretia."

I disagreed. I thought at least one probably did. The killer wouldn't answer any direct questions anyway, so I pushed past him into the kitchen, giving him no chance to stop me. "Um, since Ruthie's not here, I'll help tidy, okay?"

"Be my guest."

Marley, Dominic, Emilia, Sam, Cooper, and Chip chatted by the stove, Chip waving a glass of what looked like scotch. Adrenaline surged in me as I slid out of their line of sight, grabbed a smock, and opened the door of the housekeeping closet. I stepped around a stack of old Inn towels that had spilled to the floor, grabbed a feather duster, and moved through the lounge. I didn't want to tip my hand, let any suspects know that I was watching. I didn't know what to do except listen, hoping to see or hear something that would lead to Lucretia, some slip of the tongue that would lead to the killer. The lounge was empty so I took a deep steadying breath, lifted some room keys into the pocket of my smock, and ran up the stairs to the third floor.

I took some fresh towels from the housekeeping closet, steeled myself, and knocked on Cooper's door. I'd seen him downstairs in the kitchen, but still my heart pounded. I opened the door with the pass key and flicked on the light. The room was empty and I saw nothing helpful.

I let the door close softly behind me and remembered Jenira's evasiveness when I asked about the locations she'd filmed her movies. I knocked on her door and called, "Housekeeping."

When there was no answer, I slipped in.

Jenira's closet door was ajar and her trunks lined up by the door. She'd packed. I turned over the airport tags on the handle of her bag and found what I wanted. KRW. Poland. I was sure she'd been in *Voices in the Ice*, had seen first-hand the dangers of dry ice. I left the room, almost forgot to return the towels to the closet, then went downstairs, where I returned the keys and hurried into the lounge.

If I expected a drawing-room scene from an Agatha Christie denouement, I was disappointed. The air in the lounge was more exhausted inconvenience than suspicion and guilt.

Chip sat at the bar, staring at the screen of his cell phone as if it had wronged him. Dominic set a tray of appetizers on the coffee table and nodded to me as he headed back to the kitchen. Evan Smith entered from the lobby, heaped a plate, and gave me a brilliant smile. "Gotta make some calls," he announced to the room and headed toward the stairs.

On the couch, Sam dozed with his hands jammed in the kangaroo pocket of his sweatshirt. Emilia sat next to him, huddled in a brown lambswool throw. She gave me a small smile as I entered, and I pretended to busy myself clearing glasses. Cooper handed her a cup of tea and she took it with a grateful look, then he settled in a chair next to her with his laptop.

"I am a bit tired," she was saying, "even after my nap."

"You were outside all day at the shoot," Cooper said.

"And you didn't sleep well last night, Emilia." Sam opened his eyes and leaned forward, concern in his voice. "You were sleepwalking again. I found you in the hallway around midnight."

"I was sleepwalking?" Emilia's hand shook, spilling tea onto her wrap. "I had no idea. I thought I'd slept so soundly."

Sam squeezed her knee with the hand I'd seen her bandage so tenderly. "You've done so every night since we've been here. No wonder you're tired."

Cooper's head jerked up from his laptop. "You walked in your sleep on Saturday night?"

"I," Emilia stammered, "I had no idea. I was so tired and jet-lagged. What did I do, Sam?"

"I heard you trying to open our door," Sam said. "Nothing to worry about. I didn't wake you, of course, just helped you back to bed. You're not supposed to wake sleepwalkers."

Emilia's wrap fell from her shoulder as she set down her cup, her face blank. "When it's my turn, I'll have to tell the police officer."

Jenira crossed the lobby from the dining room, her cell phone to her ear, and threw a sour look into the lounge. Chip lifted his glass to her and downed its contents in one swallow as she headed for the stairs.

Chip gave me a welcoming smile as he poured more whiskey into his glass, and I grabbed a bar towel to wipe up some of the alcohol he'd spilled. Emilia went to the piano and began a moody classical piece as the brothers bent over the appetizers. I wanted to question each of them alone, but didn't know how to start, and my stomach clenched with worry for Lucretia.

"My lawyer called." Chip's words slurred as spoke into his glass, more to himself than me. "As expected, Diantha left everything to Sam and Cooper, and I have no recourse. Little old Chip's the cheese standing alone. Good thing I always looked out for myself." He raised his glass. "Well, Diantha taught me to do that.

"Jenira was raving about your ice cream, Ice Cream Lady." He knocked back his scotch and poured another. "I should be reviewing the dailies, but I'm too bloody drunk to care."

I decided I didn't have time to beat around the bush

and blurted the first question that came to mind. "Did you throw away a script on the night of Diantha's murder?"

He chortled. "Did you find it? Leave it in the dumpster, my dear, that's where it belongs. You didn't hear that little tiff, did you?"

I shook my head as he leaned close. "You ever see someone throw away their future? That's my delusional little princess, Jenira. Wanted me to do some practically X-rated script called *Meteor*." He pronounced the word as if it left a sour taste in his mouth. "What do meteors do? They crash and burn. That would be her career." He made a bomb-dropping gesture and swayed on his barstool. "Talk about biting the hand that feeds you. She came to me with that script and I knew she'd do anything to change my mind, even put on a pink bikini under her robe so I'd get the message, but Skylark has been very, very good to me. I opened the window and tossed it out like a Frisbee!" His voice rose and he pressed his finger to his lips with a chuckle. "I was being dramatic, but Jenira brings that out in people. I'm glad it's in the dumpster. That's where it belonged, and that's where her career's going if she does ever get that thing made. She doesn't understand that she already got her stroke of luck and that pretty girls who can act are a dime a dozen.

"I warned my brothers to stay away from her"—he glanced at the group on the couch, his words slurred—"but Jenira's very persuasive."

Brothers? Plural? "Brothers?"

"Slip of the tongue, don't mind me, I'm a gossip." He waved me closer, the scent of alcohol strong on his breath. "Sam and Jenira met when Cooper was filming some disaster of a movie in Europe. He happened to be over there for some skateboard competition in Krakow."

My eyes widened and Chip winked. "They were discreet, but I know sparks when I see them; Skylark doesn't have me direct for nothing. But it's over. Sam and Jenira hardly look at each other now."

Maybe that was by design. I'd seen her walking at the festival with . . . a guy in a hockey mask and fright wig.

"Did one of the brothers wear a fright wig and hockey mask to the festival?" I whispered.

Chip snorted. "Sam's favorite costume since Magistrate's! Coop would never cover his pretty face—that would discourage the girls." He looked over at Cooper, who leaned over the piano as Emilia played and Sam texted. "Except the one he can't have."

Chip lay his head on his arm. "I'll take a nap right here." He made a snoring sound, but I shook his shoulder.

"Diantha made a lot of donations to Magistrate's School while you were there," I whispered. "Why?"

He didn't lift his head. "She was putting out fires. They would've been dish-enrolled," he slurred, "kicked out if she hadn't. Cooper was always in trouble with the ladies and Sam there ran his own drug ring for a while. Used to deal by the lake, had his own dispensary at the canoe house. Same place Coop used to bring his girl-friends."

By the lake . . .

His eyes drifted shut. "I thought the bloody cops would be here by now."

I ran from the room into the hallway, pushing past Marley as I ran out the kitchen door.

Jack had said he'd check out all the places kids go. He knew all the places Penniman kids would go, not Magistrate's School kids. The killer would choose a place he knew well, knew would be secluded, especially since Magistrate's had a homecoming game tonight.

It was also a place Lucretia would feel comfortable. She'd spent hours with her grandmother at the Girl Scout camp on the point near Magistrate's canoe house.

I pulled my phone from my pocket and raced through the parking lot and graveyard as I dialed, praying Jack would pick up and not let the call go to voice mail.

He picked up. "Jack—"

But it was his voicemail recording. I swore as I wrenched open Ruthie's gate.

"Come on," I muttered as I waited for the beep to leave my message. "Jack! I have another place for you to check. Magistrate's School canoe house on the lake. Hurry!"

I bolted up the steps and threw open Ruthie's kitchen door. Ruthie, Flo, and Brandon startled and Brandon half-rose from his seat. "What's happening?" Ruthie gasped.

"Ruthie"—I sucked in air—"I need the car keys."

Without a word she handed them to me and I dashed outside. My abrupt departure left the dogs yelping wildly. I threw myself into Ruthie's car and drove as fast as I could down Long Meadow Road. I prayed I'd find Lucretia well, but I was convinced the bold young woman had played with fire and been burned. The tires squealed as I turned into the narrow lane at the lake that led to the scout camp. When I'd checked the jogging-trail map earlier, I'd seen that the access road to Magistrate's canoe house was two miles farther down Long Meadow. I remembered an overgrown path from the scout camp to the canoe house, a little-used shortcut. I knew I could take it and get there faster than by driving.

If the path still existed.

A chain barred access to the camp road. I slammed the brakes and threw the car into park, not bothering to shut the car door after I jumped out. I raced along the lakeside trail, hoping my memory would serve.

Past the camp's dock, I dove into the dark woods, pushing through thick branches of pine and laurel that crowded the sides of the rarely used trail, using the security lights of the distant buildings to guide my steps. My feet slid on slippery pine needles and low branches whipped my arms as I scrambled through the undergrowth.

Magistrate's canoe house was a small redwood structure tucked into a stand of pine trees, with a dock extending into the lake. Up a short trail was a larger boathouse for rowing shells. The windows of the canoe house were dark, the only illumination a pale circle of light from an overhead fixture over the door facing the dock.

"Lucretia! Lucretia!" I shouted.

Flashlights bobbed in the distance and voices carried on a frigid gust of wind. As the dark forms approached and swarmed the small building, I could make out Jack and security guards from Magistrate's.

A painfully bright beam hit my eyes, blinding me and making me stumble as I stepped onto the dock. "Hey you! Stop!" a voice shouted.

I threw up my arm to protect my eyes, then put up both my hands. "It's me, Riley."

Jack ran up to me and gripped my arm. "What are you doing here? I got your message. You should've stayed home." Tension clipped his words.

"I think Lucretia's here," I panted. "Both Collins brothers used this as a meeting place when they were students at Magistrate's."

He released my arm, his expression grim. "Stay here!"

The security team unlocked the canoe house door and ran inside, their footsteps thudding on the wooden floor. I bent at the waist, my hands on my thighs, trying to catch my breath as the security team turned on the interior lights and raced through a long, narrow room. Through the open door I could see canoes lining the walls and the searchers checked inside each one.

"No one here," one called. "We'll check the boat-house up the hill."

Jack walked past me on the dock, looking out at the dark water, hands on his hips. I didn't speak. If this search turned up nothing, I'd be responsible for wasting precious time. My head bowed, I joined him as he shined his flashlight beam on the water. I turned my beam closer to the dock. Several life jackets bobbed on the surface. "Look!"

"Check the water!" Jack shouted as he dropped to his knees, grappling for the sodden jackets. My breath caught. *Lucretia could be in the water.*

As a security guard pushed past me to join Jack, I turned away, sickened by the thought that Lucretia might be beneath the black surface of the lake. My legs trembling, I faced the front of the canoe house and headed toward two long storage benches that flanked the door. I remembered similar ones at the scout camp—they were used to store life jackets.

Life jackets.

I ran to the bench to the right of the door and lifted the lid. It was filled with neatly stacked life jackets. A sense of dread washed over me. With a cry, I ran to the other bench, crouched before it, and threw back the lid.

A pungent chemical smell made me wince, and my breath caught in my throat. The limp form of Lucretia Collins lay inside.

Chapter 34

J ack called for an ambulance on his radio as I
 brushed back Lucretia's hair and pressed my fingers to her neck to check for a pulse. It was weak but
steady.

Jack and I lifted her out of the bench and lay her on
the rough planks of the dock. I fell to my knees beside
her, trembling with adrenaline and horror. Her hands
and legs had been bound with electrical tape. Part of a
strip of tape that had been placed over her mouth hung
loose in tatters. Scrapes on her cheek told the tale—
she must've rubbed her face against the rough wood at
the bottom of the bench to tear the tape away.

Lucretia murmured and I smoothed her hair from her
brow.

Jack knelt beside me. "What was that, Lucretia?" Jack
said as he gently took her hand. "Say it again? Who did
this?"

She mumbled and coughed.

"Lucretia, who did this to you?" I leaned close as
emergency responders ran toward us, their heavy footsteps making the dock sway.

Her voice was less than a whisper as she uttered one word. "Sam."

I called Flo and told her that Lucretia was being transported to Eastern Hospital. She said she and Brandon would take Ruthie there right away.

I hung up before she could ask any questions.

"Do you think she'll be okay?" I asked as Jack retrieved a rag from inside the bench. I recognized a worn towel from the Inn and heard Ruthie's words about Yankees never throwing anything away. Jack sniffed it, winced, and dropped it back inside. "Chloroform. You can find the recipe online. People think it simply knocks people out like in the movies, but exposure to that stuff can kill."

"Lucretia's a witness," I said. "I think she saw the killer at the window of Diantha's room the night of the murder and I think she tried to blackmail him."

I shivered. *She'd be a witness if she makes it*. If we hadn't found Lucretia, she'd have died, her body inside that horrible bench until the school opened the canoe house the following spring.

"She's a tough girl." Jack met my eyes, but his worried tone told me he was trying to convince himself.

"I have so much to tell you," I said, my thoughts returning to Lucretia's workroom. Could there be hard evidence there? I recalled my search and thought there was. "Jack, Lucretia has sketchbooks in her workroom. You need to see them."

I headed toward the path to the scout camp.

"Where are you going?" Jack called.

"I have Ruthie's car—"

"I'll send someone for it later," Jack said. "Come with me. It'll be faster with the sirens and we can talk as we go."

As Jack's police SUV raced past the ivy-covered walls of Magistrate's School, everything I'd learned poured out: the pumpkin in Diantha's room, the accident on the film set in Poland, the airport tags, the wrapping paper. I could see him making connections, and he nodded when I told him that I thought the killer hadn't worked alone.

"Makes sense," he said. "They took a lot of risks."

"Lucretia took risks." I leaned my head against the cool window glass, watching the darkened woods flow by as I grappled with my feelings. If only Lucretia had felt she could trust me. "And she lied."

Jack shot me a glance. "What do you mean?"

"When she told me she dropped off the pumpkin at the Inn the night Diantha was murdered, I asked her who she gave it to. She was vague, told me she handed the pumpkin to some guy. By the time she spoke to me, she knew Sam was the killer and she knew she'd handed him the pumpkin. She's an artist, she notices things. I shouldn't have believed her. By the time she talked to me, she'd already decided to blackmail him."

At Ruthie's house, the SUV had barely come to a stop before I jumped out and led Jack to Lucretia's workshop. Ruthie's dogs barked and whined as we passed the house, where lights still burned in the kitchen. Inside the workshop I groped for the chain to one of the overhead lights and rushed to the table where I'd seen sketchbooks. I flipped pages to her most recent sketches. She'd documented each of her pumpkins with a sketch of its buyer, but the last page was covered by black swirls and the image of a man standing at a window.

"Jack, look." I stepped aside so he could see.

The face of Sam Collins stared back at us.

Chapter 35

Jack's SUV jerked to a stop as he parked in front of the Inn. He gave me a warning look and said, "Stay here," but I don't think he really believed I would. He keyed his mic as he ran up the front steps.

As soon as he was inside, I jumped out and hurried around the building. I ran up the back steps into the kitchen, and just as the door closed beside me, I saw a squad car pull into the parking lot.

Though I was practically vibrating with adrenaline, I managed to slip unseen into the back hallway as Marley took a beautiful golden-brown tart from the oven. What a lovely last meal Sam Collins and his accomplice were going to miss, and the food in prison wouldn't be nearly as good. The wistful notes of a piano concerto flowed around me as I stood in the service hallway outside the lounge and wondered how this last scene would play out.

Cooper still stood by the piano as Emilia played. Chip had poured himself onto the couch in the corner of the lounge, his head lolling onto its back, and Dominic sat by the window, texting. I wondered if he was still texting Mary Anne. Despite my worry for Lucretia, I felt a lightness I hadn't in days. The cloud of suspicion would be lifted from Mary Anne and she could get on with her life.

Jack and Rob crossed the lobby to the lounge. Rob's expression was stony, no longer the solicitous innkeeper trying to keep peace for his guests.

"Finally," Chip yawned, "the cops are here. Let the grilling begin."

Emilia hit a discordant note as she turned abruptly from the piano.

"I'm looking for Sam Collins," Jack said. "And Jenira Ford."

Emilia's hands fluttered to her throat. Cooper put a hand on her shoulder.

"Sam went to our room to make a call," Emilia whispered. "I'm sure he'll be back any minute."

"I saw Miss Ford go to her room earlier. I'll get her." Rob strode to the stairs.

Muffled shouts and a commotion outside drew us to the windows in time to see Sam sprint from the spa entrance and run toward one of the production company's vans. One cop tried to intercept him, but Sam flung him aside and wrenched open the van door. Another cop pulled Sam out of the van and Sam responded with a flurry of vicious punches before being wrestled to the ground. Sam almost threw him off, but the first cop joined the second and together they pushed Sam against the van. Sam struggled but was cuffed, and moments later he stood in the lounge, held between the two disheveled but stern-faced officers. Sam's body language was relaxed, almost insolent.

"Sam!" Emilia rushed to him. "What's going on?"

"No worries, Em, I'll be fine." Sam dipped his chin and his hair fell over his face, but not before I saw defiance tighten his jaw.

Rob rushed into the lounge. "Jack, she's gone. Her bags are too."

Marley wheeled a tray with the scrumptious-looking tart and coffee service into the lounge. He stopped short when he saw Sam and the police. "What did I miss?"

Laughter filled the kitchen of the farmhouse. "Tillie's being hailed as a hero? I can't believe it!"

Caroline, Flo, Gerri, Pru, and I crowded around the kitchen table. It was past midnight, but no one showed any signs of wanting to go home.

I'd been at the police station giving my statement when Tillie's red VW bug rolled up in front of the building. She'd opened the back door, and a very confused Jenira Ford had stepped from the vehicle into the waiting arms of the police.

"Jenira was following the plan she and Sam had made and was heading to a private airfield in Woodstock," I said. "She had no idea the police were looking for her, but Tillie had heard the APB on the in-ear Bluetooth radio she'd taken to wearing while acting as Jenira's protection detail. Tillie turned around and brought Jenira right into the waiting arms of the police."

Punchy with exhaustion and red wine, we raised our glasses. "To Tillie!" "Hear, hear!"

"Sam asked for his lawyer and clammed up," I said. "All the evidence against him for Diantha's killing could be called circumstantial, but he had Lucretia putting him at the scene. He actually tried to pin Diantha's murder on Emilia and kept talking about her sleepwalking." I suddenly recalled something odd I'd seen the first day I'd worked at the Inn: an empty bottle of Benadryl in the men's room off the lounge. Sleepiness is one of its side-effects. Sam had thanked Ruthie for making

Emilia a smoothie, and I was certain he'd doctored it and given it to Emilia, who was already exhausted from their long flight, to ensure she'd sleep through his visits to Diantha's room.

Flo patted my hand, pulling me from my reverie. "But he'll go down for Lucretia's kidnapping and attempted murder."

"Do you think Jenira knew Sam kidnapped Lucretia?" Caroline asked.

I shrugged. "I don't know. I think Sam was taking care of a loose end."

Pru said, "Most importantly, Lucretia's going to be okay."

Gerri sniffed. "I still can't believe such tawdry crimes happened right here in Penniman."

Flo turned to me. "Let me get this straight. When did this start? When Jenira met Sam on that film set in Poland?"

This crime had been years in the making, I thought, *with Diantha's sons simultaneously spoiled and ignored.* "I think it started when Diantha announced her intention to marry Dominic. She told her sons she planned to change her will after the wedding. Sam managed to fly home just in time and had to act fast."

I thought of the airline tags for the airport in Krakow on both Sam's and Jenira's luggage. "Sam had met Jenira when she was working on *Voices in the Ice*. He'd gone to visit Cooper, who'd worked on it as assistant director. Sam and Jenira started their affair while she was still dating Cooper. Cooper and Jenira broke up officially soon after." I thought of the unlocked door between Jenira and Cooper's rooms. "But I think he still had feelings for her.

"Emilia told me she and Sam met in chemistry class. After the *Voices in the Ice* tragedy, he saw the possibilities of using dry ice to kill Diantha. There was a stack of boxes of dry ice right here at the Inn because Dominic used it in his molecular gastronomy and Diantha wanted it for the fog machine. When Emilia bought that roll of wrapping paper, Sam saw a way to get the ice to Diantha's room without causing suspicion.

"He, or Jenira, wrapped the Styrofoam boxes." I remembered seeing Sam on the stairs when I'd first met him. He said he was going upstairs to take the wrapped box to the gift room. I think he'd been taking it out of the library and was heading for Diantha's Little Room, but he saw Ruthie and me coming and made up a quick lie about carrying the heavy box to the gift room.

"He hid the wrapped boxes under Diantha's bed. At the party in the lounge that night, Jenira left at one point, saying she was going to talk to Chip about *Meteor*. She knew he'd never go for it, but she caused a scene and therefore had a memorable alibi and a good story for why she stepped out of the party. Chip threw the script out the window and I found it in the dumpster.

"After leaving Chip, Jenira ran to Diantha's room. Remember, Chip's room was out of the way, at the end of the hallway near the stairs. She unwrapped the boxes and, probably inspired by Chip's dramatic gesture, tossed the paper out the window, blocked the window with a towel, and pulled the drapes to make the room as air tight as possible."

"So each of them took turns leaving the party to prepare Diantha's Little Room," Caroline said, "because a long absence would be noticed."

I nodded. "Sometime during Diantha and Dominic's party, Sam took delivery of the pumpkin from Lucretia. I think he and Jenira ordered the pumpkin to have a ready excuse in case one of them was seen going into Diantha's room. Diantha loved Halloween, and what a nice touch for her room a personalized glowing pumpkin would be. Sam dashed in and opened the boxes. That's how he hurt his hand. Dry ice can burn if you come in contact with it. I saw Emilia bandage his hand and he told her he'd hurt it skateboarding."

"There was one other person at the Inn with a burn on their hand. Marley." I considered how satisfying it would've been to see him go to jail. "But he didn't stay the night in the Inn, so I had to exclude him. Also he had no reason to kill Diantha. He was eager to ingratiate himself and be part of the new restaurant."

"Forget Marley, get back to the murder," Flo said.

"The harder part was at three a.m. when Sam entered the room to dispose of the boxes."

"That would be a risk, wouldn't it?" Caroline said. "Dry ice is solid carbon dioxide. The fumes take oxygen away, right? He'd have to hold his breath for some time."

"I think Sam was confident in his athletic abilities," I said. "I saw pictures of him free diving—"

"Free diving?" Pru said.

"It's a sport where you see how long you can hold your breath and how deep you can dive under water without oxygen tanks. He ran into the room, holding his breath, and threw open the window."

"But first made sure Diantha was dead." Caroline's hand went to her throat.

Swirling my glass, I said, "Then Sam tossed the boxes out the window, and probably pushed the towel out by mistake." It had been the open window and the pristine towel in the dumpster that had made me think there was more to Diantha's death than natural causes. "Unfortunately for him, Lucretia happened to be running across the parking lot. The sound of the boxes landing in the dumpster made her turn and look up at the window."

"Poor Diantha," Pru said quietly.

Gerri said, "I wonder what'll happen with the Inn now?"

After everyone left, my eyes fell on a vase of roses and daisies on the dining room table. I inhaled the sweet scent of the flowers. "So Jack stopped by?"

"He did," Caroline called from the kitchen. "Only for a second though, on his way to the pond to look for Lucretia. After he left, Liam and I went out looking too."

"Liam was here?"

At my puzzled tone Caroline joined me in the dining room.

"That bouquet's for you, Riley, from Liam. You didn't get my text?"

I vaguely remembered my phone vibrating with a text when I was at Ruthie's house.

"While you were busy saving Lucretia's life and catching a killer," Caroline continued. "I was sweeping the porch steps and playing with Rocky when Liam arrived to take you on your date, carrying those beauties. Jack stopped by a few minutes later."

"Oh no!" I moaned. "My date! I can't believe I forgot again. Poor Liam! I have to apologize."

Caroline smiled. "You were a little busy. I think he'll forgive you."

As I lay in bed later, I pictured what Jack had seen: Caroline and Liam on the steps of our cozy farmhouse, Liam handing her a beautiful bouquet of flowers in the light of our carved jack-o'-lanterns with Rocky romping in the foreground. It was a scene right out of a Skylark movie. Smiling, I rolled over and hoped Jack was jealous.

Chapter 36

T he next day at the shop was busier than I expected
    for a blustery November day, but the citizens of Pen-
niman were gathering for gossip as well as hot fudge
sundaes.

My phone buzzed and I stepped into the workroom
to take a call from Ruthie.

"Riley, I wanted you to know that Lucretia's doing
well and the hospital will release her tomorrow."

I sagged with relief against the wall. "I'm so glad to
hear that."

"That girl's supposed to rest, but her friends keep texting her at all hours." Ruthie complained, but I could hear
the tenderness in her voice. "And Brandon came by and
dropped off some ice cream. Such a nice boy."

"He is." I smiled as Brandon passed me with a pan
of a new creation and set it in the dipping cabinet. He
handed Flo a tasting spoon.

"Lucretia says she wants to talk to you when she's discharged. Is it okay if she stops by?"

"I'll be here."

I couldn't wait to hear Lucretia's side of her ordeal. I

hung up and joined Brandon and Flo as she took a bite. "So what do we have here?"

"Behold." Brandon pointed to a lumpy dark gray mixture, unappetizing in both color and texture. "I'm not sure if I'll call it Kitchen Sink or Leftovers of the Gods. Since we're closing for the season, I used all the leftover bits—pretzels, sprinkles, marshmallows, cherries, pineapple, butterscotch swirls . . ."

Dear God.

Flo licked her spoon. "It's not bad."

"Want a taste?" Brandon held out a loaded spoon.

I waved him off. "Maybe later."

Just before closing time, Mary Anne stepped into the kitchen and threw her arms around me. Her dark hair was shiny and sleek, her lips brightened with her customary deep-red lipstick. She looked more herself than she had in weeks. "Riley, I can't thank you enough for everything you did for me. I know the cops had me pegged for Diantha's killer. I don't know what would've happened without you uncovering the truth about Sam and Jenira."

"I was glad to help."

"You can help me again." She handed me an order for an ice-cream cake. "I had a special request at the Inn for a party the day after tomorrow."

"I'll drop it by tomorrow night. I'm having dinner at Dad's," I said. "Are you going to keep working at the Inn?"

"Yes. Dominic said the Inn had too many sad memories, so he's moving on. Rob's made me head chef. And Dominic did the right thing and told his publisher that the cookbook should be published under my name also."

"That's wonderful," I said.

Her expression darkened. "Guess what? I overheard

Cooper talking to Emilia. Sam had replaced her medications with plain-old vitamins."

"That's awful," I breathed.

"With all the stress of Sam's arrest, Emilia went to see a doctor and he discovered the switch." Mary Anne shook her head. "Good news is she should be feeling better soon. Chip and Cooper are staying around to sort things out and are going to keep an eye on her."

Bitterness rose in my throat. Emilia's body would heal, but what about her heart after this betrayal by her husband? Prison was too good for Sam Collins.

"You have to let me do something nice for you," Mary Anne squeezed my hand. "After you close for the season, come to the Inn for dinner and bring Caroline, your staff, your whole family. My treat. I want to make you a feast. It's the least I can do."

"I'd love to, but . . ." I hesitated. "Won't that be awkward? With Chip, Cooper, and Emilia there?"

"On the doctor's advice, Cooper's going to take Emilia to the Farrow Center." The Farrow was an exclusive, secluded, and discreet rehab center on the outskirts of Penniman. "They've booked a cottage up there, Chip, Cooper, and Emilia. There's tons of security and no one will bother them."

"I'm glad."

"It's all turned into a media circus at the Inn as you can imagine. This picture's all over the news." Mary Anne turned her phone screen to me and I recognized the pool at the Inn's spa. The image was grainy but clear enough that I could make out Sam and Jenira locked in a not-very-Skylark embrace. A headline above blared *Skylark Sweetheart Embroiled in Murder Plot*.

"Whoa!" I said. "I wonder what'll happen with the movie now."

"Chip said Skylark corporate's through the roof. They

can't run with *Bound for Love* with Jenira involved, but they liked your dad's bookshop," she chuckled. "And Sprinkles. So they'll reshoot with Jenira's role recast."

As Flo, Brandon, and Pru left and I turned out the shop lights, Jack pulled up in his SUV. Rocky prowled at the steps, meowing piteously as a gust of wind whipped dried leaves against the window, so I let him in. I watched Jack and Mary Anne speak briefly, then she held out her hand and he shook it.

Jack ran to the door. "Do you have a minute?"

"Sure. Do you want to come up to the house—"

"This is fine," he said, so I held the door wide. "I want to ask you about Caroline."

I led him into the front of the shop and we took seats at a café table next to the window. I didn't turn on the lights. His serious tone made me think this conversation would go better with only the dim light from the parking lot.

Ask me about Caroline? Was he asking about marriage? My heart had jumped at his words, but I was also filled with trepidation. Caroline was so besotted, I knew if he asked her to marry him she'd leap into his arms. I wanted to joke, *"Are you asking me to grant permission?"* but his knitted brow made me sink onto my chair, made me wonder where this conversation would go.

"She doesn't have anyone else," he said. "You're her family."

Even in the dim light, I could see that Jack's eyes were troubled. Rocky materialized at my feet and I pulled him into my lap. Some people are more comfortable unburdening themselves without eye contact, so I kept my head down as I stroked Rocky's fur and let the silence stretch. Rocky, however, watched Jack with unblinking attention.

Jack cleared his throat. "Five years ago, I was shot when I was out on patrol." He gestured to his shoulder. "I'd let my guard down. I was engaged to someone else at the time and it was too much for her. She couldn't stand living with the worry. When I was shot it proved to her that her worry was justified.

"I don't know if I can ask that of Caroline. Have her be worried every moment. Cop's spouse isn't an easy job. Maybe what we have's enough . . ." The rasp in his voice told me it wasn't enough for him. Rocky turned to me expectantly, as if waiting for my reply.

Jack was a protector by nature, that's why he went into police work. I didn't know what it was like to be married to a police officer, but Jack was right about one thing. I knew Caroline. I knew that under that unassuming, sweet demeanor was a strong, devoted heart. She never shirked hard work. She'd survived unimaginable hardship as a foster child, uprooted more times than any child should endure, all her worldly belongings shoved into a plastic garbage bag. She knew what she wanted. She wanted Jack.

I looked up and waited until he'd meet my eyes. "Jack, if Caroline's worried about you, she will be, married or not. But more important, you can't decide for her that your current relationship's enough. I can't decide that for her either. So ask her. Let her decide for herself."

Chapter 37

The following night when Caroline and I stopped by the Inn to deliver the ice-cream cake, the road in front was packed with cars so I pulled into the parking lot. As we exited Sadie, the Inn's back door banged open. Rob flung Marley out the door by the back of his chef's white jacket, yelling, "And never come back!"

Marley regained his balance and stormed down the stairs.

"You're making a big mistake, Rob!" Marley shook his fist and mounted his huge motorcycle. The engine left a blisteringly loud echo as he blasted out of the parking lot. Caroline and I shared a glance then headed up the stairs.

Rob shot his cuffs and held the door wide. "Ladies."

"What was that about?" I asked.

Rob blew out a breath. "I'd gotten a phone call a couple of weeks ago from a senator who shall remain nameless, accusing me of selling photos of him with a person who was not his spouse. Of course, I denied it. But five minutes ago I got a message from some rag in California addressed to the Inn's email, saying they wanted more photos. This was attached." He showed me the photo of Sam and Jenira in the pool Mary Anne had shown me earlier.

I recalled the phone conversation I'd overheard and Marley's skulking around the hotel. "He was selling photos of the guests."

Rob straightened his tie. "Not anymore."

Mary Anne greeted me, and when I handed her the box with the cake she blushed to the roots of her hair. "I still feel so embarrassed about what I did to your cake. Can you forgive me?"

"Just take good care of this one," I said.

A t Dad's house, Paulette opened the door before Caroline and I stepped onto the porch.

"Riley, another birthday gift came for you at the shop!" Paulette's tone was eager as she handed me a small cardboard mailing box. The leap of pleasure I'd felt when I took the box from her hands was extinguished when I recognized the handwriting.

"Open it!" Paulette said as she took our coats. My apprehension grew as I opened the cardboard box, revealing a gift wrapped in Venetian marbled paper—*carta marmorizzata*—in shades of green and blue, and tied with a gold bow.

Paulette sighed. "Isn't that the most beautifully wrapped gift. From someone special?" Her avid eyes made me realize she thought it was from Liam. I'd called him earlier to thank him for the flowers and he'd been sweet enough to ask for a raincheck, but I didn't think my chances were good with the insanely busy vet.

Caroline coughed and said, "Is that your lasagna, Paulette?" She'd recognized the traditional Italian pattern of the giftwrap, met my eye, and said with exaggerated excitement, "Let's have dinner and solve the cipher first!"

Gerri and Flo waved from the dining room. "It does smell delicious."

I tucked the gift in my bag, resolved to enjoy Paulette's vegetable lasagna and not let this unwelcome surprise spoil the evening.

And I did enjoy dinner. After we cleared our dishes, Dad placed the Bible Lucretia had found in the basement of the Collins Homestead in the center of the table and I took the stack of letters out of my bag.

I'd invited Flo and Gerri to join us. As board members of the Penniman Historical Society, I felt they should be present at any discovery of historic interest.

Flo's eyes were wide with excitement and she rubbed her hands together. "I feel like we're going to summon a demon."

Gerri snorted and settled her silky blue scarf around her shoulders. "Hardly."

I wasn't sure Flo was far off the mark. The message in the letters had been carefully coded. A cipher required coordination, planning, and craft. I doubted such subterfuge would be required of anything but dark deeds.

Caroline took the Bible and carefully turned to the section I'd bookmarked.

Dad settled his reading glasses on his nose and scanned the list of letters and numbers I'd gleaned from the old Collins letters. "So we're looking for the words associated with this chapter and these verses?"

"Yes," I said. "The books of the Bible are organized into chapters and verses. I'm pretty sure the letters took advantage of this format to send coded messages."

Gerri took a fancy fountain pen from her purse and opened a notebook. "I'll be scribe."

"Okay," I said, "the underlined letters and numbers on the first letter spelled out L K 2."

Flo's eyes brightened. "Oh, Luke chapter two. The Christmas story."

"I should've asked you first," I laughed. "It took me a while to figure out what that meant. I found additional underlined numbers in other letters."

"This print's tiny." Caroline squinted at the page. "I can barely read it." Dad handed her a magnifying glass and she took it with a laugh. "I feel very Sherlockian! Go ahead, Riley."

"Count the words from the start of the verse." I called out the numbers that I'd copied, and she counted to the corresponding word while Gerri wrote them down.

"Inn . . . shepherd . . ."

"That's it? Hardly makes sense." Paulette stood, her disappointment clear. "I'll us get us some coffee and cake." The rich scent of coffee brewing surrounded us as we pondered the words.

"And the last word." Caroline looked up from the page, her eyebrows raised. "Sword."

"Sword? Didn't expect that," Dad said.

"Inn, shepherd, sword?" Gerri's expression was puzzled.

"Well, it beats me." Flo rubbed her eyes.

I scanned the last letter again, turning the paper side to side. Using Dad's magnifying glass, I was able to make out faint markings. "Wait, I missed some letters. P—L-R-A—I. and there's an eight underlined, too."

Gerri frowned as she scribbled the letters.

"Unscramble the letters," Dad said. "They spell April."

"April eighth," Caroline said. "Something with Inn, shepherd, and sword was supposed to happen on April eighth."

"Sword," I mused. "is a weapon."

"At the Inn . . ." Caroline said.

"Shepherd, sheep, a lamb led to slaughter," Flo said, her eyes wide. "Gerri, George Washington was in the area in April 1776, wasn't he?

"A shepherd leads, right?" Caroline said.

"John Collins, scion of the Collins family, was planning an assassination. I knew he was a Tory." Gerri's voice rang with vindication. "The Collins family were traitors!"

As we excitedly discussed this theory, I cleared the Bible and letters, putting them on the fireplace mantel for safe keeping while Paulette served slices of pumpkin cake, fragrant with cinnamon, cloves, and nutmeg.

"Dad, what did your friend say about Lucretia?" I'd asked Dad to talk to a friend who was an expert in the forgery of old books and papers.

Dad smiled thanks as Paulette handed him a cup of coffee. "He was impressed not only by her talent but her level of research, how she made her own inks from natural ingredients, how she sourced them, how she used a quill."

I remembered how Lucretia had asked Brandon to bring her goose feathers from the farm, making him an unwitting accomplice to her scheme.

Dad continued, "Of course the old paper she found in the cellar of the homestead—"

"Was a gift to her criminal tendencies?" Gerri interrupted.

"Made it hard to dismiss the authenticity of the forgery," Dad said mildly.

"That's a question most people know to ask. 'How old's the paper?'" I said. "Most organizations don't have the money to do testing, but Diantha's friend at Magistrate's School was able to get the paper in Lucretia's George Washington letter authenticated. It was convincing." I suspected Dr. Blood had been another spider in Diantha's web, which is why I asked Dad to reach out to his friend.

"They'll have to take that cache of paper," Gerri said, her tone indicating that Lucretia was already lost to the criminal underworld. "Like taking a lock jimmy away from a car thief."

I wondered if Lucretia had anticipated this development and stashed some paper away.

"So what'll happen to her?" Paulette said.

While I hoped Gerri was wrong and Lucretia wasn't destined for a life of crime, she did need a crash course in ethics. Wanting to help her grandmother didn't justify blackmail.

Dad said, "My friend has offered to take her under his wing. She's talented. Best if she uses her powers for good instead of evil." He waggled his bushy eyebrows. Paulette hit him with the back of her hand but laughed.

"Like a hacker," I said. "Get the best on your team to play defense against the bad guys."

"Exactly."

Paulette frowned. "She should still face consequences."

"Oh, there are consequences," Flo said. "Lucretia has community service. She has to dust the historical society every Sunday afternoon for the next six months."

Gerri interrupted, "And I'll be there to make sure it's done properly."

Dad turned to me and mouthed, *Ouch.*

Chapter 38

The following Saturday was the shop's last day until spring, and the line ran out the door as we erased flavor after flavor from the chalkboard. There was a lull around four when Lucretia and Ruthie came in. Lucretia's expression was uncertain and her skin pale, but she gave me a hug and her embrace was strong. "I'll never be able to thank you enough, Riley."

"I'm happy I could help. I'm so glad that you're okay." She joined Brandon in the workroom and my heart warmed when I saw the approval in Ruthie's expression.

"Can you step outside for a moment?" Ruthie said.

I nodded and shrugged on my coat. "You're not going to ask me to work at the Inn again, are you?"

She gave a short bark of a laugh. "Only if you want to. Some good news. Cooper came by and said he's not going to change anything at the Inn. He's going to let us stay in our house, and Rob says I can work at the Inn as long I like." Ruthie pressed a tissue to her eyes then jammed it into her pocket.

"That's good news, isn't it?" I led her to a picnic table.

"Cooper and Chip came by the Inn to pick up some equipment while Lucretia was helping me. Cooper, well, he told me he'd noticed a resemblance . . ." her voice faltered, and I waited as she struggled to compose herself.

A rush of details flickered through my memory. The sheet music. The comment by the Magistrate's waitress. Diantha's hiring of private investigators to follow Cooper's girlfriends. The fact that Rob rented the Collins house to Ruthie and Lucretia.

Through the door, I could see Brandon and Lucretia laughing as she tried Kitchen Sink. Deep-dyed black tips emphasized her honey blonde roots, the same shade as Diantha's hair, the same shade as Cooper's.

"Rob confirmed it for me. Jamie and Cooper met when she went to her music teacher's house by the lake. He was prepping for a singing role in the school's play, and Jamie'd been invited to play with the school orchestra."

Ruthie pulled the collar of her coat tight around her neck. "You have to believe me, I never had any idea who Lucretia's father was. Jamie was so secretive." Her eyes welled. "When she told me she was expecting, I wasn't as supportive as I should've been. She said she didn't want anything further to do with Lucretia's father. But when Cooper saw Lucretia, he said something to Rob, and Rob told me.

"I don't know what I'll do, if I'll tell her. Rob, he always knew. That's why he's always been so kind to me and Lucretia, helped me with the house, and a job."

"Rob knew." Of course. He'd confessed to me that he'd kept all Diantha's secrets.

At my troubled expression, Ruthie said, "Rob says he figured it out long ago. Cooper almost got kicked out of Magistrate's for"—she sighed—"meeting too many girlfriends down at the lake. One of them told the headmaster in retaliation when he broke up with her. Diantha made a big donation to make sure Cooper graduated and there wasn't any scandal."

That wasn't the only donation she'd made.

Ruthie dabbed at her eyes again. "I don't know what to do. Being abandoned by your own mother and father and his family . . . how could any child handle that? Cooper's open to DNA testing and wants to make things right, but I don't know if Lucretia cares. He said no matter what she decides, he's going to help out with Lucretia's schooling, anonymously if need be." Her head dipped to her chest and her voice was thick with tears. "I don't want to make any more mistakes."

Lucretia shrieked from inside the kitchen, "This is the worst thing I've ever tasted!" which was followed by peals of Brandon's laughter.

I wrapped Ruthie in a hug. "Lucretia knows her own mind, and no matter what, she has you." *And Rob*, I added silently, thinking of how he'd kept this secret, a testimony to his devotion to Diantha. I also thought of Lucretia's hard work, her determination to pay for Ruthie's house. If she had caring people to help her stay on a good path, she'd be fine. Now that she was on Gerri's radar, the poor girl would be watched like a hawk. "She'll be fine."

Chapter 39

Back at the farmhouse later that night, Caroline and I curled up on the couch in the parlor with cups of hot cocoa. Rocky and Sprinkles sprawled between us. I'd put Liam's flowers on a high shelf, out of reach of the curious cats.

Caroline threw me a worried look as I opened the note that accompanied Paolo's beautifully wrapped gift. "Are you sure you don't want to read it alone?" she asked.

After everything that had happened, I felt a page had turned, and I could face my memories of Paolo without fear of rekindling any dangerous feelings. I'd already tossed his first letter, unopened, in the trash. "I'm sure."

Riley,

  As you did not call me nor join me at the place I suggested in my earlier letter, I can imagine that you do not wish to see me. I understand. I wished to make amends and tell you of my extreme desolation that my actions caused you pain. I am a gentleman and will not force a meeting upon you.

I snorted.

I am no coward. [Just a liar and a thief, I thought] *and I had wished to talk with you face to face, to apologize with the utmost humility, abase myself and beg for forgiveness.*

As it is not possible, I leave you with a gift as a sign of my sincerity. I beg you, don't throw it in the fire. It is irreplaceable.

It is not stolen.

I remain your servant,
Paolo

I handed the letter to Caroline and unwrapped a book. "*Arsène Lupin. Gentleman Burglar.* Perfect." I turned to the title page. "First edition and it's signed."

Caroline leaned over to see the signature and whistled. "1907! That must be worth a lot of money. Do you think he stole it?"

"He says he didn't." I gave her a wry smile.

A tiny bit of newsprint peeked from the top of the next page. I turned the page and a trimmed newspaper clipping fell out. The clipping was in Italian, of course, but two words jumped out. *Figurina romana.* Roman figurine.

The photo showed the figurine Paolo had stolen from my office at the embassy in Rome cradled in the white-gloved hands of a police officer. It had been discovered via a tip to the police, left in a trattoria in a box addressed to the Ministry of Culture.

"My Italian's rusty," I said, but the photo was clear and I could translate the words that jumped out. "*Comando Carabinieri per la Tutela del Patrimonio Culturale*"—Carabinieri Art Squad.

"My Italian's nonexistent," Caroline said as she read

the clipping over my shoulder, "but he gave the figurine back. He took a huge risk of getting arrested."

"He could still be arrested," I murmured as Rocky climbed into my lap, though the thought didn't kindle as much satisfaction as it would've earlier.

"Actually." Caroline raised her eyebrows. "You have to admit, that was quite the romantic gesture."

I'd run the article past a friend who spoke Italian—"trust but verify" was my motto with Paolo—but I had to agree with Caroline. As I cuddled Rocky, I caught sight of the flowers on the shelf. "Quite."

"Have you decided?" Caroline said. "About the gelato-making class?"

Rocky's bright eyes blinked up at me as I scratched under his chin.

"I've already booked my ticket to Rome."

Author's Note

Historians know that George Washington stayed in New London, Connecticut, in April 1776. It's not far from New London to the northeastern corner of Connecticut where "Penniman" is located, so it's possible the "Father of Our Country" could've visited the area and had need of an inn.

Perhaps.

Recipes

Heavenly Hot Fudge Sauce

So good you'll want to eat it with a spoon!

⅔ cup semisweet chocolate chips

¼ cup unsalted butter

1 cup half and half

7 tablespoons unsweetened cocoa powder

¾ cup granulated sugar

¼ teaspoon salt

1½ teaspoons vanilla extract

Mix together the cocoa powder, sugar, and salt and set aside.

Melt the butter and chocolate chips together in a small saucepan over medium-low heat, stirring constantly.

Slowly whisk the half and half into the butter and chocolate mixture.

Whisk in the sugar, cocoa powder, and salt mixture until well combined. Keep whisking over medium-low heat until the mixture comes just to a boil. Lower the heat and simmer for another 2-3 minutes, stirring continuously.

Remove from heat and stir in the vanilla extract.

Pour into heat-safe container and let it cool. Serve warm over ice cream or pound cake. Keeps in the refrigerator

for 2 weeks. When you're ready to use it, set it in a bowl
of hot water (not submerged) to warm.

Fast and Fabulous Hot Fudge Sauce

Quick and easy, this recipe is a snap to whip up when
you have a last-minute need for a tasty ice-cream or cake
topping. This makes four servings; it is easy to double.

1 cup sugar

1 cup heavy cream

1 cup dark cocoa powder

1 stick (½ cup) salted butter, cut into 8–10 pieces

Put all the ingredients in a small sauce pan over
medium heat. Stir constantly until the butter melts and
everything combines into a velvety smooth mixture.

Pour into a heat-safe container (mason jars work well)
and cool. Use while still warm or store it in the fridge
and rewarm in a bowl of hot water until it's the temperature you like.